Accidentally Engaged

An Enemies to Lovers Romance

Single Dad Billionaires

Mia Mara

A hot neighbor and a future baby daddy? Yes please!

Hudson:
I know she secretly watches me from her window when I work out by my pool.
Behind her quirky, good girl facade, she can't help herself.
Especially when I give her the show of her life. No shorts.
It turns me on to think about what's going on in her tight jeans.

But I know I shouldn't. It's not fitting for a single dad or a fertility doctor of my reputation.
And I need a nanny... last minute.
She's the only one who can help me out.

When I finally work up the nerve to ask her, she's out on the driveway arguing with her parents.
Something about her having a fiancé? Damn...
But then they're all looking at me.
And I'm suddenly accidentally fake engaged!?!

So I'll play her fiancé.
Be nice to her parents.
Kiss her in all the right places.

There's one catch. She wants a treatment for a baby.
Hell yeah!
But I make my own rules.
I'll get her pregnant... the real way.

Chapter 1

Hudson

Thursday

The drive home from the clinic was supposed to be cathartic. It was my alone time, my personal time, the time of the day when I wasn't Hudson, the dad, or Hudson, the doctor. No matter how much I loved my son and my job, I needed this moment of the day to decompress, to shift gears.

However, as I clutched the steering wheel with white knuckles in the thick Boston traffic, it felt anything but.

Things had been going well for too long. I knew that. I knew there'd be highs and lows, calm and unrest, but I just didn't have the energy today. Not after I'd had to sit an optimistic woman down and tell her that the treatment wasn't working, that it likely wouldn't take, and watch as she cried against her husband's soggy shirt. Not after I'd spoken to prospective parents who had lost their son—three years old, the same age as my Jamey—and wanted to try again. I didn't

1

like having to give bad news to my patients. It hurt, especially when most of my job was giving the best news that couples wanted to hear. That was the highlight of my day, my week, my profession. I lived for it, I loved being able to tell them they were expecting. But after today, I needed the promise of a relaxing evening.

Instead, I'd gotten a cryptic text from Jamey's nanny. "I need to talk to you when you get home," she'd said.

I knew the drill already.

Driving past row after row of flashy houses and fancy cars, I pulled into my driveway, pressing the button on the sun visor that opened up my three-car garage. Beyond the house, the sky was drenched in blood-orange, little strips of fleshy pink freckled between the thin clouds. The day was winding down, soon to be over, and I'd have to start all over again tomorrow, fresh in the knowledge of whatever Jenny was going to drop on me when I walked through the door. I positioned my Porsche next to my other two vehicles—a Range Rover for towing the boat and a Mercedes AMG. I dropped my forehead against the curve of the steering wheel, measuring my breaths to keep myself calm as I savored the last few seconds I had before having to switch back to dad-mode.

One. Deep breath in.

Two. Exhale.

Three. Deep breath in.

Four. Exhale.

My fingers found the handle of the door before I'd gotten to five. Clearly, my body had decided it was go-time.

I clutched my phone and its goddamn ambiguous text message in my palm as I walked up the driveway, sidestepping an upturned bucket and a miniature, plastic excavator.

The latch on the door turned as it registered my phone in its proximity.

I blew out a breath as I turned the handle, the rush of air tickling the scruff that had grown on my upper lip. *Definitely need to shave tonight.*

"Daddy!"

"Hey, hey, finish your carrots first!"

Jamey's little emerald eyes lit up in excitement as I stepped through the door. He sat at the kitchen island, his tiny feet swaying back and forth, thudding against the marble with each kick. He shifted in his seat, clearly making a move to hop down from the high-top chair, but Jenny flashed a single, pointed finger at him and he calmed.

"What did I say, Jamey? Carrots."

"Sorry, Jenny," he mumbled, picking up a baby carrot and dipping it into a tiny bowl of ranch before stuffing it in his mouth. He grinned at her with food between his teeth.

I chuckled as I dropped my keys into the basin by the door, kicking off my shoes with my toes. "Hey, bud," I called, jogging across the wooden floor toward the two of them. Jamey's carrot-ridden grin turned to me, little flecks of ranch dressing on his lips, and he giggled as I rustled his mop of dark brown hair. *Almost as dark as mine. Almost.*

I only hoped it would get darker.

"Hey, Dr. Brady," Jenny said, lifting herself from where she leaned on the counter. Her skin wrinkled as she furrowed her brows at me. "Did you get my text?"

I plucked a baby carrot from Jamey's plate and stuffed it in my mouth in an effort to seem nonchalant. Showing that I was nervous about whatever she was going to tell me wouldn't help the situation. "Yeah," I replied, speaking around the crunching between my teeth, "what's up?"

The flesh of her cheeks turned a shade darker, pinkening the skin. "Can we talk in private?"

I nodded. Shucking my jacket off my shoulders, I threw the neckline of it over Jamey's head, and he giggled playfully as he popped himself out of the collar. "Why don't you go watch some PAW Patrol while Jenny and I chat, okay? You can finish your carrots later," I said to him, giving him a little peck on the top of his head.

"Okie dokie," he said. Before I could stop him, he scooted his butt to the edge of the chair and hopped off—something I'd told him numerous times not to do—and landed on shaky footing before taking off toward the living room.

His footsteps echoed through the quiet kitchen until they disappeared around the corner, the room instead filling with the distant sound of the PAW Patrol theme song. I sang along in my head as I looked across the counter at Jenny.

"The floor is yours, Jen."

She took a deep breath, her nervousness palpable in the air. "I need to quit."

"Well, I figured that much," I sighed, pulling the chair out from the counter and plopping myself into it. I picked up another one of Jamey's carrots but put it back down when I realized it was wet. *What had he done to it...?*

"I need to quit today."

Well, fuck. I hadn't expected that.

"Today? You can't even give two weeks' notice?" I snapped, immediately regretting the harshness of my tone when she physically recoiled. I took a deep breath to calm myself. "Sorry, it's been a long day. I didn't mean to snap at you."

She relaxed a bit as she crossed her arms over her chest.

"I know it's last minute. I'm sorry. I was offered a role on Broadway for a musical I auditioned for a few weeks ago, and I just can't pass it up. They need me to relocate to New York City this weekend."

"Jesus, *they* couldn't have given you two weeks' notice?" I asked, trying to keep the conversation light.

"Apparently not. I got the call this morning after you left, otherwise I'd have told you then," she explained. She leaned one hip against the counter. "I'm really sorry, Dr. Brady. If I knew anyone else that could help you out I'd make that my number one priority, but all my other nanny friends are booked solid."

I sighed as I gave her an exasperated smile. What the fuck was I going to do? My mom lived nearby, but she had her own life, her own job, her own time. I couldn't expect her to take on Jamey full-time while I was at work, and I wasn't about to put him in daycare—not after the horror stories I'd heard. *If Becks hadn't taken off...* No. Nope, absolutely not, I was not about to go down that rabbit hole.

"Is there any chance I could get my last paycheck today?" Jenny asked, completely pulling me out of my thoughts. I was grateful for it. "It's just, I need the money for my moving fees and my flight..."

"Yeah, of course." I pulled my phone and wallet from my pocket and slapped them on the countertop. "Do you want cash or Venmo?"

———

I held Jamey in my arms, his small frame wrapped around the muscles of my hip, as Jenny's car rumbled to life. I could tell he didn't quite understand, and in his limited knowledge, he probably just thought that Jenny was going away for a little while and he'd see her again soon. Maybe at the grocery store like where we'd run into his old nanny, Caitlyn, as she worked behind the deli counter. Or maybe how we'd occasionally see Patty, our old neighbor who'd moved out last year, at the park walking her dog.

I knew he didn't get that it could be the last time he saw her because he wasn't waving goodbye like I was. He wasn't even watching as Jenny reversed down the drive. His gaze was drifting far to the right of the porch, locked on something that I couldn't see because his tiny noggin was in the way. "Wave goodbye," I whispered to him, and he snapped his head toward me instead, confusion written all over his face.

"Why?"

"Because she's moving away," I said softly.

"So?"

"So, you won't see her for a very long time. You liked her, didn't you?"

He nodded his head, his little tufts of hair flopping about his face.

"Then give her a wave. She liked you, too, munchkin," I sighed, wrapping my thumb and forefinger around his wrist and lifting his hand with it. He gave a little wave as she drove off.

Jamey wiggled his feet, his signal to me that he wanted to be put down. As his socks hit the concrete of our entranceway, he glanced one more time toward the right of the house before turning and walking back inside. I followed his gaze again, but nothing was there—just the bright blue Nissan Altima parked in the driveway of our new neighbor's house, the one that had moved in after Patty had left. I hadn't gotten the chance to meet her yet, but I'd heard good things from the neighborhood Facebook group.

I followed Jamey inside and through to the living room where PAW Patrol was still playing on the television. Immediately, he was glued even though he'd seen the episode at least twenty times. I could almost recite it by heart.

Dropping onto the couch beside him, I tucked him into my chest, letting my mind drift to the sounds of children's television. It was shocking how easy it had become to tune it out when I needed to.

I needed someone to watch Jamey. I'd already sent an email to let the others at the office know I wouldn't be coming in tomorrow and to shift my appointments to the other doctors at the practice, but that only bought me an extra day. I had tomorrow and the weekend to find someone that could look after him during the week.

If only he had a fucking mother.

My grip on the couch turned rougher, and I was careful not to let it affect the side of my body that Jamey was snuggled up to. *Don't. Don't think about her. You'll only end up more frustrated,* I thought to myself. *You can't change the past. You can't make her be a mother if she doesn't want to be.*

I'd be a liar if I tried to say it hadn't wrecked me. Becks' running away had fucked me up for far too long, and even now, I found the idea of an actual relationship daunting. I was thankful that Jamey was too young to remember his mother—she'd left just over two years ago, just after Jamey had turned two. I was also thankful that he looked absolutely nothing like her. That was a godsend, really.

7

I had enough money to not work if I needed to. In fact, I could never work another day in my life and be fine. I could be a stay-at-home dad if it came down to it, but I loved my job, and even on my toughest days, I didn't want to give it up. I loved being able to help women get what they craved, what they'd always known they wanted, and I was good at it. But faced with this new dilemma I had no idea what I was going to do. I was fucked. Completely, utterly fucked, and despite my doctorates, I wasn't smart enough to come up with an idea out of thin air.

"I'm gonna get some housework done, bud," I said, slowly sliding out of his embrace. I needed a distraction, and PAW Patrol wasn't going to cut it. "Shout if you need me."

Jamey nodded, his eyes never leaving the screen.

Despite how messy of a child Jamey was, Jenny always did a spectacular job of cleaning up after him and making sure he helped her with his messes, so as I found myself pacing the kitchen, there wasn't much to do. The dishes were done and put away, a final load running in the dishwasher. In the distance, I could hear the laundry tumbling in the dryer. The countertops were spotless, save for the plate with half-eaten carrots and dipping pot of ranch, so I figured I'd start there.

Wiping the soggy carrots into the hidden trash can, I noticed it was almost full to the brim. Perfect. Another job I could do.

I left the plate and the dipping pot in the sink and tugged the strings of the trash bag until it closed. "Jamey!" I shouted, lifting the bag out. "I'm just taking the trash out, I'll be back in a minute!"

"Okay!"

As I stepped out the front door, I noticed that the sky had turned mostly dark, with only a low-level blue light remaining. Soon, it'd be pitch-black and the streetlights would come on, casting the neighborhood in a warm glow that could only be described as suburban.

Lifting the lid of the trash can, I noticed something moving out of the corner of my eye. I followed it, tracking the movement as a head of brown hair bobbed behind the blue Nissan Altima, heading toward the mailbox at the end of her driveway.

She appeared behind the back of her car, keys in hand, not even giving me a passing glance. *That must be the new neighbor*, I thought to myself. Her long hair swayed behind her as she walked, moving back and forth along the small of her back. She was of average height, her slender frame covered only by a pair of lounging shorts and a tank top, definitely not the right clothes for the slight chill in the air, but my god, she looked like heaven in them.

I watched as she unlocked her mailbox and sorted through the letters, her bare feet planted on the asphalt of the road. She was almost mesmerizing to look at—stark blue eyes that I could see even from where I stood, a button nose, full lips. She didn't seem to notice me, and somehow, that made her all the more enticing. My blood pressure dipped, my mind getting the better of me and sending blood where it didn't belong. My cock twitched to life as my eyes followed her, zeroing in on that pretty mouth and the perfect body beneath it. *What I would give...*

No. You don't want to go down that road again.

I truly didn't. I didn't need the stress of that in my life. But from what I'd heard, she worked from home. Someone in the Facebook group had said she ran her own business and had recently started after a string of babysitting jobs as well.

No. That would be insane, right? I didn't even know

her. I couldn't imagine a stranger watching after my son. But she *was* next door, and she *was* beautiful, though that shouldn't matter. That couldn't matter. I could keep that separate if she agreed.

She looked up from her handful of mail as she came up the driveway, her bright blue eyes catching on me. She stopped dead in her tracks, as if she could sense every ounce of attraction I already felt for her.

Salvation.

Chapter 2

Sophie

Friday

The drive to want something you don't have can be absolutely fucking maddening. Hence why I had a glass of Chardonnay clutched between my fingers, a lipstick stain already smeared across the edge of the rim.

The back of my heel slid on and off, clacking against the floor as I tapped my foot along to the beat of the pop song playing over the speakers of the bar. "I really don't think it's that big of a deal," I mumble, staining the glass once more.

"You don't? What? How?" Lisa's brown eyes narrowed, her bobbed, blonde tresses flying about her head as she shook it. "Sophie. You're twenty-six. And single. And hot."

I rolled my eyes and glanced around the room, no longer feeling entirely comfortable looking at her. "What does that have to do with anything?"

"I can't believe you want to throw that all away by having a goddamn baby," she scoffed, the ice in her glass tinkling as she stirred her mixed drink.

"Having a child doesn't negate any of that."

"Oh, it absolutely does," she refuted, that tiny bit of venom hiding just beneath the surface of her words. God, I loved her, but she could be so intense sometimes. "Who am I supposed to go out with if you have a crying, shitting, bundle of 'joy' in your arms? You'll leave me behind."

I looked back at her, my gaze flat. She was so dramatic. "Don't be absurd, Lisa. Babysitters exist."

"For newborns?"

Another annoyed stare from her, another stain on my glass as I sipped. "I mean, yeah. I wouldn't use one right away but..."

Lisa groaned as she leaned back in her seat, her tiny frame slipping down the leather booth, her lower lip pouting. Was she really using the puppy dog look on me? She hadn't done that since we were kids.

"I know you're not as annoyed as you seem," I cooed, the edge of my lips tilting up in a smirk.

She sighed exasperatedly. "Well yeah, I am annoyed. I know you've always wanted to be a mom, but *now*? Really? We're in our mid-twenties, for Christ's sake!"

I reached across the table and took her perfectly manicured hands into mine. "I've thought about it a lot, dingus. I know what I want. I'm ready. I'm successful, I have a home, stable income... I'm ready. I don't need a man to make it the perfect time." It was true. I had given it a lot of thought. In fact, I'd been thinking about it since I graduated college, and it wasn't until the last few months that I really felt like I could do it. I ran my own business, I worked from home, it all added up.

But the main reason was the intense need, almost down to my bones, that longed for a child.

"Please say you'll support me," I said quietly.

Lisa's lips pressed into a thin line as she sat up, using my hands for leverage. "Of course, I'll support you, Soph." She bit down on her lip, smearing lipstick across her teeth. "But how are you even going to get pregnant? I thought you had... what's it called? Poly something."

"Polycystic ovarian syndrome."

"Yeah! That."

I nodded as I sipped the last of my chardonnay. I lifted the glass toward the bartender, silently requesting another.

"I do."

"I thought that was supposed to make it difficult for you," Lisa said, her eyes going soft. She knew it was a touchy subject for me, and had she known what I'd been doing for the last few months, she likely would have wanted to hold me while I cried. I didn't want to put that on her, though, so I'd kept her in the dark until now.

"It does. I've, uh, been going to the sperm bank for a few months now," I explained, my tapping foot growing wilder in my nervousness. "I've tried multiple times but it's never worked."

I made a point not to look at her. I didn't want to see the sympathy written all over her face.

"I have an appointment next week at an IVF clinic," I finished.

Lisa's eyebrows rose in shock, her jaw dropping open just a hair. "How would that even work without a man?"

I couldn't help but laugh. What did she think I was going to do, grab a random guy off the street and start fucking him while doing the treatment? That's not how any of it worked. "Well, when couples do it, the guy gives his sperm in the same way a donor would. They put the egg in a weird little dish thing and force the sperm toward it, pretty much guaranteeing a fertilized egg. It's the implantation afterward that can be iffy."

"So you're going to use a donor for that, too?"

"Yeah," I grinned. "It'll be like baby roulette. Who's will it be? Nobody knows."

Lisa snorted as she nearly choked on her drink. "And your parents are okay with this?"

I tapped the rim of my glass, smearing the lipstick stains, and pulled my lower lip between my teeth. "I haven't exactly told them." A waiter rounded the edge of the table and deposited another glass of wine in front of me, swiping away the empty one.

For once, Lisa fell silent. She stared at me with widened eyes, the clinking of ice in her glass a thing of the past. It was never a good thing when she felt like there was nothing she could say.

"They wouldn't approve," I elaborated, hating the words already as they fell from my lips. My parents were old-fashioned, and not in the fun, fancy drink way. No, they were heavily religious; they believed that marriage was the key to a healthy life, and a woman having a child outside the confines of a stable, godly relationship was unholy. I'd written off that shit years ago, but I'd be lying if I tried to say the kernels of their beliefs didn't live inside of me just a little bit, screaming from the depths of my mind that I was fucking up.

I didn't want to live my life according to them.

"I'll tell them eventually when the time is right." I lifted the glass to my lips and took a hearty gulp of wine, desperately needing it to chase away my worries. "They'll probably disown me, though."

She raised one brow at me. "Doesn't your brother have a kid?"

"Yeah. With his *wife*. Aaron wouldn't dare defy my parents, not in a million years. You should have seen how excited they were when they found out," I sighed, the temptation to drop my forehead against the rim of the wine glass gnawing at me. "I highly doubt they'll feel the same when I have to tell them I'm having a baby with a stranger."

Lisa pursed her lips as she gave my hand a gentle squeeze. "I'll cover for you, you know. As long as you need it. Plus, you could always design some sick-ass clothes to hide the bump."

I couldn't stop the sly grin from spreading across my cheeks. I'd studied fashion design in college, and now that I was able to run my own small business from the comfort of my home, I could absolutely design some interesting clothes to hide it. Babydoll dresses all around.

"How's the business doing, anyway?" She asked, a quick and easy way to change the subject to something she knew was the opposite of one that caused worry. My business was doing great. In fact, it was so stable that I'd been able to purchase my first home in a fancy neighborhood, surrounded by large homes and expensive cars. It was a condo, but that didn't matter. It still felt like a step in the right direction.

"Great." I grinned as I pulled my phone from my purse. Unlocking it, I slid it across the table, my shopfront open on the screen. "Business is booming. I can hardly keep up, to be honest. I'm up five hundred percent from last month since I hired a new marketing guy. He really knows what he's doing."

"That's insane," she gawked, her eyes glued to the

screen of my phone. "Soon you'll need to hire little foreign children to make your designs."

I sent her a seething glare as I snatched my phone back from her. "Don't even joke about that."

Chapter 3

Hudson

Saturday

The feeling of eyes on you while working out isn't exactly the most uncomfortable sensation but feeling it in your own backyard is a little offsetting.

The rope slapped against the ground beneath my feet with every jump, the sound ricocheting off the stucco of my home. I'd lost count at that point, no longer knowing where I was in the set; I could hardly focus. My thoughts were spiraling, considering every option I had about finding childcare for Jamey, but that goddamn sensation that someone was watching seemed to wrap them up in barbed wire.

My mom had agreed to take Jamey for the day, and I was more than grateful. As much as I loved having weekends with him, I needed time alone to think, to plan, to focus on what the fuck I was going to do. I'd spent the morning trawling nannying websites and local childcare facilities, hoping to strike gold and find someone as good as Jenny. But I couldn't find a damned thing. Deep in the suburbs of Boston, my only options were pre-kindergarten and cheap daycare, neither of which I wanted to subject my son to. Everyone and everything else was booked solid months in advance—the drawback of living in a wealthy area, I suppose.

Sweat dripped down my body as I tried to recall what number I was on, but it was entirely pointless. The counts had been forgotten long ago, somewhere along the line of thinking that I could become some kind of evening fertility doctor, if those even existed. Normally, working out calmed my stress, but today of all days, it only amplified it beyond a reasonable degree.

Tossing my jump rope to the side, I walked on shaky legs out of the shade and into the blistering sun. I placed my hand above my eyes like an army cadet to shield them, deciding then and there that if someone was watching me, I wanted to know who. If it was going to keep me from being able to de-stress, I had to find the source.

A few of my neighbor's windows in the house that sat to the left of mine were within eyeshot of my backyard, though I'd never known the Traeger's to spy on my property. They were elderly, in their late eighties, and spent most of their time downstairs. I couldn't see anyone behind the glass of the upstairs windows and, considering my house backed up against a lake, that left one other option.

My new neighbor.

My cock twitched in my shorts at the thought of her watching me. Did she like what she saw? Was she glued to the pane of glass, unable to take her eyes away no matter how much she wanted to? Was she wet thinking about me? I knew I was in great shape—I made an effort to keep as fit as possible, and the muscles that resulted weren't bad to look at. I got hit on frequently, be it at the gym or even in my office, with the occasional woman sending me a heated glance even in front of their husband. I never paid any attention to it but my new neighbor... she was dangerous.

Shifting my gaze as nonchalantly as possible, I made sure to keep my eyes hidden from her as I glanced up at her windows. *Nothing in the top left... the middle? Nope. Top right.*

There you are.

I could see the lower half of her upper body, her arms across her chest and hands clutching a mug of something steaming. Her long brown hair settled around the swells of her breasts, the curled ends hanging about her waist. I imagined her nipples hardening below her shirt, and that did nothing to help my growing arousal. I didn't dare look higher to see her face. No, better to leave her thinking that I had no idea she was even there, for now, anyway.

I could have more fun with her that way.

I kept my eyes glued to her small frame as my hand inched toward the tie of my shorts. *Do you want to see more?* I could feel the little drops of sweat beading and sliding down my bare chest, my back, and there was nothing better than a dip in the pool after a hard workout. And considering Jamey wasn't here...

Blood pooled between the hard lines of my waist, hardening my cock and creating a tent in the fabric that did little to hide what lay beneath. That small, sensible part of me that knew that she was my only real option for childcare screamed at me to stop, but her gaze on me was too much, too exciting for me to quit. I wanted to tease her, to excite her, and considering she still hadn't moved, she clearly wanted that, too.

Removing the protection my hand granted my eyes in one quick motion, I pushed my shorts down my thighs, letting them drop to the ground with a wet *thwap.* My length was swollen, twitching, red—and most of all, unmissable.

I looked directly at her.

I wished I could see the blush spreading across her freckled cheeks as she physically jumped, the hot liquid in her cup sloshing and dripping down the side. Her immediate instinct told her to run, to hide, to pretend as though she hadn't been caught, but it was clear she fought it as she kept her gaze directly on my naked form. Her eyes were widened with fear, her lips parted, and god, all I wanted was to shove my aching cock between them.

I gave her a little smirk as I motioned with one hand toward the pool. *Care to join me?* I mouthed, over-expressing each word so she could get the message from where she stood.

Slowly, she lifted her fingers and placed them in front of her lips to hide her spreading grin. Caught red-handed.

Naughty, I mouthed, unable to keep my laugh at bay. It seemed so ridiculous, her watching me—adorable, but ridiculous. She'd had every opportunity to introduce herself in the last month she'd lived here, and yet, *this* was how she chose to do it? Granted, she probably had no idea she'd be caught. I couldn't help but wonder how many times she had watched me before.

The urge to touch my aching cock was overwhelming, but I didn't give myself—or her—the satisfaction. No, if she wanted that, she had to earn it.

Turning my gaze toward the rippling water, I hoped

she'd stay to watch as I took a running start before diving into the pool. The cool water was a shock to my system, forcing the air from my lungs and the blood from my dick. Resurfacing took more effort than I thought, the worry that she'd disappeared and left me hanging sitting like a rock in my mind, and as my head crested the surface, I found myself staring again at her window.

Still there, but smaller, as if she'd backed away. Her shoulders shook with what I hoped was laughter, and as the droplets washed away the sweat from my hair, I couldn't help but join her. My head tipped back, dunking the strands again, as I let out a laugh that did more to clear my head than the exercise had. For the first time in nearly forty-eight hours, I felt like I could breathe, like I didn't have this horrible, annoying thing weighing over me.

Somehow, it was because of her. Because of her and her wandering eyes and her playful laugh; because of her and her confidence; her determination not to shy away when she'd been caught.

Lifting my head from the water once again, I looked toward her window, only to find it empty. Immediately, the stress rushed back in like a tidal wave, pulling me under and drowning me.

Why had I done that?

She was the only realistic option I had. The idea that I might have just thrown that entirely out the window formed like a pit in my stomach, roiling my guts and chasing away the last of the blood that pooled. How on earth was I supposed to face her now, to ask her to watch my son, no strings attached? If she didn't already know I was attracted to her from the way I looked at her the other night, she had to know now.

In the distance, under the shade provided by my back

porch, my phone buzzed incessantly. I scrambled up the steps of the pool, wrapping a towel around my waist to not terrify the Traeger's if they wandered upstairs, and jogged over to my phone. I hoped for a miracle, for a stray nanny to have found my number, wanting to offer their services, but as I picked my phone up in my damp hand and dragged my dripping thumb across the screen, it was a text from my mom.

A photo and a short message. *Jamey loves mint-chocolate-chip ice cream now.*

Chapter 4

Sophie

Sunday

The scraping of cutlery on porcelain had always ground my gears, but today, it made my anxiety peak much higher than the usual limit.

My parents sat across from me, their knees knocking against each other beneath the kitchen table. They'd insisted on paying me a visit and checking out my new condo. Dad wanted to make sure it was "up to scratch," as he put it, which seemed like the kind of thing one would do *before* their daughter set up a mortgage, but whatever.

The afternoon sun shone harshly through the windows that looked out at my back porch, glinting off the polished countertops and illuminating the little specks of dust in the air. I watched as they danced, floating amongst each other, and wished I could feel as weightless as them.

No matter the topic of conversation, I found my mind spinning. When they would tell me about Aaron's baby girl, my stomach tumbled, my own broodiness overwhelming, and the idea of having to tell them what I was doing made me nauseous. When they would tell me about literally anything else, like their planned cruise to the Bahamas next year or their bingo nights, my mind filled with thoughts of my next-door neighbor and what I'd done yesterday. I still couldn't believe I'd stayed in that window. I couldn't believe he'd offered me to join him, buck naked in the midday heat and glistening with sweat. Even from a distance, I could tell how large he was. It made my mouth water even now.

"Soph?"

I blinked away the thoughts fogging my mind for a moment as I turned my head toward my dad. "Sorry, I missed that."

He laughed the way he always did when something tickled him—full-bellied, head tipped back. "I asked if you'd made any plans to see Aaron and Michelle. You'd love Brynn."

God dammit. Back to babies again. I wrung my hands under the table, fighting the urge to say what bubbled on the tip of my tongue. "Uh, no, not yet. I've been so busy, you know, with the business. Haven't had a chance to think about it."

"We're going up there next week if you'd like to join us," Mom piped up around a mouthful of macaroni and cheese. Aaron had moved to Bar Harbor, Maine, a couple of years ago after meeting Michelle on one of those dating apps. It was a lovely place, but it was quiet, and I didn't quite understand the pull of it when there was so much more to do even here in the suburbs of Boston.

I rolled my lips between my teeth. "Uh, yeah, maybe. I'll have to see if I have time."

"Oh, come on, sweetie. You can make time to meet your

little niece, right? She's at that cute stage where they stop lookin' like a raisin and start lookin' all plump—"

"Martin!" My mother's open hand slapped him lightly in the gut. "Brynnie does *not* look like a raisin."

Dad laughed again as he grabbed for my mother's hand, planting a little kiss on the back of her palm. "I know, darling. That's what I was getting at."

I chuckled as I imagined a newborn, wrinkled skin and fragile, weightless in my arms. I'd seen the pictures of Brynn that Aaron had sent me, had seen the ones Michelle had posted online, but in my imagination, it wasn't Brynn in my arms. No, it was a brown-haired little girl, a mini-me with bright blue eyes and olive skin, her tiny fingers wrapped like a vice around my finger. The ache in my chest from the intense want for her to be real nearly stole the breath from my lungs.

"Why do you look so sad, bug?" Mom asked, evaporating the image from my mind within a second as if it were only passing smoke. "I thought you'd be excited to hear about Brynn."

"No, I am, Mom. And I'd love to meet her."

"Then what's going on with you?" Her hand snaked across the table, finding mine. I hadn't even realized my fingers were balled into a fist until she loosened the grip I had. "You don't seem like yourself."

I could be honest. I could say what I'm feeling without giving anything away, right? I took a deep breath, forcing a small smile across my lips. "To be honest, Mom, I'm just a little jealous."

Her head tilted, her brow furrowing as she blinked at me in confusion. "Bug, you're only twenty-six. And you're single. You've got to focus on finding someone and getting married before you even start to want that." Dad fiddled with his watch, clearly a little uncomfortable with my admission.

"I know," I sighed. "It's just... I'm so ready for it. It's just a little hard knowing it's not within reach yet, and that when it finally is, it won't be easy." *Not a complete lie.*

"Oh, bug." Mom flashed a sad smile at me as she squeezed my knuckles together, something that should have been reassuring but just felt wrong. "I'm sure when you find the right man, God will make sure it isn't hard for you."

I wasn't sure if she caught the flinch that rippled across my face in the blink of an eye. I didn't need a man to get what I wanted, and I definitely didn't need a god to make a miracle happen—not unless they wanted me to be turned into some kind of Mary figure. I needed IVF, I needed sperm from the donor facility, and I needed myself. That was it.

"Right, sorry sweetie but it's getting late and we've got bingo tonight," Dad said, an effort to clear the awkwardness in the air. He stood, picking up his plate and Mom's as well. "You're welcome to join us next week at church if you'd like. I know it's across town, but it could help you."

After taking the plates from my dad and picking up my own, I scraped the leftover bits into the garbage disposal. It was enough to distract me for all of two seconds. "That's sweet, Dad, but I've got plans. Maybe the week after," I lied.

Dad nodded. Placing his hand on top of my mom's blonde mop, he ruffled her hair, annoying her the way he always did and the way she loved most. "Come on, darling. Let's get going."

Mom pushed her chair back from the table, the squeak along the tile floor making me want to grind my teeth. Despite only being in their mid-fifties, Dad still offered her his hands, hoisting her up the way he always did.

"I'll walk you guys out."

The warmth of the outside air hit me like a wall of bricks as I opened the door, completely at odds with the coolness of my house. I had to squint to keep the sun from burning my retinas as my dad walked out, my mom following behind, looking back to make sure I was close to her. Across the lawn, in the still heat of his driveway, my neighbor was bent at the waist over the innards of his Mercedes. My breath caught in my throat from both the humiliation of yesterday and the fact that he was topless and sweaty. *Again.*

"You know, Soph," Mom started, her voice quiet, "I really think coming to church on Sunday would do you some good. I understand how you're feeling."

I could barely pay attention to her. My thoughts were twisting and spiraling, my gaze fixed solely on the way his muscles flexed as he twisted a wrench, tighter and tighter. It felt like the bolt was inside of me, fixing me in place.

"I went through a similar thing in my early twenties, bug," Mom continued, her voice sounding further and further away. *If only I was on the hood of his car. Would he fuck me like that?* "My friends started getting married and having babies. I knew how unholy it was to fall pregnant outside of marriage, so I went back to church, started praying for a man. Blessed be, I found your father a month later."

He looked directly at me as he stood up straight, his abs flexing from the movement, wrench still in hand. A wry smirk spread across his lips. *He's eavesdropping.*

"I don't want you to fall down the beaten path, sweetheart. It's important to keep your morals—"

My head spun around to face her, finally picking up on her words. "Beaten path? I want a child, Mom, not heroin."

"I know, but it's so easy to get swept up in one-night-stands and such these days. I worry for you, honey," she said quietly, one hand on the door handle of their white Ford F150. Her phone dinged in her handbag, and she quickly fished it out. "Oh! Would you look at that? It's Aaron and little Brynnie."

She held the phone out to me. A photo of my grinning brother and an equally ecstatic little girl in his lap, her hands clapped together and her mouth a huge smile. The hole in my chest grew a little bit wider, a little bit deeper, a little bit more empty.

The words fell out of me before I could stop them.

"I'm doing IVF," I whispered quietly. A rush of relief flooded me, but the moment my words were processed by my mother, the solace turned as sour as her face. "Mom—"

"You're *what*?" She pressed, her voice turning cold, angry, bitter. The slight wrinkles on her face deepened, anger making her look older. "You don't even have a boyfriend, Sophia! Are you telling me right now that you're actively trying to become pregnant?"

I swallowed what little saliva remained in my mouth. It went dry, filling with what felt like sand, and the brightness of the sun became far too overwhelming. Had I been transported to the desert? "Mom, calm down—"

"Did you hear that, Martin?"

I was going to be sick. I could feel it in the back of my throat, that familiar sensation of acid clouding my better judgment. "I'm engaged," I said, the words hollow on my tongue, the lie flowing from me so easily that I hadn't even considered how ridiculous it was.

Her lips went flat, her head tilted to the side. A look that said *I don't believe you*. "Oh yeah? And why haven't we heard this before? Where's the ring?"

"I..." I fiddled with my hands, feeling for a ring I knew I wouldn't find. *Shit. Think, Sophie, think.* "I didn't want to tell you until I knew it was serious. And then I got so wrapped up in the move and getting my business going. I know I should have told you guys earlier. I'm sorry. My ring is upstairs."

Mom's brows creased deeper as she looked me up and down. Dad stood on the driver's side, his gaze fixed on me, a hint of suspicion in his eyes. I had to make this work. I had to make them believe it. I wasn't ready to lose them, not yet.

"So, who is he, then?" Dad asked, his voice less angry than Mom's.

"He..." I bit my lower lip, wracking my brain for any sort of explanation I could come up with. I could make someone up, but of course they would want to meet him. It was better than nothing, I supposed, I could figure something out between then and now. But...wait. No. I can't.

I have to.

My pulse was pounding in my throat as I took a step, my bare feet crunching in the grass between our lawns. Another step, and I wanted to throw myself off a cliff. But I'd committed to what I was about to do. I couldn't turn back, not after I crossed the property line between our houses, not as he stared at me in confusion, those green eyes blazing. Not after I took his grease-covered, massive hand in mine, and not even after I began pulling him toward my parents with my eyes locked on his. *Please. Please, go along with it. I know you were listening.*

To my immediate surprise, he doesn't fight me. He comes without a second thought, a filthy rag in one hand and my fingers in the other. *You owe me,* he mouthed, a sly grin on his face.

He planted his croc-covered feet in the grass in front of

my mom, dropping my hand so he could rub the sludge off his with the rag. "Afternoon," he said to her, and *fuck me* his voice sounded like browned butter, thick and heady. "You must be my dear fiancée's parents."

He was *listening. I knew it.*

He held out his cleanest hand.

Mom shook it, her suspicions lessened.

"I'm Hudson," he beamed. "I'm sorry we haven't had the chance to meet yet. This one," he jutted a finger at me, "was so nervous to tell you about me that she had me over there working on her neighbor's car."

"Hudson," Mom enunciated slowly as if she was tasting every letter of his name. "When did you—"

"Pop the question?" He finished for her as his gaze slowly slid to me. It made my heart hammer in my chest the way he looked at me, as if he were some kind of professional actor, doing his best to show love as he looked at his 'fiancée.' "Couple weeks ago. I took her to the Gardner Museum. She was so busy staring at the statues in the garden that she didn't even realize I'd dropped to one knee." He laughed. How did he know I liked that museum? Lucky guess?

He wrapped an arm around me and I stiffened, the display of affection catching me off guard. No matter how much I wanted this to work, no matter how well I tried to play my part, all I could think about was what I'd seen out my window the day before, and what hid beneath the shorts he was wearing.

He placed a kiss on the side of my head, right above my ear. Although I felt like I couldn't breathe, I knew I was because I could smell him all around me—sweet and thick like rum, with a hint of citrus and wood. The small bit of sweat he'd built up did nothing to mask it.

"Right, well, I guess congratulations are in order," Mom said slowly, glancing between me, my father, and the man to my left who I now knew was named Hudson. I wasn't sure if it was worse now that I knew his name. "We should come over for dinner soon. Get to know one another."

"Absolutely," Hudson grinned. "I'd love that."

My parents hopped into their truck. As they pulled out of the driveway, they stared me down, confusion and surprise the only words capable of describing the vibes they put off. Hudson held me to him in silence until they were no longer within sight, until we couldn't even hear the hint of the engine anymore.

I slithered out from under his arm the moment it felt safe to do so.

I didn't know what to say to him. How to thank him, to tell him how much it meant to me, how much he'd saved my ass by playing along. I wanted to form the words, I could feel them on the tip of my tongue, but each time I tried to open my mouth, it felt like it'd be sewn shut.

"You don't need to thank me," he said calmly, as if reading my mind, the words coming so easily to him. I was jealous.

"Okay," I whispered. It was the only word that I could manage.

If only I could have said more before turning and bolting back inside my house, sick from the stress and embarrassment of the entire afternoon.

Chapter 5

Hudson

Monday

The chair below me squeaked as I rolled across the small clinical room. According to my planner, in approximately five minutes, I'd have a new patient walking through the door. That in itself wasn't entirely unusual, but I'd be lying if I said the name on the patient file didn't make my cock twitch to life.

Sophia Mitchell.

The possibility that it was her was small. There were thousands of women named Sophia across Boston, and I doubted all of them went by Sophie. But just the mention of her name—the name I'd come to know from eavesdropping on her yesterday—was enough to excite me.

Why was I so intrigued by her to begin with?

My foot tapped incessantly against the vinyl floor. At any moment, a nurse would bring this patient through my door, and I had to chill the fuck out. The likelihood that it was her was so small, so absurd, that it would be a horrible twist of fate for her to end up in my room. And if it wasn't her, I needed to stop thinking about how many ways I wanted to take her, because a half-erect dick poking out of my scrubs was not a good first impression for an IVF doctor.

The door handle wiggled and pulled free. I sucked in a sharp breath.

God fucking dammit.

My throat was suddenly filled with a lump, chased by my quickening pulse. Sophie, dressed in a little yellow sundress and sandals, stared directly at me, eyes widened in what I could only assume was horror. She turned to the nurse, her face paling and making her freckles stand out more than they already did. If I wasn't so stunned myself I would have taken the time to appreciate how beautiful she looked.

"Is this a joke?" She asked quietly, her pretty mouth barely forming the words.

Janice, the nurse, stared back in confusion. "Uh..."

"It's alright, Jan. I'll handle it," I said, the words feeling hollow. She glanced between me and Sophie, the concern dripping from her features. She nodded to herself, seeming to accept the situation, then turned and headed out of the room, leaving me alone with a horrified Sophie in my doorway.

"It's a prank. This has to be a prank," she whispered, her fingers shaking as they touched her lips. I remembered she did the same thing when she saw me notice her watching me from her window, and... *fuck*, now I was back to thinking about that.

"I can assure you, little voyeur, that I had no idea that

the 'Sophia Mitchell' on my appointment calendar was you," I said, and like a freight train full of boulders, the regret of calling her out hit me. The moment it processed for her, her cheeks heated, red as a sunburn, and she honestly looked like she wanted to murder me.

I'd probably let her.

"Come on in."

Her shoulders rose and fell with each exasperated breath. Her nostrils flared with every exhale, and if we were in one of Jamey's cartoons, she'd be physically steaming. "You want me to come in there? With *you*? And talk about my in vitro fertilization treatment? Absolutely not."

"Come on. I'll keep it professional," I insisted, already knowing deep down in my gut that I absolutely could not do that.

"You just called me a voyeur," she spat, a little hint of venom in her words. "You call that being professional?"

She was right. I could admit that. "Won't happen again," I said, raising my right hand and crossing my left over my chest. "Scouts honor."

Her eyes narrowed, suspicion clouding her vision. "You were a scout?"

"Well, no, but—"

"Ugh," she scolded in disgust, turning on the ball of her foot. "I'm out of here."

I was on my feet before I could even make the decision. I bolted to the door, each step matching two of hers, and caught her wrist in my hand only a meter from the doorway.

She swiveled again, bright blue eyes blazing as she glared up at me. I held her wrist tight enough to ensure she wasn't going anywhere, but loose enough not to hurt her. Not only did I not want a medical malpractice lawsuit on my hands, but something about her made me want to hold her, comfort her. "Listen to me," I said softly, my gaze flicking down the hall to ensure we were alone before landing back on her captivating stare. "You've set aside your time and your money to be here. You want this. There isn't a better treatment facility in Boston, and you know that. Get your money's worth, Sophie. Talk to me."

Her face softened a little, though still etched with annoyance and anger around the edges.

"I've looked at your file," I continued. I pulled her toward me, just an inch, and she let me. Her breath hitched, her pulse below my fingertips a steady, too-fast drum. "I know why you're here. Let me help you."

She steeled her jaw as she mulled over her options. I could practically see the gears turning in her mind.

"I can help you," I whispered. "I *want* to help you." I meant it. Truly, from somewhere deep in my iced-over heart, I wanted to help her. I'd seen patients like her before, I knew how hard it was.

Slowly, she wiggled her wrist from my grasp and rubbed the skin I'd covered. "Fine," she murmured, "But you're not putting anything inside of me."

I snorted, unable to contain the chuckle sneaking up my throat. "Deal," I said firmly. I tried to disguise my grin.

———

"So, you have polycystic ovarian syndrome, correct?"

She nodded her reply. The conversation was heavily

one-sided, with me asking questions about her health and her giving short, one-word answers or nothing at all, and for once I found myself wishing that my patient would have a conversation with me during the questioning process.

"Did your mother have any issues with pregnancy?"

"No," she said. I waited for more, but she didn't open her mouth again. *For fucks sake.*

"No problems at all? That's unusual. Often reproductive issues like this are hereditary."

"If she did, she never told me. She had my brother, Aaron, when she was twenty-three. Then me four years later." Her gaze was fixed on one of the posters on the wall —a mother holding her baby, smiles on both of their faces, and below them, quotes from thank-you notes our office had received. My patients always stared at that one, always imagining themselves as the mother in the photo, but it broke my heart to watch her do it.

"Okay. Let's get some bloodwork done to check your hormone levels and see what's going on there, alright? In the meantime, we'll need to do a pregnancy test to ensure you're not currently pregnant as the medications we'll need to put you on could interfere—"

"I'm not pregnant," she cut in, her words like a knife.

"I understand. But we need to double check, okay?"

She crossed her arms over her chest as she slowly dragged her gaze back to me. "Fine. Whatever."

Quickly, I shot a message to Jan, requesting she take Sophie for her pregnancy test before we got into the nitty-gritty. Might as well get that out of the way before I said what I needed to next—I knew she wasn't going to like it, but it was standard procedure for our PCOS patients. "We'll also need to do an internal ultrasound to make sure there are no cysts inside your uterus."

Her face paled as she stared me down, her lips parting just a hair as she breathed in. "I don't feel comfortable with that."

"I'll schedule it with our ultrasound technician. I wouldn't be the one to do that," I explained. Relief washed over her face, and I kicked myself for hating how much she clearly didn't want me to touch her. *I can change your mind.*

"Fine."

A knock on the door cut the tension. Jan poked her head inside, a little plastic cup held in one hand.

"Jan's going to take you to do your test, then once we have the results we can continue."

Sophie didn't look at her. Instead, she looked at me, something unreadable in those bright blue eyes, something similar to fear but not quite the same. I could put the pieces together from my years as a reproductive specialist, I knew the look, despite it being so specific, so different. I knew she didn't want to take the test, and I knew exactly why. She didn't want another negative. Didn't want to see it, to hear the words. Didn't want it to hurt her again.

"I know," I said quietly, pursing my lips together for emphasis. "We have to check, Soph."

Slowly, agonizingly slowly, she nodded her head before picking herself up and defeatedly following a confused Janice out the door. And even though I had a mountain of paperwork to deal with and could have spent the next ten minutes getting things done, I couldn't do anything except think about her every second she was out of my room.

———

. . .

"I'm sorry for yesterday."

My leg bounced again as I stared at the screen, ticking off boxes. It was the first time she'd spoken since coming back from her pregnancy test, and I didn't want to make a big deal out of it. "That's unnecessary," I said blandly, trying my best to keep my eyes off her body as I ticked 'physically fit.'

"I want you to know that I don't expect you to actually have dinner with my parents," she said. She was wringing her hands in her lap, something she'd done yesterday before running across our joined lawns and grabbing me the same way I'd done to her ten minutes ago. I wondered if it was her way of dealing with nerves. "I'll figure something out. Tell them I got pregnant and that you died or something."

I hid my smirk with the back of my hand. "Already planning my death, Soph?"

The glare she leveled at me told me that yes, she definitely was.

"Honestly, it's fine," I continued. I wrapped my fingers around my knee, forcing my leg to stop bouncing. "I don't mind pretending to be your fiancé. I'm happy to have dinner with your parents if you need."

"There's really no need—"

"Consider it a favor." I turned my chair toward her. I knew what had to be done—a favor for a favor. My mom couldn't take Jamey forever, and it was already becoming a hassle after only a few days. "And besides, I already know how you can pay me back."

Confusion rippled across her face before making the stark shift into angered shock. Her brows rose, her nostrils flared again, and god fucking dammit if I wasn't already confused about how I'd upset her again, I'd be transfixed on how cute she looked when she's mad.

She stood from her chair, purse clutched in one fisted hand. My mind spun, combing through thought after thought at how I'd said something offensive. "Are you fucking serious?" She hissed, the words icy and frigid, wrought with annoyance and a lack of patience. "What kind of woman do you think I am?"

I could physically feel it click in my mind.

"Whoa, whoa, hold on." I rolled my chair back a foot, putting some precious distance between us. "That's not what I meant—"

"Bullshit." The laugh that seeped from her wasn't one of joy or humor. No, it was angry, filled with contempt and shock and disbelief within herself. "Is this what you do with your patients? Get them all drugged up on whatever magic fertility potions you guys use and then fuck them?"

I wanted to laugh. It sounded like a joke, but from the look on her face, I knew damn well it wasn't. "Absolutely not. Can you let me explain?"

"No need," she seethed, taking one step toward the door. "I hope you enjoy bad reviews and legal action."

"Sophie—"

Metal crashed against metal. The chair she'd been in toppled, clanging against a cart with the blood testing kit atop it, sending it spinning. Her foot had caught, and I stood, crossing the distance faster than I thought I could. Down, down, down, she went toward the floor at lightning speed, and I couldn't think of anything other than grabbing her and wrapping my arms around her to avoid the fall.

With one hand on the small of her back and the other wrapped around her wrist as I'd done before, I held her minimal weight. Heart pounding and eyes wild, she stared up at me, her lips parted in shock and confusion as to how we'd ended up in the position we were in.

The temptation to press my lips to hers overwhelmed me at once, like a grease fire spreading, one that could only be tamped down, not put out. It was wrong and unprofessional, but there was a pull there, one that had hit me the first time I'd seen her that night checking her mail, one that hadn't left me since. She was intoxicating, even in her anger.

Righting us before I could get the chance to give in to temptation, I made sure she was steady on her feet before putting space between us again. I needed to breathe, to calm down, to regain control of myself so I didn't end up with a class-action lawsuit on my hands.

I pushed my hands through my hair, smoothing back the loose tendrils that had escaped around my face. "I just wanted to ask you to watch my son."

Her hand was on the door handle, a second from leaving, but she didn't look away from me.

"His nanny quit. I can't find anyone else. You're next door, and I heard you had babysitting experience and worked from home," I rapid-fired, hoping it would clear up the confusion long enough for her to stay. My breath was heavy, quick. *Why do you affect me like this?*

"You just want me to watch your kid?"

I nodded.

"Can I think about it?"

"Of course."

She turned the handle. "Okay. I'll, uh, make another appointment for my bloodwork."

I nodded as she opened the door, unable to take my eyes off her as she squeezed through, the door held half-closed by the chair on the floor. Despite everything, the IVF, the fake engagement, her goddamn hotheadedness, her angering curiosity—I just wanted her to come back. I wanted to drag her back in, wrap my arms around her, kiss her and fucking take her on the examining table, shredding the paper covering it like confetti as I buried myself inside of her.

This was bad.

This was really, horribly, fucking bad.

Chapter 6

Sophie

Tuesday

E ven the late-morning light filtering in through my upstairs window couldn't erase what had happened yesterday from my mind. The anxiety and adrenaline still pumped through my system, and I'd barely gotten any sleep last night. Instead, I'd spent the entirety of the early morning hours tossing and turning in bed before turning on the television, mindlessly flipping from one show to another trying to distract myself. I'd resisted the temptation of my vibrator not once, not twice, but three fucking times, because despite how insane it all was, I was annoyingly turned on by every thought of Dr. Brady.

Dr. Hudson fucking Brady.

Why was I bestowed the worst luck?

I wasn't one to feel regret often nor was I one to back myself out of opportunities. But as I paced across the tile floor in my bedroom, eyes glued to my full-length mirror across the space and the person reflecting back at me, I found myself wishing I hadn't acted the way I had yesterday. I'd jumped to conclusions—logical conclusions, to be fair—and painted him in a bad light. I'd accused him of arranging the entire thing as if he somehow already knew my intentions and plans. I'd been surprised, angry even, to see him the moment that door had opened.

And I'd closed it without a second thought.

The temptation to look out my window and into his backyard gnawed at the back of my mind even though I knew he wouldn't be there. He'd be at the practice, as the receptionist had so happily relayed when I asked for an appointment to do my bloodwork.

I stopped in front of the mirror, taking in every inch of my disheveled form, wrapped tightly in my plush robe. My hair, thrown up into a bun on the top of my head, had mostly fallen out of its ponytail holder and fell in strands around my face. The same face with sunken eyes and dark circles beneath them, my tell when I hadn't slept well.

Turning to the side, I kept my gaze locked on myself, and much like I did every morning, I imagined what I would look like with a little bump for a stomach, and then a larger one, and larger still until I pictured myself nine months pregnant, walking like a beached whale and complaining about how I was over it. I placed a hand against my flat abdomen, wishing I felt something, *anything*, but as that fucking pregnancy test had confirmed yesterday I wasn't pregnant.

I wanted to throw up, and I wished it was morning sickness.

After a shower, I made myself lunch because I'd woken far too late to call it breakfast, and forced myself to think about anything other than Hudson as I sat down to get some work done.

By the time an hour had passed, I'd drafted a new pattern for a dress that would sit nicely over a baby bump. I had to constantly remind myself that the dress would look nice without one as well because I desperately needed to keep my hopes grounded in realism. I knew Hudson was the best fertility doctor around. I'd done my research, and I'd searched up other clinics before landing on his, but I couldn't get my hopes up. It would be a miracle if I ended up pregnant at his hand.

Nope. No, do not think about him like that.

But I'd already gone down that road. I'd already spent the entire evening thinking about him, his hands on my body and in my hair, his cock inside of me and filling me so wholly that I never wanted to be empty again. I never should have looked out that stupid, godforsaken window.

I snorted at the idea that going to church with my parents would somehow erase that.

As I hand-sewed appliqués onto a custom dress a customer had ordered from me, my thoughts drifted again to my parents, and I ended up feeling slightly nauseous with the regret of involving Hudson at all, and the embarrassment from running across our lawns, barefoot and over-whelmed. It was one of those things that would undoubtedly keep me up in the middle of the night for years to come, long after I'd forgotten about Hudson and long after I had my own little one.

Grounded hopes, Sophie.

But realistically I did need a fake fiancé. At least until I managed to get pregnant. Then I could, theoretically, kill him off or make up a sob story about how he cheated on me so I left him. The idea of looking after Hudson's kid wasn't exactly unappealing. I'd seen him playing in the front yard before, had waved to him a few times, and found myself wanting to know his name and what he likes, found myself wanting to mother him the way I felt with practically every child I came across. Being broody had sent me down that spiral.

A knock at my door startled me, ripping me from my thoughts. I pressed pause on the playlist I had going and hopped up from my chair, nearly poking my finger with the needle as I stabbed it into the little pin cushion on my wrist. *Must be the shipment for that new chiffon I ordered.*

I slid across the smooth floor toward the door in my socks, my damp hair piled into another, neater bun on top of my head. I didn't mind delivery drivers seeing me makeupless, clad in my satin shorts and crop top, nipples poking at the cotton fabric. I'd been caught in less before, and considering I worked from the comfort of my own home, alone, I didn't see the need to dress up for them. But as I pulled the door open, I found myself deeply regretting my decisions.

Dr. Brady—Hudson—stared at me from my front stoop. The temptation to shut the door in his face was so powerful but I restrained myself.

I watched his eyes as they wandered up and down my body, from head to sock-covered toe, and felt more exposed than I did when I'd been caught staring at him through my bedroom window. He stood in his blue scrubs, his muscular arms on display and the fabric hugging far too tightly on his powerful thighs. His black hair, normally pushed back and away from his face, hung around his temples in waves, brightening the heavy green of his irises.

"What do you want?" I asked, the intended venom in my words nowhere to be found.

"I'm sorry to bother you," he started, pushing the loose

strands away from his face, making me almost miss them. "I had to leave work a little early today to relieve my mom of babysitting duties, and I figured I'd check in with you before heading inside. Can we chat?"

No. I should have said no, I should have shut the door. I could've hidden away, claimed I was too busy, but that stupid little part of myself that found him far more intriguing than I should have opened the door wider, gesturing with my hand to come in. Stupid. So, so stupid.

Hudson followed me inside. He closed the door behind him as I hopped back up on my stool, threading my needle once again, trying not to think about the fact that he was in my fucking house, too close for comfort again, stepping over some kind of boundary.

Unless fertility doctors had suddenly started making house calls.

"Have you given any thought to watching Jamey?"

Jamey. That was his name. It fit him perfectly. "Uh, a bit, but I haven't decided yet." I held the needle between my front teeth as I picked up another appliqué and held it against the dress form.

"I don't want you to feel like you have to say yes." He stood near the door, hands in his pockets, the muscles of his forearms flexing. I wondered if his hands were in fists. "I know you work from home, and that you're good with kids. It would work out well if you're up for it. I'd pay you, of course, and I think it would help with the whole fake fiancé thing."

He'd already told me this. Had he really stopped by my house just to reiterate what he'd said to me yesterday?

"I know this doesn't exactly help with the situation, but my parents are leaving for a cruise on Friday, and I really, really need someone to watch him. I've tried shifting my appointments around and getting the other doctors to take some of them, but I just can't make it work."

I glued my gaze to the appliqué, knowing damn well if I looked at him and those annoying, fascinating, puppy-dog-eyes any longer, I'd lose any sense of mind I still had. "I need to think about it, Dr. Brady."

"You know you can call me Hudson, right? You're my neighbor."

"You're also my doctor, apparently," I quipped.

Pain shot through my thumb and I gasped, realizing I'd shoved the needle right into the tip. I pulled it free, hissing in my breath, as blood pooled around my nail bed, smearing itself across the appliqué. The very, *very* expensive appliqué.

"Fucks sake," I mumbled, shoving my thumb into my mouth to control the bleeding.

I could hear his footsteps as they approached. My back steeled, my body going rigid, and I shoved the needle into the dress form in annoyance.

"Are you alright?"

"Fine," I said around my thumb, the word muffled and pointless. Hopping off the stool, I shuffled across the room to the open-plan kitchen, knocking the water faucet on with my free hand. Of course, he followed me.

"Are you bleeding?"

"No," I lied. I shoved my thumb under the running water, rinsing away the evidence.

The way he stared at me was fucking criminal. A combination of worry and smugness, the classic, manly 'let me help you.'

"There's blood on your lip."

I licked the drop of blood away. "No there isn't."

He leaned against the glazed wooden countertop across

from my sink on his elbows, lifting his head to get a better view of my thumb. "Stab it with the needle?"

"No," I lied again.

He reached into the little pocket on the front of his shirt, plucking out a band-aid and a little square of gauze. The perfect timing couldn't have annoyed me more.

"Why do you even have that?"

He chuckled as he flipped the handle for the faucet, turning off the water. "I'm a doctor, Sophie."

"Yeah, a fertility doctor. Surely you don't need band-aids every day." I sucked in a breath as he reached for my hand, grabbing my thumb and dragging my arm across the counter toward him, making my pulse skyrocket. He placed the gauze against the tiny puncture wound, drying it off. If his being in my house was crossing a boundary, then this was at least ten steps over the line, no matter how much it made my stomach flutter.

"I have to do a lot of blood work," he said, the words coming out slow and calm. The blood pushed out through the wound again, just a drop, and he wiped it away with the gauze. "And Jamey isn't the most coordinated."

I watched with bated breath as he unpackaged the band-aid, pressed the padded square against the hole in my skin, and wrapped the little flaps around my nail with gentle precision. It was such a nonchalant, normal thing, but it felt like something more, like I was being taken care of. That was a dangerous thing to feel with him, especially with more on the line than I originally thought. Not only was he my doctor, but now, he wanted me to be his nanny. And somehow not cross the boundaries that would be necessary for either of those things to work.

"Don't want you to get more blood on that pretty little

dress you're making," he murmured, finally letting go of my hand after what felt like far too long to be casual.

"Thanks," I whispered.

He nodded as he pulled himself back, creating a barrier once again. "Please think about it, Sophie. I'll keep looking around in the meantime, but I'll need a decision fairly soon."

I brought my arm to my chest, rubbing the skin around my wrist where he'd held it not once, not twice, but three fucking times now. "Okay."

Chapter 7

Hudson

Wednesday

The woman taking up the entirety of my screen, with her thick black hair and her rosy-red cheeks was nice enough, I'd give her that. But even as she spoke of her extensive experience with her younger siblings and her string of babysitting gigs throughout her teenage years, she didn't grab me.

Not like Sophie.

This was the third interview I'd done between appointments, and during every single one, I'd found my thoughts spiraling back to her. I couldn't remember the last time I'd fawned over a woman like I was with Sophie—not even my ex-wife. It had been easy with Becks, natural, but there'd never been that intense pull, that keep-me-up-in-the-middle-of-the-night ache. It was beginning to freak me out. I'd told myself over and over for the last two years that I didn't want another relationship, that I didn't need love to be happy. I could fuck and date and have fun and that was all I needed. But Jamey was getting older, was starting to realize that he didn't have something most other people did, and I knew it would break my heart worse than Becks did when Jamey eventually asked me why he didn't have a mom. I dreaded that day.

"Dr. Brady?"

Shit. I blinked away the thoughts, refocusing on the screen of my laptop, and a very confused... *what was her name? Emily?* staring back at me. I scrubbed my face with my hands, trying to chase away any lingering thoughts so I could focus. "I'm sorry, what did you say?"

"I asked how soon you would need me," she dead-panned. There was an air of impatience in her tone, and immediately, that told me everything I needed to know. I required someone patient, someone kind, who could handle my toddler and more importantly, me.

Someone like Sophie. Oh my god, I had to stop. Sophie was less patient with me than Emily, but that only excited me more. "Uh, if I were to hire you, I'd need an immediate start. Would that be something you could do?"

The video feed stuttered, pixelating her face for a moment, but her words came through clearly. "Oh, I'm going on vacation this weekend. I won't be back until next Friday."

I held my phone between my thumb and middle finger, spinning it around as I tapped it against the particleboard desk. "Unfortunately, Emily, I don't think that'll work."

The video feed sputtered back to life. She looked annoyed, with her thin, dark brows furrowed and her eyes squinted. "My name is Olivia." *God dammit.* "And you should really include the timeframe in your job posting so we don't both waste our time."

I sucked my teeth, forcing the annoyed words I wanted to say to stay behind my lips. This was going nowhere. "I did," I quipped. *You should have read the fucking requirements.* I shut the laptop, effectively ending the call, and rolled my desk chair back, needing to get myself away from the failed interview. I just couldn't deal with it anymore today—it was going to drive me insane, especially if I couldn't stop thinking about Sophie.

———

"Honey. I love you, but you can't just spring things on me."

I gnawed on the flesh of my cheek, my scrubs feeling too tight against my skin. Her voice sounded patient, kind, but so frustrated over the crackle of my cell phone. I wondered if Jamey had been a handful today. "I know, Mom," I sighed. "I'm sorry. It's a last-minute thing. I should only be an hour late at most." I hated lying to her. Genuinely. Even when I was a kid, I had a hard time keeping secrets to myself.

"It's fine. Just try to give me a heads-up a little earlier next time, okay? You know I love watching Jamey, but I've got to get home and pack."

"I know. I'll try to get out as quickly as I can." Another lie, and my palms became sweaty. I wiped them on the blue fabric covering my legs.

"Okay. Love you, Honey."

"Love you too."

I hung up the call and grabbed my bag from under my desk. Making my way down the hall and out the front door,

I shoved away the thoughts of nannies, my mom, and Sophie. I needed good ol' Hudson and Nathan time, a nice glass of whiskey, and a silent mind. I figured I'd only get two of those, though.

I'd sent him a text an hour ago, asking if he was free for a drink after work, about two minutes after hanging up the call with the last interviewee. I needed to unwind, and I had a distinct feeling that if I tried to at home, even after Jamey went to bed, I'd just find myself in front of Sophie's house.

That on its own was enough to send me into madness.

The drive to the bar was surprisingly quick despite the traffic, and as I parked my Mercedes, the buzz of seeing Nathan hit me. It had been at least a month, if not more. I didn't see him nearly enough, and Jamey always asked about him. We'd gone to university together, both studying medicine and the female anatomy—he'd ended up as a gynecologist.

His big-ass head was easy to spot as I walked inside the bar. His familiar caramel skin wrinkled with a smile as I stepped up to the bar, settling myself on the barstool next to him. Eyes as bright as Sophie's, and just as blue, met mine.

"Hey, man," he grinned, his left hand patting the space between my shoulder blades. "Long time, no see."

I gave him a half smile as I rattled off my order to the bartender: Lagavulin, neat, two fingers. "I know. I almost feel bad asking to meet up, though. I've got some shit going on and good god, do I need to talk about it," I laughed. "But, more importantly, how's Izabel? The girls?"

"Yeah, yeah, good, man. Iz just got a promotion at work, so that's exciting. Devin's entering the school's talent show this year, so it's been non-stop practice with her singing some Taylor Swift song every second of every hour. I've invested in a pair of really nice noise-canceling headphones." He knocked back a shot before requesting another, and I hoped he didn't think this was going to be a get-wasted-and-forget-our-problems kind of evening. "And Caroline is finally out of diapers, thank God."

"I completely understand that struggle," I chuckled. I took a heavy sip of the fiery alcohol, coating my throat enough to push the thought of Sophie's pretty lips to the side. "Jamey was still wearing pull-ups at night until he was two and a half. I'm so happy that I never have to look at another diaper again."

The slow, easy jazz playing over the speakers, mixed with the drink in my hand, was enough to relax the tension in my shoulders, my neck. I hadn't even realized how much I'd been straining them, and I knew damn well I would feel it when I worked out next. I rolled my head to the side, forcing a crack from my spine.

"So what's going on with you, Huds? What's driving you so insane that you needed to see me?"

I groaned and scrubbed my face with my hands, trying to figure out where to even start. I needed to talk about all of it—from the fake engagement to finding Jamey a nanny—and deep down I knew I needed to talk about how I couldn't get Sophie out of my fucking head.

———

Nathan's silence hung in the air like a goddamn storm cloud.

I gritted my teeth as I lifted the nearly-finished glass of

whiskey to my lips. I knew what was coming. "Just say it, Nathan."

"Have you considered..."

"Yes," I interjected.

"...that you might..."

I swallowed, letting the burn soothe my spiraling thoughts.

"...like her?"

There it is. "Absolutely not." I set my glass down, my grip on it far too tight, almost dangerously so. I didn't want to consider that, but of course, I had. It had been floating around in my head for days now, always there, hiding in the recesses of my mind and poking me with a fucking stick.

"Look, I know that's not the kind of thing you want. I know that thinking of anyone like that after Becks is difficult for you—"

"Don't." I sucked in a breath through my teeth, wishing I hadn't finished my drink so quickly. "It's not even an option."

"Maybe playing house with the girl isn't such a bad idea. Maybe it'll help you get over some of that pent-up anger over Becks. Don't close yourself off, Huds."

Dragging my tongue along my incisors, I slid the glass across the bar toward the bartender. He lifted it toward the shelf, offering me a refill, but I shook my head, making the move to get up. I had to get home. I had to relieve my mom, I had to see my son, and I had to talk to Sophie. *Wait, where did that come from?*

"Hudson—"

I turned to Nathan, a tight smile across my lips. "Thanks for the advice, really. But I've been closed off for years now, and I don't expect that to change anytime soon."

———

The sky was already pitch-black by the time I pulled up my driveway. My headlights illuminated Sophie's condo, casting beams of light straight into her lit living room, creating shadows that gave her presence away.

Even though I knew my mom had seen me arrive, even though I knew Jamey would be bouncing in excitement because I was home, I couldn't bring myself to walk to my door. I didn't even realize what I had done until the car door shut behind me and I was halfway across my lawn, my sights set on Sophie's door, that gnawing sensation in my brain gaining control of me.

Before I could blink, I was on her porch, hand raised and ready to knock, hovering an inch from her door. *What the fuck am I doing? I should go home. I shouldn't be here.* Soft footsteps echoed behind the door and I froze, unable to back away.

The handle twisted and I dropped my arm. I hadn't even knocked yet, *had she been watching me?*

Sophie's face was backlit as she pulled the door open just enough for her head. Even in the low light, her eyes shone like fucking diamonds. "What are you doing here, Dr. Brady?"

A lump caught in my throat at the sound of her voice. *So goddamn perfect.* "It's Hudson. And I just wanted to check in with you."

"I haven't made any decisions yet, and I'm kind of busy right now."

My lips tipped up at the edge. *Caught.* "Busy?"

Her gaze hardened as she looked me up and down. "Yes. Busy."

"Doing what, exactly?" I pressed, taking a step toward the door. She backed up, making a move to shut it, but I slid my foot between the door and the frame, stopping that action dead in its tracks.

"Dr. Brady," she hissed.

"It sure seemed like you weren't busy when you came to the door," I continued, leaning one hand on the handle. "I didn't even knock, Sophie. Were you watching me? Again?"

The blush that spread across her cheeks was obvious even in the low light. Her mouth parted, her breath caught, and fuck, why did she have to do that? Why did it twist something in my chest, turning me more neanderthal than modern man? All I could think of was her under me, over me, those perfect lips parted so perfectly—

"That would be incredibly inappropriate," she breathed, taking another step back, relinquishing her hold on the door. The warm glow of the room lit her features, increasing the desire I felt for her.

I stepped through, letting myself into her living room, the door opened wide behind me. "Probably about as inappropriate as me showing up at your house unannounced," I said, my voice dropping an octave without me even trying, "or stripping off my clothes when I knew someone was watching."

Another step back, and she collided with the back of the couch, her hand grabbing onto the plush fabric to hold herself steady. "Dr. Brady."

"Hudson," I corrected again.

"I haven't made a decision yet about Jamey."

Do I make you nervous?

I slid my lower lip between my teeth, nodding my acceptance. "And the fake engagement?"

She breathed in, slow and steady, and I wondered if it was to calm herself or just to feign confidence. "I don't know yet," she whispered. "Give me a day or two."

I couldn't keep my eyes off of her as she crossed one leg over the other, holding her thighs together. She was wearing shorts, the same ones she'd worn when she'd picked up the mail last week. Her legs, long and lean and dotted with the occasional freckle, swam around in my mind. *What would they look like wrapped around my hips?*

"Do you have a piece of paper?" I asked, my voice much lighter than I expected considering the images running through my head. "And a pen?"

She blinked at me, her brows furrowing, but nodded. I watched her body as she padded across the floor on bare feet toward her massive work table, covered in strips of fabric, two different sewing machines, and a roll of brown paper. She plucked a pen from a desk organizer and tore off a small sheet of paper from the roll, laying both out on the desk. She motioned for me to come closer to her, to use the pen and paper, and all my cock wanted to do was take that in a way I knew she didn't mean.

Pen clutched in my shaking hand, I scribbled out my phone number in my neatest handwriting and my name below it.

"Call me when you decide, Sophia."

I didn't wait for a response. I had to get out of there before I did something I knew I'd regret later.

Chapter 8

Sophie

Thursday

I'd spent yet another night tossing and turning in my bed, hardly getting an ounce of sleep. I stared at the time on my phone, watching it tick by, minute by minute, and then hour by hour. By the time it had reached seven a.m., I knew I wasn't going to get anything more than maybe a nap later on.

I hadn't been able to stop thinking about Hudson all night. He'd called me out last night—I *had* been watching, since the moment his car pulled into his driveway, and even before that. I glanced out my window far too many times between the hours of five and six p.m.

Rolling out of bed, I slid my robe over my shoulders and tightened the strap, not wanting to give Hudson anything to look at if he decided to spy on me, too. I made my way down the stairs, eyes bleary and puffy from my lack of sleep, and started on a cup of coffee.

I could feel the slip of paper taunting me.

Out of the corner of my eye, I could see it, sitting right where he'd left it before he'd walked out without even saying goodbye. His shockingly neat handwriting for a doctor was angled toward the door, and it was almost as if I could feel him through it, waiting desperately for me to call him.

A part of me wanted to help him. To call him, to tell him I would watch Jamey, that I could handle the extra workload on top of my business. I could, and I knew that because I'd spent at least an hour doing the math in my head while I was trying to sleep.

But the other part, the more wary part, knew it wouldn't be a good idea. That part knew I was attracted to him, worryingly so, and that the tension between us would eventually need an outlet. But did I want to get involved? Especially when a little boy was caught in the mix? As far as I could tell, he didn't have a mom around. Would he get attached? Would I?

My head spun as I leaned against the counter, sipping my coffee. Hudson was an enigma, and a goddamn annoying one at that. Did I want more of that in my life? More stress, more confusion, on top of trying for a baby? No, absolutely not.

So why did I type those stupid fucking numbers into my phone?

It rang once. Twice. Three times, and the phone crackled to life. But the voice on the other end wasn't what I was expecting—no, it was much smaller, much higher, and much cuter.

"Hi, Grandma!"

I didn't know what to say. It was Jamey, definitely, but why did he think I was his Grandma?

"Hello?" He asked when my silence hadn't been enough for him.

"Uh, hi, Jamey. This isn't your Grandma," I said, biting my lip to keep from laughing.

"Why?"

I chuckled, glancing over toward Hudson's house. Through an open window, I caught a glimpse of a tall, muscular form, covered by a thin, tight-fitting long-sleeve shirt and blue scrubs on his bottom half. He looked like he was picking up something from the floor. "Can you bring the phone to your dad?"

"Okay," he chirped. I could hear the sound of shuffling, followed by tiny footsteps. "Daddy! The lady said she's not my grandma!"

Hudson's deep voice was too muffled to hear, but he was standing straight now from what I could see, his back to me as he looked down at his son.

"I dunno. Why isn't it Grandma?" Jamey complained.

More muffling, more shuffling, and the phone switched hands. I watched him as he looked at the number on the screen before raising it to his ear.

"Hello, Sophie." *That's the voice I wanted to hear.*

I watched as he turned toward the window, his eyes locking with mine through the reflective glass. I bit down on the nail of my thumb, searching for the words I wanted to say, but coming up empty.

"I'll do it," I said quietly.

His sigh of relief was audible even through the phone, and I could see every drop of stress melt away in his body. "Does that mean the uh..." He lowered his voice. "...fake engagement is a go?"

Sighing, I leaned forward with my elbows on the counter, toward the window. "I don't know yet."

He took a few steps toward his, sidestepping something on the floor, and looked directly at me. It made goosebumps pop up all over my skin, forcing a shiver up my spine. "That's okay. When can you start?"

"Today." I glanced at the time on the microwave and looked back at him. "Give me thirty minutes to get dressed and grab my stuff."

"Perfect. I need to leave at eight-thirty, so I can at least give you a tour of the house and show you where everything is before I need to go."

"Okay. I'll see you then."

A short pause. It felt like an hour as he stood there, eyes locked on me, a little grin spreading across his lips. "Sophie?"

"Yes?"

"Are you doing that on purpose?"

What the fuck is he—

I glanced down, confused. My cheeks warmed as if I'd been drinking when I realized that the top of my robe had come loose, and in my leaning position on the countertop with my biceps against my chest, I'd parted the fabric on one side.

My entire left breast was out.

"Oh my god."

His laughter boomed, forcing the butterflies in my stomach to take flight and make me nauseous. "It's okay, really," he choked through his fits of chuckles.

I covered myself immediately, standing straight to glare at him for even daring to look. "Fucking perv."

"We're even now," he grinned, but even with the sun reflecting on his window, I could still see a tint of red on his cheeks. "And that freckle on your nipple is cute."

"Oh my god, I'm going to kill you."

62

His smile spread wider, and I turned, no longer wanting to look at him. It would be hard enough seeing him face to face in thirty minutes; I didn't want another second ruined by his creeping stare. "I'll see you in half an hour," he said, and the call dropped.

———

It had never felt more important to cover myself up.

Knowing damn well I'd be on my hands and knees playing with a four-year-old for at least half the day, I went with my tried-and-tested black joggers, a tight-fitting tank top, and a loose, white knit cardigan that I assumed I'd need to take off if Jamey insisted on painting or something.

It also left everything to the imagination for when I had to see his father.

Sliding my slippers on, I grabbed my laptop from its spot on my workstation, making my way out the door and across our conjoined lawns. The sun was already blazing in the sky, warming up the day and chasing away the chill in the air from the night before. It wasn't enough to calm the shaking of my hands, though.

Hudson opened the door before I could even approach, and I wondered if he had one of those fancy doorbells with the live video feed that alerted when someone was nearby. I did my best not to make eye contact as I shuffled past him and in through the open door, a timid Jamey hiding behind his father's legs.

"Jamey," Hudson said softly, turning at the waist as he closed the door behind me. I watched every muscle in his abdomen ripple as he twisted, the tight white shirt doing little to hide what lay beneath. "This is Sophie. She's going to watch you today."

I set my laptop down on the entryway table and knelt down to his height, getting a good look at him. He looked so much like Hudson it was crazy. Same bright green eyes, same dark mop of hair on top of his head. It was a little lighter than Hudson's, though, and I wondered if that came from his mom. He was absolutely adorable, and I felt that familiar, hungry ache break open just a little bit more in my chest. I wanted one like him.

"Hi, Jamey," I grinned, holding out my hand for him to shake. He backed away a little. "I'm your neighbor. You've waved at me a few times, remember?"

"Yeah," he said softly, so quietly I almost didn't hear him.

"I know it's a bit scary to meet new people." I glanced up at Hudson, trying not to pay attention to how I was nearly at eye level with his hips and what sat between them. "I don't want you to feel like you have to be okay with it right away, alright? We can hang out when you feel comfortable. Until then, I'll be around, just like your dad, keeping an eye on you."

Jamey nodded as he buried his face into the back of his father's scrubs.

I stood up straight, taking a solid first look around the massive house. The floor was a dark hardwood, polished to a shine, complimented by the varying grays on the walls. The kitchen, which sat at the back of the house, looked as though it was carved straight from marble—marble countertops, marble flooring, even the sink appeared to be marble. The room to my left was the one I'd seen Hudson in that morning, and I could hear children's cartoons playing on the television in there. I found myself wondering what Hudson's room looked like, and immediately wiped the thought from my memory. *I'm not mixing these things together. I can't.*

"How about you go finish your cereal, okay bud? I'm just going to show Sophie around the house," Hudson said, his large hand resting firmly on his son's back.

Jamey's eyes popped open as he looked up at his dad. "Don't show her my room! I want to."

I couldn't keep myself from watching as Hudson's smile grew, lighting up his annoyingly handsome face. He looked so much less intimidating when he was being a parent. Being happy.

"Okay, okay, I won't show her your room," he laughed. He ushered Jamey toward the room to our left, and Jamey left a solid chunk of space between him and me as he passed. I knew it would take him a little bit to open up to me —I was used to that, considering the string of babysitting jobs I'd done before starting my business. He was on the shy side, and I could definitely break through that with enough time.

Luckily, I had all day.

Hudson walked me from room to room on the ground floor of the house, from the kitchen to the living room, to the *second* living room, the piano room, the spare room, his office, the garage with his three fancy-ass cars. He showed me the laundry room and how it connected to the gym, which I'd assumed he didn't have from how he'd been working out outside the day that I... *no, do not think about that, Sophie.*

He was incredibly professional when he needed to be, and I wondered if it was an act he was putting on because I was in his home, looking after his child for the day. I was an unknown nanny—he hadn't even asked for any references, for Christ's sake. He clearly wanted to make a good impression, and so did I.

"So, where do you keep the first aid kit? Just in case."

Hudson turned to me, one foot on the first step of the staircase. The mask slipped, only for a second, and I caught a glance of something unreadable in his features. "It's, uh, in my room. I'll show you."

I nodded wordlessly and followed him up to the equally large second floor. There was a huge open landing that overlooked the kitchen and second living room of the downstairs area, and surrounding it was a slew of doors. The one toward the end was larger than the rest, a grander double door, and I could only guess that was the master suite.

Hudson pushed the doors open, and holy hell, his room was massive. A large, black, four-poster bed sat in the middle of the far wall, the sheets barely messed up from when he'd gotten out of bed. The wall that faced his backyard was glass, two massive hanging curtains lining the edges, looking out over the expanse of his property and across the lake. From where I stood, I could almost see my own bedroom window through it.

Could he see into it from the corner of his room?

Heat warmed my cheeks as I silently followed him through the room and into his adjoining ensuite bathroom. Marble again. The tub, the sink, the floor. The glass shower sat recessed into the house's front wall, large enough for a hockey team to shower together, with two rainfall shower heads on either end and a marble bench that stretched the length of it. It made my shower-tub combo look tiny in comparison.

Don't imagine him in it.

Don't imagine you in it with him, Sophie.

"Here we go," he said, cutting through the heated

images beginning to form in my head. I'd never been more grateful to hear him speak.

He held up a medium-sized basket, filled to the brim with medical supplies. I'd been expecting a simple, fold-open box with the basics but really, I should have assumed more from a doctor.

"Anything you could possibly need is in here."

"Yeah, if I can find it," I quipped, looking through the clear sides into the layers upon layers of band-aids, gauze, alcohol wipes, medicine, burn cream... goddamn, I could fit my whole house in there.

He leveled a glare at me as he slid the box back under the sink cabinet. "If you need anything at all, or there's an emergency, or you get confused—"

"Yeah, yeah, call you. I know the drill, Dr. Brady."

His jaw hardened. "Hudson."

———

Slowly, painstakingly slowly, Jamey came out of his shell.

The shy little boy I'd met earlier that morning had come up to me around ten a.m. and asked if I'd paint with him. I had enough time in my schedule for the day, so I was happy to join him.

By noon, he finally showed me his room. It was decked out with science toys, from a working telescope to a constellation tracker. His ceiling had been painted black, and little, glow-in-the-dark stars were stuck all over it, glowing bright when he turned the lights off and shut his black-out curtains.

Around one o'clock, he begged me to make him lunch. I'd made mac and cheese with chicken nuggets, and he'd squealed in excitement when I served it to him.

At three, he asked me to play tag with him in the back-yard, and I had to pretend that I couldn't run as fast as I really could. I let him win most of the rounds.

When the clock finally struck five, we were so deep in a game of hide-and-seek that I'd hardly gotten any of my work done. Jamey had hidden somewhere that I couldn't find, and my exploration had left me more familiar with the house. I'd found a closet that I thought was a room, filled with junk and boxes, and when I'd gone searching behind them for the four-year-old in question, I'd accidentally knocked one of them over.

The contents spilled onto the floor, and in my desperate attempt to reassemble the box of random items as best I could, I couldn't help but notice a small wooden frame lying face down. On the back, scribbled in pen along the MDF backing read: *Becks and Jamey, Jamey's First Birthday.*

The sinking feeling in my gut told me I shouldn't look. It told me that it would be an invasion of privacy, a crossing of a boundary I desperately needed to put in place. But I couldn't help myself.

I picked up the frame, turning it over in my hands.

A gorgeous blonde woman smiled brightly for the camera, a baby boy with a thick mop of black hair in her lap. Jamey was mid-clap with cake smeared across his fingers and his mouth, a discarded birthday candle off to the side of the frame. The woman—Becks, I'm assuming—was the polar opposite of me. Clear, unfreckled skin. Bright blonde, almost white, hair. Sharp brown eyes, creased at the edges from her wide smile. She was stunning.

The sound of footsteps in the doorway didn't make me

turn as quickly as it should have. In my defense, I thought it was Jamey, finally coming out of his hiding spot to announce that he had won. But when I turned, the photo still clutched in my grasp, I found Hudson.

I could feel every ounce of blood drain from my face as I took him in, all six-foot-something of him. "I-I'm so sorry," I muttered, fumbling as I tried to put the frame back into the box before he could see. There had to be a reason she was in here, in a box, hidden from the world. There weren't any photos of her around the house.

Hudson swallowed, his jaw twitching as he watched me. My brain scrambled under his stare, all sense leaving my mind.

"Who...?"

"Becks," he said, his voice quiet, almost solemn. "Jamey's mom."

"Is she...?"

"No." He shook his head as he took a step toward me. There was nowhere for me to go without knocking anything else over. "Last I heard, she is very much alive and on the other side of the country. Out of our lives."

Even in his scrubs, even as unreadable as he looked with his hair falling around the edges of his face and his chin hard set, his closeness made something low in my gut spring to life. I'd been caught doing something I absolutely shouldn't have, so why on earth was I unable to tear my gaze from his perfect lips, his straight nose, his glaringly green eyes?

"I'm sorry," I whispered again. I didn't know what else to say.

"Sophieeeee! I win!"

Little feet padded hard against the wood floor as Jamey raced down the hallway. He stepped around his dad, not

69

even saying hello, and latched onto my hand with his two little ones.

"Come on, come on, come on. It's your turn to hide."

Hudson's face softened as he watched Jamey put all of his tiny strength into dragging me toward the doorway. "You little squirt," he started, leaning down and grabbing Jamey beneath his arms. He lifted him high, flipped him around, and brought him into his chest. "Didn't even say hi to me. You've wounded me, bud."

Jamey giggled as his dad placed little kisses on his cheeks, his head. "Hi, Dad. Sophie's really bad at hide-and-seek."

Hudson turned his sights on me as he settled Jamey into the crook of his hip. "You know, last I checked, if you're the seeker you shouldn't be hiding in a closet full of junk."

"Oh, I wasn't, I was looking for—"

"A likely story." He gave me a wink, and if I wasn't already flooded with adrenaline, I might have collapsed. "Come on, Jamey. No use in all of us hanging out in here. We can leave Sophie to snoop all she wants."

"I swear I wasn't—"

"I know." He laughed, full and true, and I wondered if he really hadn't minded at all. He shifted Jamey's weight as he watched me, a leftover grin holding his lips apart. "Do you want to stay for dinner after I get home tomorrow night? If you can watch Jamey, I mean."

He wants me to watch Jamey again? After catching me deep in his personal things? "Oh, uh, yeah, I can watch him."

"And dinner?"

I bit my lip as I looked between the two of them. Jamey's eyes were locked on mine, big and round as he stuck out his lower lip, silently begging me to stay. I didn't want to say no to that alone, but it was Hudson's voice and the way he looked at me as if I was some kind of savior from above, that made me say yes.

I knew it was a bad idea. A horrible one, in fact, a boundary-crossing one. But god fucking dammit, I couldn't help myself.

"Okay."

Chapter 9

Hudson

Friday

The alert on my phone woke me up from what had easily been the best sleep I'd had in over a week. I could breathe again, I could think again, without the constant worry of finding someone to watch Jamey. Had I tossed and turned a little thinking about someone I absolutely shouldn't have been thinking of while I stroked my cock? Yes. But I'd gotten some real, serious rest afterward.

The curtains along my windowed wall parted automatically, drawing back and illuminating the room with the fresh morning sunshine. I grabbed my phone from my bedside table as the alarm beeped quietly from somewhere under my bed. Apparently I must have snoozed it too aggressively.

I opened the notification on my phone, my bleary, sleepy eyes not focusing. Immediately, my screen filled with the live video feed from my front door. Sophie stood there, bouncing back and forth on her toes in what I could only assume was nervousness, her laptop clutched in one hand and her sweater clinging to her chest. In the haze of sleep, I watched her for a moment, my eyes devouring every inch of her. *Those fucking leggings.*

It took me far too long to acknowledge she was there.

Finally, I pressed the talk button on the feed. "Hey," I said, the gruff of sleep heavy in my voice. Her brows furrowed as she looked for the source of the sound, eyes finally landing on the little camera pointed at her.

"Are you still in bed, Dr. Brady?"

"No," I lied. I pushed the covers off, my hardened length springing up from morning wood, and brought my phone along as I started my search for literally anything to cover my naked body. "Been up for hours."

She snorted as she rolled back and forth from heel to toe. "Can you let me in, then?"

I glanced at the time. Shit, it was eight-fifteen. *How long had she been waiting?* I tapped the screen, unlocking the door with the click of a button. "Come on in, Sophie. Just don't come upstairs."

"Gladly."

Exiting the app, I heard the door downstairs open and close. Down the hall, Jamey's door opened, and tiny feet padded heavily on the wood as he raced down the stairs. Clearly, he'd been up for a little while, but surprisingly he didn't wake me up, which was something he usually did.

Sliding on the first pair of boxers I could find, I thought of puppies and baby chickens as I raced to put on my scrubs, desperately attempting to drive away my blaring erection. I brushed my teeth while combing my hair, nearly dragging a toothpaste-laden brush through it, then raced down the stairs in record time.

Sophie stood at the kitchen sink, her back to me, as she chatted with Jamey about what he wanted to do that day. My gaze locked onto the way her leggings rounded her ass, hugging her form so enticingly it was a fucking sin.

"Daddy said there's a fair. Can we go to that?" Jamey asked around a mouthful of cereal, his bare toes pressed firmly against the marble island in front of him. "Please, Sophie? Can we please?"

"A fair?"

Jamey's eyes lit up as he noticed me. "Daddy!" He twisted in his seat, his little feet dangling from the high-top chair, and slowly climbed down the way I'd taught him before taking off in my direction. Wrapping my arms around his small frame, I lifted him up, holding him to my chest as he giggled.

"Morning, bud." I pressed a kiss against the side of his head, just above his ear. "Why didn't you wake me up this morning?"

"I was busy."

Busy? I couldn't help the laugh that crawled up through my chest. Sophie turned to us, wiping her damp hands on the kitchen towel she'd slung over her shoulder. She raised one brow as she took in my disheveled, just-woken-up look.

"What could you have possibly been busy with?" I asked him, burying my nose in the mop of his hair.

Jamey's voice dropped, so silent I could barely hear him. "I made something for Sophie."

He made something for Sophie.

I pursed my lips together to hide the smile I knew I couldn't keep down. He'd warmed to her *that* much already, enough to make her something? It was probably a picture he colored or some badly folded-up piece of paper he thought looked like a flower. Whatever it was, I knew it'd be adorable. I nearly flinched as I felt something inside of me crack, only a hair, but I shoved it away before it could form into a thought. Jamey had made something for Sophie. He liked having her around, he liked her watching after him.

Would it be so bad if I liked that too?

I pulled Jamey back, over-expressing my surprise with my face. "You made her something?" I whispered. He nodded quickly, ferociously, his baby teeth on full display. "That's so nice of you. I'm sure she'll love whatever it is."

He wiggled his feet, asking to be put down, and I obliged.

"Sophie," I called, watching as her gaze snapped to me and out of whatever daydream she'd been caught in. "I've got to get to work. I'll pick up some pizzas on my way home—"

"Pizza?"

Jamey's shriek was enough to make my ears bleed. That boy loved pizza so much he would probably die for it, and I realized the fatal mistake I'd made in my exhaustion—I knew that Jamey wouldn't shut up about pizza until he got to eat it. Poor Sophie.

"Pizza!"

I grinned as I grabbed my keys and slid my feet into my work Crocs. "Good luck with him!" I called over my shoulder.

———

Ten minutes after I'd walked through the doors of the clinic and settled myself in my office, my phone buzzed in my pocket. I knew it was Sophie without even looking. I had a patient coming in at any moment, but I couldn't stop my twitching hand from fishing out my phone. I wanted to know what she'd said, wanted to text her back. I wanted to chat with her.

Jamey won't shut up about pizza.

Please send help.

I snorted. I really shouldn't have said anything about pizza in front of Jamey, but my damn filter wasn't working very well that morning. I quickly shot back a reply.

RIP to your sanity, little voyeur.

Three little dots danced on the bottom of my screen immediately, telling me she was typing out a response. I watched them with far too much anticipation and far too little regard for the fact that my office door had opened. I only noticed when two pairs of shoes appeared in my line of sight, one heeled and one in leather loafers. I pocketed my phone immediately, apologizing for my actions, but I didn't mean a single word of it.

The sun was only just beginning to set as I loaded my Mercedes with three large pizzas. I didn't know what to get Sophie and knew damn well that my anticipation to see her would only get worse if I called or texted to ask, so I'd gone with my gut and gotten her plain ol' pepperoni.

Despite having a fairly good day at work—I didn't have

76

to deliver any bad news and instead only gave good news and good outcomes—it still felt like purgatory. I'd found my thoughts weaving back toward Sophie, thinking about her in my house with my son, looking forward to seeing her when I got home. It was enough to drive me insane. I'd nearly had to jerk off in the toilet at lunchtime because I couldn't stop thinking about her goddamn ass in those leggings earlier that morning.

As I drove the short distance between my house and the pizzeria, I told myself that I'd make sure Sophie would be out of the house before Jamey went to bed. That left us two hours from the time I walked in the door until she definitely had to leave. I knew it wasn't a good idea to be alone with her. I didn't trust myself not to cross that boundary line we needed.

The boundary line *I* needed.

Jamey was on me the moment I walked through the door, nearly knocking the pizzas out of my hands as he ran into my leg. "Pizza!"

He wrapped his little arms around the muscles of my thigh and calf, securing himself to me, and I walked across the entryway with him standing on my foot for support. Sophie stood in the kitchen, her brown hair a mess and freckles shining in the reflection of the setting sun. She looked exhausted.

"Thank god you're home," she sighed, leaning forward on the island and burying her face in her hands. "He's been nonstop talking about pizza for... geez, it's six? Ten hours."

I laughed as I set the boxes down in front of her. "I'm sorry," I said, my lips tipping up on one side in a smirk. "I thought you were capable of handling a four-year-old."

The smack she levied against my chest surprised me. "I am. But you sabotaged it."

"Oh, don't be so dramatic, Sophie. He couldn't have been that bad." Jamey unlatched himself from my thigh and ran to his spot at the dining table, practically vibrating in excitement.

"He hasn't eaten anything since breakfast," Sophie deadpanned.

"What? Why?"

"He refused to eat until he got pizza."

I chuckled as I took out a plate for Jamey, loading it up with a couple of slices of cheese pizza and a little dipping pot of ranch. "I'm sorry," I admitted, actually meaning it. "I won't tell him we're having pizza again that early in the day."

She slid her hands down her face, groaning as she stood up straight. "Thank you."

"Wine?"

"God, yes."

———

I'd done exactly what I told myself I wouldn't. I'd let her stay.

Jamey had spent the entirety of dinner talking our ears off, telling me about his day with Sophie and how much he loved her. They'd played something he'd named tickle monster, which in reality was just hide-and-seek but if you were found you got tickled. They'd apparently also played hair salon, and Jamey had tried to braid Sophie's hair, thus explaining Sophie's messy tresses.

He'd been so exhausted from his excitement that he'd

passed out on the couch ten minutes after we finished eating. I'd insisted that she could head home as I held Jamey limp and asleep in my arms, but she'd said she wanted to finish cleaning up, that she didn't feel right about leaving the house a mess. It wasn't a mess though, and I should have pushed her to go home. When I'd come back downstairs after getting changed into lounge clothes and tucking Jamey into bed, Sophie was on my couch with a new glass of wine in her hands.

I was in serious, horrendous trouble.

"I thought you were heading back to your place?"

She rubbed the skin of her neck, a little blush rushing to her cheeks. *It's just the alcohol. Don't get your hopes up.* "I thought we could, like, chat. Or something. I don't know." *Fuck.*

"You want to hang out with me?" I smirked, plucking my glass from the side of the sink and filling it anew. "You could have just asked."

She rolled her eyes as I plopped down on the sofa next to her. "I just thought that since I'm spending so much time here, we should probably get to know each other better. I mean, I could be an axe murderer for all you know, and you have me watching your son."

"Hmm," I pondered, taking a sip of my wine. "I don't get axe murderer when I look in your eyes though. Stalker? Maybe. Voyeur? Absolutely."

Her blush spread further, covering her cheeks and creeping down her neck. "That was an accident."

"Oh, come on. We both know it wasn't an accident."

She went silent as she stared into her glass of wine, watching her reflection ripple in her unsteady hand, before suddenly breaking out in a half-winded giggle. It was odd, seeing her like that. The wall she seemed to have put up had come down half an inch, erasing the uncomfortable tension that was building. "You're right," she admitted, hiding her smile behind her glass. "It wasn't an accident. But it was a mistake, so we can move on from it."

We should *move on from it. So why don't I want to?*

"Can I ask you something, Hudson?"

My gaze locked on hers the moment she said my name. I hadn't needed to correct her, and I wondered if it was just the three glasses of wine she'd had or if it was something more. Either way, it set off an alert in my gut, a stirring of blood where it shouldn't go. "Yeah," I breathed.

"Do you ever think about having more kids? I mean, you work in a fertility clinic. Surely seeing all those happy faces makes you want to feel it yourself," she said, her blue eyes flicking between my own and my lips. "I know it would for me."

"No," I answered, and judging by the flinch she gave, it wasn't the answer she expected. "I'm happy with Jamey. He's my entire world, you know? I'd do anything for that little squirt. So I don't really see a need to change that. Being able to give that good news to my patients is enough for me."

She nodded as she took in my answer, processing it like she did when she'd realized I'd gotten her pepperoni pizza. *That's my favorite,* she'd said. *How did you know?*

"Have you given any more thought to the fake engagement?" I asked, trying to cut the silence with the first thing that popped up into my mind. "It's the least I can do in exchange for you watching Jamey."

She lifted a single brow. "I thought you were paying me."

"Well, that too."

For a moment she seemed to get lost in her thoughts

again. I'd never wanted to read someone's mind more in my life as I watched her part her lips, her tongue running across the length of her teeth. "I just don't know if we can pull it off."

"Yeah, that's fair," I lied, putting on my best smile as she looked back at me. *I just want to push her buttons. She looks so fucking hot when she's annoyed.* "It's just not believable. I'm way out of your league."

Her mouth popped open, her brows furrowing. "Asshole," she laughed, shifting herself until she was on her knees facing me, the plush cushion dipping below her. "I am *so* within your league. In fact, I'm out of *your* league. You wish you could get a fiancée like me."

"You think?" I chuckled, downing the last of my glass. I was going to need it. "Is that why you flashed me from your window yesterday morning?"

She struggled to keep her laughter at bay, her mouth going into a thin line that tipped up at the edges as she tried to hold it back. "Now *that* really was an accident."

Her hand reached out to push me, her body moving too fast for the glass of wine she held. The blood-red liquid tipped over the edge, half landing on my chest and half landing on the black sofa beneath us, creating an even darker patch of dampness.

When I looked back at her, she'd paled. "I'm so sorry," she said, her eyes wide and her hand stuck in place against my chest. "Oh my god. Oh my god, okay, uh, I'll clean this up."

"Sophie—"

"No, no, I've got this." She set the remaining wine on the table and scrambled from her seat, rushing to the kitchen. She came back with a roll of paper towels clutched in her hand, the panic on her face only growing. "I can buy you a new shirt. The couch, though…"

"Sophie, the couch is fine—"

"How much was your shirt? Actually, don't answer that." She unspooled a few strips of the absorbent material and balled them in her hand, pressing the wad into the damp patch on the couch. "Just send me a link or something, it'll be fine."

Without thinking, I wrapped my hand around her wrist, holding her hand in place against the couch. Her pulse raced below my fingers. "Sophia. It's fine," I said sternly, dragging her attention back to me. "I got a black couch specifically because Jamey spills shit all the time. You can't even see it. It's fine."

She blinked in confusion as she slipped her hand from my grasp. I didn't fight her on it. "Okay, but your shirt, Hudson. There's wine all over your fucking shirt." She grabbed another handful of paper towels and pressed them to the drying stain against my chest, and suddenly, *my* pulse was the one racing.

I grabbed her wrist again, holding her hand to my chest, only the thin wad of paper between her hand and me. She stilled. "I'm a parent," I said slowly, sitting up just a hair to bring myself an inch closer to her. I could smell her perfume, thin and light, floral. It was intoxicating. "I assume everything I wear will eventually end up with stains. *It's okay.*"

"Let me fix it," she whispered, her eyes flicking between both of mine, her body leaning in toward me.

My hand moved without me telling it to, damning me where I sat, crossing every boundary I wanted. It wrapped itself around the back of her neck, taking in every inch of her soft skin beneath it like it was a script I had to memorize. The baby hairs along the edge of her hairline tickled my flesh, and she gulped, her mouth popping open enough for me to fantasize about filling it.

I pulled her to me, closing the distance between us and pressing my lips to hers.

Chapter 10

Sophie

Friday Night

Shock spread through me like wildfire, but I didn't pull away. Couldn't even consider it. My mind had made its own decision.

The moment I gave in to him, parting my lips and leaning closer, he was on me. The hand that held mine to his chest wrapped itself around my waist, tugging me fully into his lap, as his other pushed its way into my hair, closing like a vice around the strands.

He kissed like a fucking god, and I wondered if I was even breathing as his tongue delved between my lips, meeting mine. I pressed my palms against his chest, fisting his stained shirt in my hands, and committed myself to tasting him, a mix of something uniquely Hudson and the wine we'd been drinking, the wine I'd definitely had a glass too much of seeing as I'd let my guard down beyond my comfort zone.

A stinging, split second of pain blossomed across my scalp as he used my hair as leverage, tugging downward to lift my chin well above his own. His mouth left mine as he did it, his lips brushing their way down my throat, his mouth parting once again as he licked and nipped at the flesh there. I sucked in a breath.

"Do you have any idea how much I've wanted to taste you, Sophie?" He rasped, his hot breath fanning out across my skin. I moved my hand to the back of his head, holding him in place, a silent request not to leave. "You've been in my fucking head. I haven't been able to stop thinking about it."

Something low in my abdomen twisted, the blood that once warmed my cheeks heading down below. I wanted him to touch me more. Everywhere. "Hudson," I breathed, tightening my grip on his shirt.

"Calling me by my first name now, angel?" He growled, his hand sneaking under the band of my sweater, rising until it met bare flesh. I sucked in a breath, my head beginning to spin. Below my hips and between his own, I could feel a hardness begin to swell.

I nodded, the passion of his touch causing a tingling sensation to shoot straight down between my thighs. "Yes," I whispered, and his hand moved a little bit further up my shirt with my response, his fingers brushing against the lace of my bra. A lump formed in my throat, making words even harder than they already seemed with my swimming mind. "More."

Within a second, he shifted below me and I was facing him, my legs around his waist and his feet on the floor. He stood, releasing my hair and holding me underneath my ass instead, sending little electrical shocks throughout my body with just his touch alone. "You want more?" He cooed, stepping around the ottoman and heading toward the stairs, my weight almost nothing to his strong physique. "I'll give you what you want, but we need to go somewhere a little more private."

I wrapped my arms around his neck, trusting him with my body as he carried me up the stairs with shocking ease. Silently, he walked past Jamey's door, little snoring noises leaking through, and before I turned my head I already knew he was taking me straight to his room.

Even if I wanted to overthink it, to consider every downside, to reject the offer he was clearly laying on the table, my head was too full of all the ways it could go right. I didn't care if what was about to happen would make things awkward, if it made things more confusing than they needed to be. I hadn't been able to stop thinking about him, either, and I had to admit to myself that I wanted this.

My ass hit the plush mattress a moment later, the lights low and the moon high in the sky out the windowed wall. Hudson loomed above me, his lips parted and swollen from our kiss, his eyes half-lidded with lust. I could see the outline of him in his sweatpants, my attention no longer on the wine stain that ruined his shirt. "Is this what you wanted?" He whispered, his mouth hovering above my own, his arms pinning me in as I leaned back on one hand. "Is this the *more* you were after?"

I nodded, words failing me.

His lips met mine again, harder, needier. He didn't hold back anymore; his hands pushed the fabric of my sweater and my shirt up, revealing my abdomen and the lower half of my bra. He devoured my lips as if he was a starving man, his tongue tasting every nook and cranny, wrestling with my own.

Clumsily, I fingered the buttons on his shirt with one hand, trying and failing to pop them open. His hand met mine, forcing it away from them before he grabbed the collar and tugged once. I almost laughed at the drama of it, all of his buttons flying off in different directions as the shirt parted and hung loosely down the center. "It was stained anyway," he mumbled against my lips.

I dragged my hand along his bare chest as he leaned further into me, forcing me to lay back on the bed. I could feel every ripple and divot of muscle, every hard plane of skin that shivered under my touch. I wanted to feel more. I wanted to feel *all* of him.

Fingers brushed against my skin as my sweater and shirt left my body together, our mouths parting for only a second. Goosebumps spread to life along my flesh, my back arching as his hand made its way under, straight to the clasp of my bra, and released it in one quick motion. Within a second, the delicate fabric was off my body, discarded on the floor with my sweater. His lips left mine, planting little kisses along my skin as he made his way down my throat, across my collarbone, and to the swells of my breasts. His teeth sunk lightly into my freckled nipple as his mouth closed around it.

Fuck, yes.

I moaned, savoring the way his mouth moved over me, his tongue dragging along the tip of my breast. I looked down, watching the way his lips tipped up at the edges, the way his hand dragged along my side and ribcage, cupping my other breast in his hand. "You are fucking temptation," he growled, his fingers kneading my flesh.

I smirked as I pushed his shirt off of his shoulders, the fabric pooling around his elbows and exposing more of his chest, more of the man that I wanted to keep beneath my fingertips for as long as possible. Gone was the part of me that tossed and turned in the middle of the night, not sure whether being around him was a good idea or not. She could have her time in the sun; I'd take mine in the dark.

Hudson's fingers wandered down my skin, hooking themselves in the band of my leggings, grazing the flesh of my ass. He tugged them down in bursts, drawing out the moment as long as he could withstand it, my nipple sucked firmly between his teeth as he grinned wickedly up at me, a thousand promises in his eyes of how he wanted to take me, how much he wanted to taste me, how he couldn't help himself.

By the time he'd pulled every strip of fabric from my body, I'd only managed to get his shirt fully off. He'd seemed far more focused on me than himself. He stood up straight above me, taking me in, his eyes wandering the length of my bare, freckled skin, and he looked like he wanted to eat me alive.

I'd probably let him.

"What?" I asked when the silence had grown palpable, his gaze fixed on me as I laid back on the bed. The sheets felt like silk beneath my skin. "Is something wrong?"

He shook his head. "No," he breathed, leaning over me once more and grabbing me around the waist. He shifted me further up the bed so my legs weren't dangling off the end anymore. "Absolutely nothing is wrong."

Settling himself between my bent legs, he kissed along the flat plane of my stomach, lowering himself as he went. My heart hammered in my chest as he reached the swell of my thighs, sinking his teeth into the thicker flesh light enough to not leave a mark but hard enough to make me suck in air. I had grown to expect incompetence, a valiant effort but never enough from a man going down on me. A twisted part of me wanted to watch him do it, though. Wanted to watch as he tried different tactics aimlessly...

"Fucking dripping for me already."

My back arched, my hands fisted the sheets as he latched onto me with absurd precision. His tongue grazed over my clit, his lips sucking it in, his fingers digging into the thickness of my thigh with enough force to bruise. *Holy goddamn motherfucking shit.* This is what I would think of late at night in my own bed, vibrator clutched in my hand and mind wandering. This was more dangerous than I could have ever imagined.

He groaned his approval as his tongue dragged further down, circling my entrance, lapping up every bit of lubricant my body had made for me. "You taste like sin," he mumbled, and the vibration of his words made my clit begin to ache. I wanted more. More of him, more of this. "But I'm impatient, Sophie."

Blinking through the haze of my pleasure, I watched as he crawled back up my body, leaving me needy between my thighs. His pants were gone—*when had that happened?*—and as he settled himself above me, I could feel his warm length drape itself over my dampness. I reached down, eager to feel it, and wrapped my hand firmly around his cock.

His breathing grew heavy as I stroked him softly, my fingers dancing across the tip and collecting that little bead of precum. "Condom," he muttered, but his hands didn't move from either side of my head.

A sharp pang hit me in the chest, bringing me slightly back to reality. I hadn't even thought about using one, my body was plenty good at keeping me from getting pregnant on its own. "Do you... ?"

"I don't have anything." His head dropped, his forehead resting against mine. "I check myself once a month at the clinic."

"Then it's fine." I hated that it was fine. I wished it wasn't fine, but there was no use when I knew I wasn't getting pregnant without help.

"But—"

I pursed my lips as I looked up at him. Even in the dim light, his green eyes shone as if they were lit from within. "You've seen my file," I chuckled. "It's fine. I'm not on the drugs yet. There's zero chance, Dr. Brady."

"*Dr. Brady.*" The laugh that came from him was sinister. His smile morphed into a smirk as he adjusted himself, pressing his tip against my entrance. "Does it turn you on to call me that, angel? Does it excite you?" He forced my legs higher, almost touching my chest, with the forearm of one hand. "Does it make you want me even more?"

My cheeks warmed as he pressed in, just an inch, letting me adjust to his girth. He was big, no denying that.

"Answer me, Sophia, or this will be as far as I go."

Sadistic motherfucker. My mind was blank as I searched for an answer. *Does it turn me on to say it? Do I like referring to him as Dr. Brady? Is that why I hadn't stopped?* "I..."

I was going to kill him. When the sun finally rose and things were back to normal, I was going to fucking kill him. "Yes," I admitted, my voice no louder than a whisper.

I gasped as he thrust his full length inside, sinking in until almost nothing was left. My walls stretched to accommodate him, the sting almost heavenly, and as he leaned down to whisper into my ear, I think I left my body entirely. "Good girl."

Oh my god. I wanted to hate him. I wanted to hate him so badly, wanted to tell myself *you know better,* but I couldn't. I just couldn't. I buried the back of my head in the sheets as he slowly slid out, just a hint of him left, before plunging back in with enough force to make me see stars.

And then it began.

Rough, needy, and desperate, he fucked me. His cock curved upward just a hair, hitting that spot inside of me that made me feel like my world was imploding. Every inch of my skin crawled with pleasure, deep and unbridled. I moaned, jerking my head back farther, and his lips explored the sensitive spots of my neck as if I'd given them to him on a silver platter.

"You take me so fucking well," he grunted, his teeth grazing across my skin. "I could live inside of you. So goddamn perfect..."

His words echoed around in my head, making my gut knot with tension. Already, I could feel my orgasm building, but I knew his length alone wouldn't be enough to tip me over the edge. I needed more. "Hudson—"

"Touch yourself, angel. I can't reach you like this." *Could he read my mind?*

I nodded as I snaked my hand between us, my fingers crawling across my own skin. I sank them between my lips, the slickness pooling far more than usual. The base of his cock brushed against my fingertips as I began to circle my clit, little movements growing more frantic, more ecstatic. I was building, my walls clenching and gripping him for dear life.

Hudson gritted his teeth as he lifted his head, staring straight down at me. His eyes were wild, ferocious behind half-lowered lids. "Watch me fuck you as you come for me," he growled, his voice far deeper than I'd heard before. "Watch how perfectly you take my cock."

He lifted my hips higher, putting them well within view. It was as if his words held power. I couldn't stop myself from looking between us, down to where our bodies met and my hand twitched. God, he was right. We fit together too well.

"Hudson." My breathing was growing choppy. Each little inhale felt like a want, not a need, and the pressure growing was reaching its breaking point. "Fuck, oh my god—"

Everything shattered at once. The moan that ripped from my throat felt like it wasn't my own, and a euphoric bliss overwhelmed my senses, flooding me and drowning me, wrecking me far more than I was used to. I ripped my hand away, suddenly too sensitive, and tried desperately to catch my breath as Hudson's arms wrapped around me, holding my damp, electrified body to his. It was too much. But it was perfect.

"Breathe, Sophia."

His movements slowed, still firm but calmer, and those arms held me tightly as he rolled us onto the other side of the bed, flipping me on top of him. I saddled him, my mind lost to the haze, and his hips did the work for me until I could do it on my own. "Holy shit," I breathed, sinking further down on him than I thought I could.

He smirked as he shifted us higher, his back resting against the headboard in a curve. "You felt like heaven as you came," he grunted, his cock twitching inside of me. "You're going to do it again."

Twice? "I... I don't know if I can." Slowly, I rocked my hips, my clit brushing against the little tuft of hair above his cock. It was enough to make my body twitch.

"You can," he said calmly. He wrapped one hand around the back of my neck, pulling me closer to him as the other buried itself between our conjoined hips, his fingers curling up to meet the overly-sensitive bundle of nerves. I cried out, feeling far too much, but he held me in place. "You *will*."

His mouth met mine as we moved in unison, my hips stuttering from the intensity, and I used my newly freed-up hands to explore every inch of him that I could. His chest, his arms, his neck. Each teeming with corded muscles, flexed from his efforts down below. Slowly, that tension began to build again, making it too hard to concentrate on the movements of my hips. It was choppy, rushed, anguished, but he kept me as steady as he could.

Briefly, I wondered if I'd be able to see myself fucking him in the reflection of my bedroom window.

"Fuck, I'm close," he grunted, growing impossibly harder inside of me. His fingers moved quicker, dragging me closer with him, those deft little movements planting themselves in my mind so I could fantasize about it later. "Don't fucking stop, angel."

I buried my head in the crook of his neck, focusing as hard as I could on my rocking despite the rush of delirium. His groans turned darker, more intense as he tightened his grip on the back of my neck. "Hudson," I whispered, the pressure beginning to break, leaking out of me and coating his cock, his fingers.

His hips sputtered, breaking our controlled movements, but his fingers kept their pace with insane precision as his orgasm spread through him. Just knowing he had come was enough to send me over the edge, the idea of him filling me and the warmth spreading inside making the second orgasm more intense than the last.

Nothing mattered anymore—not my boundaries or his, not our working relationship or the idea of some fake engagement. All that mattered was the pleasure rocketing through my veins, his deep cries of ecstasy, and the way he held me to him as if he never wanted me to leave.

Chapter 11

Hudson

Saturday

Sophie went home last night.

I'd be a liar if I said a part of me hadn't wanted her to stay, but she'd mumbled something about Jamey getting confused as she cleaned herself up and that was the reality check. I'd gathered her clothes for her, waited as she got dressed, then walked her to her front door.

I didn't know where to go from there. It felt as though a massive, boulder-sized rock had been lifted from my shoulders. The pent-up attraction had found an outlet, and I could breathe again. I'd crossed boundaries, yes, but so had she. We could easily sneak around behind Jamey's back if we decided to do it again. We could use condoms when she started the drugs.

I tried not to think about how bad of an idea that could be in the long run.

Jamey sat in front of the television with his bowl of

cereal, some rerun of a show he didn't watch often playing. Something about a pig and her little brother. I didn't like it as much as PAW Patrol.

"Daddy?"

I looked up from my phone, meeting big eyes on a small body. "Yeah, bud?"

"Can Sophie come with us to the fair?"

My brows knit together as I stared down at him. He blinked at me, that little, puffy lower lip sticking out. As much as I wanted her to go with us, and as much as I wished I didn't, I really didn't want to bother her. "Oh, bud, she probably has plans today."

"Why?"

I chuckled as I placed his empty cereal bowl on the coffee table. Gently, I pulled him into my lap, tucking him in against my chest. "Because today is Saturday. Adults like to make plans on Saturdays."

"Why?"

Oh, god, not this game again. "Because many of them don't have work. You know how sometimes you go to birthday parties on Saturdays? It's because your friends don't have to go to school on those days. Same thing."

"Why?"

Don't. Don't get annoyed. "How about this," I offered, placing a little kiss on the top of his head. "I'll call her and ask if she wants to come with us."

His face lit up as he looked up at me.

"That doesn't mean she'll say yes." I didn't want to get his hopes up, but good god that kid knew how to sway me. It didn't help that I wanted to call her, too.

———

. . .

With thirty minutes until the fair actually began, Jamey managed to blow off some energy by running circles around a family of ducks in the Boston Public Garden, far too close to the water's edge for my comfort.

"Jamey! Can you play a little further away from the water?"

I turned toward Sophie, surprised that she was thinking the same thing as me. I hadn't expected her to be on Jamey-watch when she'd agreed to come with us, but there she was, worrying about him the same way I was. We sat beneath the shade of the George Washington statue that sat in the middle of the park, likely appearing in tourist's photos as they snapped away at the image behind us.

From the moment she'd walked across our adjoining lawns to hop into my Range Rover, she'd stolen my breath. The weather was warm, and she'd chosen her outfit perfectly—high-waisted denim shorts that hugged every curve of her lower half, paired with a white, tight-fitting crop top. It made her freckles stand out more than normal, and with her deep brown hair tied up in a ponytail and a pair of sunglasses resting on her nose, I found myself wanting to see everything I knew lay beneath her clothes.

She'd made a passing comment on the way to the park about my car, asking me if I'd had custom work done on it. I assumed by that point she realized I had money, more than the average doctor, so I'd told her outright that I'd ordered it fully customized from the manufacturer, with all the bells and whistles. She'd seemed afraid that she might spill the iced coffee clutched in her hand by that point.

She was doing a really good job acting as if last night hadn't happened.

Jamey clung to her side instead of mine as we maneuvered our way around the fair. He was too small for every ride apart from the merry-go-round, and Sophie offered to ride it with him since he was nervous about going alone. I didn't get the chance to offer before she did, and Jamey practically screamed with excitement that Sophie was joining him.

In one hand, I held the massive bear Sophie had insisted upon winning for Jamey. She'd gotten so competitive. I was worried she'd end up cursing out the poor kid running the booth if she didn't get her fifth basketball in the hoop, but she'd looked so adorable frustrated that I probably would have just laughed.

Jamey waved at me with every pass he made on the merry-go-round. Sophie, bless her, was mounted on a metal horse next to him, one of his hands in hers. I hated how much it made my heart swell to see how well they got along, how much Jamey liked her and vice versa, but deep down I knew it was a good thing. Jamey hadn't liked any of his previous nannies as much as he liked Sophie, and I wanted so desperately for him to have fun, to be looked after by someone that cared about him while I was at work. If only his new nanny wasn't pure sin wrapped up with a bow.

When the ride was done, Jamey ran from the exit, his arms outstretched toward me as he cut through the sea of people. I picked him up as he got to me, settling him on my hip, and his smile was enough to break my heart in two. "Daddy, that was so fun."

"Merry-go-rounds are definitely top-tier rides," Sophie grinned as she saddled up to us.

"Well, I'm glad you two had fun." I lifted Jamey higher, placing his legs on either side of my neck, his hips pressed to the back of my head. He loved being up on my shoulders. "I think some cotton candy is in order."

"Cotton Candy!"

Sophie's expression dropped as she looked at me. "You better pray they have cotton candy. This is the p-word all over again."

———

Jamey had eaten the entirety of his cotton candy before begging us for ice cream. We'd got him a single scoop and taken him back to the park, away from the crowd of people and to the open field where he could run off every ounce of sugar he'd consumed so I wouldn't be up all night with a sugared-up toddler.

He'd finished his scoop and gone back to herding the ducks, leaving me and Sophie alone as we sat under one of the biggest trees in the park, the view overlooking the entirety of the small green space in the heart of the city.

"I've been thinking about the fake engagement thing," Sophie said quietly, almost as if she didn't want Jamey to hear, but there was no way he could hear anything over the sound of his own excited shrieking.

"Yeah?"

"I'm thinking it might be worth it." She looked up at me, her blue eyes latching onto mine like they had last night. *For fucks sake, don't think about that now.*

"So does that mean you want to do it?"

Blush spread beneath her freckles as she playfully hit me in the chest. "Yes. But don't say it like that."

I laughed as I leaned back against the tree. *Would this mean I needed to get her an engagement ring?* I wondered to myself. Considering my background, I'd have to splurge and make it look convincing if her family decided to look me up. I couldn't have them thinking I'd gone out and bought a ring from Walmart.

"I guess that means you're my fiancée now." I joked, bouncing my shoulder against hers. "We should probably start planning the wedding."

"Oh shut up." She giggled as she stood up, brushing the dirt and grass from her shorts. "What we *should* do is rescue those poor ducks from Jamey's torment."

Chapter 12

Sophie

Sunday

"Let me get this straight. You slept with your IVF doctor?"

I rolled my eyes as I shoveled a massive bite of avocado on toast into my mouth. "Don't be so dramatic, Lisa. He's my neighbor and I'm his son's nanny."

She blinked at me as her brows came together, her short blonde hair swishing about her jaw in the wind. "Please don't tell me you think that makes it sound better."

I didn't answer her, cutting off another section of toast, making sure to get some of the poached egg on my fork.

"Oh my god, you do," Lisa laughed, covering her mouth as she leaned back in her chair. "And you're pretending to be engaged. Do you not think this could be, oh, I don't know... problematic? For, like, *everyone*?"

"How?"

"Sophie. You catch feelings so damn easily."

"I do not," I said around a mouthful, the words muffled.

"You absolutely do. Remember Derek? You knew him for like two days and told me you were falling in love with him. You cried when he said he just wanted a hookup."

The sound of my fork scraping against the plate made me cringe more than remembering Derek did. "This isn't like that."

Lisa's lips pursed together as she leaned forward on the table, her elbows resting against the metal. "Babe. Come on. I love you, but you sound like you might already be falling for this guy—"

"I'm not." It came out too quickly to be something I'd thought hard about. Suspiciously quick. She definitely picked up on it based on how she raised one singular eyebrow at me. "I'm not! We fucked once, Leese. Just two adults doing the deed. It probably won't happen again."

"And you're... okay with that?"

"Of course. He's a dad, and he doesn't want any more kids. He's my doctor. I'm his nanny. It would be weird."

Lisa sucked her teeth before she took a hefty sip of her mimosa. She'd always been at least a little protective of me, even when she insisted I get with whoever and do whatever. This time, shockingly, was no different. "Did you use protection?"

I snorted. "No. Don't need to, for now at least. I'm not on the drugs yet."

"So there's no chance?"

"No. And to be honest, I don't really want to talk about how I don't need birth control," I sighed. I'd tried not to let it get to me over the last couple of days, but it had been there, right at the back of my mind, ruining any chance of fantasizing about how fucking amazing Hudson had been.

"Okay. We don't have to talk about it." Lisa cut a square

out of the center of her stack of pancakes, shoving a massive bite into her mouth. "Is he hot at least?"

I couldn't help but laugh. I wanted her to meet him, pictures wouldn't do him justice, but I pulled my phone out regardless. "He's like a Greek fucking god, Lisa. It's annoying. Here, I took a picture of him yesterday at the fair."

Lisa snatched my phone from my hand, her eyes glued to the screen immediately. "God damn."

"I know, right?"

"Wait, I'm sorry, rewind. You went to the fair? With him and his son?" She clicked the side button, blackening the screen. "Why?"

I shrugged. "He invited me."

Lisa's silence settled over the table, unnerving me. I hated it when she went silent. When she spoke again, her voice was low, slow, and calm. "You went with him to the fair, off duty, because he invited you."

"Yes."

"The day after you had sex."

"Yeah."

"Sophia Elizabeth Mitchell, you are fucking falling for him." She aimed her fork at me, a little jab. "And I think you already know that. Why are you denying it?"

I could feel the heat rise in my face as I looked down at my food. I didn't think I was falling for him. I'd put up a wall between us, making sure that I didn't get too tempted by his charm, his wit, his looks. If that wall was crumbling... *no*, I couldn't think about that. No way. It wouldn't work. "I'm not," I insisted. "I barely know him."

"That's made zero difference in the past."

"Respectfully, Leese, you're not inside my head. I just like hanging out with his kid. I *do* want a baby, so it shouldn't be that surprising."

"I still don't get that—"

"I'm not asking you to. I'm just asking you to support me. Hudson doesn't want another kid, so why would I let myself fall for him? That would be insane. I'd be setting us up for failure." I picked at the poached egg on my plate, moving it around in the avocado. I'd suddenly lost my appetite. "I love you and I appreciate your protectiveness, but I'm fine. I'm handling it."

She tapped her knife against her plate, contemplating my words. It didn't appear that they'd sunk in, not from the expression on her face. "Alright," she sighed, taking another sip of her mimosa. "Just... be careful with him. I'll pick up the pieces if you need me to, but for your own sanity, Sophie, try not to let him sink his teeth into you."

But he already has. Literally. Not metaphorically, right?
Maybe that, too.

"Guess you'll need to buy a ring, now," she joked, trying to lighten the mood a hair. It was sweet of her. And fuck, she was right.

"Shit, I didn't even think about that." I pulled my phone back out.

"No, no, let me pick it. You have awful taste," Lisa teased, and I shot her a look that said *are you fucking kidding, I'm a literal designer*, but she grabbed my phone anyway.

A few seconds later and she'd brought up a shockingly genuine-looking ring, priced at fifty bucks. It was beautiful —the kind of design I'd actually like if someone asked me to marry them, though I'd prefer one that was real and cost more than fifty dollars.

Staring at the oval-cut fake diamond and the thin, gold band that wrapped around it, I pressed the purchase button without hesitation. Worst case, it'd be good for nights at the bar when I didn't feel like being flirted with. "Fine," I mumbled, shoveling a small bite of egg into my mouth. "Maybe you do have better taste."

Lisa laughed, her full smile returning as I desperately tried not to think about how real this was all beginning to feel.

Chapter 13

Hudson

Monday

At twelve o'clock sharp, a familiar set of faces greeted me in my office.

Not the ones I would have most liked to see, though. One is tucked deep down inside, so far down to ensure that I won't think too hard about time spent with them Friday night. The other, tiny and cute and full of wonder, is always at the forefront of my mind.

Jannie and Steven Booth made themselves comfortable in the plush chairs across from my rolling one, the same one Sophie had tripped over as she'd tried to storm out. *Stop.*

Jannie had been a patient of mine for nearly a year. She'd done four rounds of IVF—one more than I'd recommended since it takes such a massive toll on the body and mind—but she was desperate, and I wanted to help her. Helping all of my patients achieve their dream of becoming parents is always the end goal.

"Alright, Jan," I started, rolling my chair a little closer to her. "We're going to do a pregnancy test today, and then another in two weeks. Are you okay with that?"

She nodded, her hands fidgeting in her lap as she held her husband's palm clutched between them. "What do we do if they're both negative?"

The one question I hated most. It was the worst part of treating prospective parents, and every single time, it made my heart just a little bit harder and wanting to break. I took a deep breath, forming my lips into a thin line as I met her worried gaze. "If they're both negative, then we have to call it quits. Your body can't handle another round of the drugs. I've already done one more than I should have with you. I'm so sorry. But let's try and stay positive until we know for sure."

Jan's expression fell as she looked at her husband, her eyes going glassy. "It's alright, honey," he said, giving her hand a little squeeze. "We can adopt if it doesn't work."

Jannie blinked away the tears building as she nodded. "Right."

"Okay, let's get that pregnancy test done for you. We'll also need to check your blood to make sure the drugs are active in your system," I said, sliding my chair back in front of my screen. I shot a message to the nurse, asking her to retrieve Jan and Steven for her test, before turning back to them. I had to shut off my emotions. I couldn't allow myself to feel what they were feeling, couldn't think about what my life would be like if I hadn't had the chance to have Jamey. "We'll call you in a few days with the results. Until then, keep taking the medicine. If it's negative, you can continue with it until your next test. If positive, stop taking it right away, okay?"

They nodded in unison. I watched with clenched teeth

as a single tear slid down Jan's cheek, carrying what I could only assume were her hopes and dreams along with it. I genuinely wished I could fix it, and I'd done everything in my power to but considering their track record, implantation was next to impossible.

———

The house was eerily quiet when I stepped through the door. From the entryway, I couldn't see Sophie or Jamey in the kitchen or the dining room, and judging from the silence in the living room, I doubted they were in there.

Toeing off my shoes, I pulled my phone from the pocket of my scrubs and sent Sophie a text.

Why isn't there any screaming or shouting going on in the house?

Somewhere, not too far away, I heard the soft buzz of a phone on silent and a very suspiciously quiet giggle.

Jamey's napping.

You'll have to find me.

Napping? Jamey wasn't one to nap this late in the afternoon. I groaned as I realized that would mean he'd be up late tonight.

You've ruined my evening, Sophia.

Here I was hoping for a relaxing night in, a glass of wine...

Now I get to spend it finger painting and watching PAW Patrol.

Another giggle, louder this time. I followed the sound

through the house, checking the living room, the laundry room, and double-checking the kitchen.

Where are you hiding, little voyeur?

Somewhere you can watch me undress?

Her answer of silence was heavy. No three little dots dancing across the bottom of my message indicating a reply, no giggles. I checked the closet where I'd found her before, holding a photo of my ex-wife and son in her hands, but came up empty. Not in the gym, not in the garage...

I pushed open the double doors that lead into my office. Sophie sat behind my oak desk, her feet propped up next to my laptop, a glass of wine in hand. Somehow, despite the impossibility of it, she looked more gorgeous than she had when I'd left this morning. Her cheeks were reddened, almost as maroon as the wine in the glass between her fingers, and her long brown hair was tied up in a messy bun. She smirked at me as my eyes drifted down her body, across the Harvard hoodie and the gray sweatpants.

Was she wearing my clothes?

"Before you freak out," she started, putting her feet down as she sat upright in my leather chair, "Jamey spilled his grape juice all over my clothes. I didn't bring anything else to wear, so..."

She *was* wearing my clothes. Sucking my teeth, I crossed the few steps between me and the desk, leaning on my palms as I bent over it. "You live next door," I said slowly, watching as the blush in her cheeks deepened. "You could have grabbed something from home."

"And leave Jamey all alone? I wouldn't be a good nanny if I left a four-year-old alone in a house."

I rolled my eyes, my grin becoming hard to hide as I stared down at her in the clothes I'd worn last night. She must've picked them up from where I'd left them on the bed.

Do they smell like me?

"You could have taken him with you."

"I..." She bit her lip as she looked up at me, those goddamn blue eyes nearly making my heart melt. "I didn't think of that."

"No," I cooed, lifting myself to my full height as I made my way around the desk. "You didn't."

"Hudson—"

I plucked the glass of wine from her hand, downing it in one fell swoop before setting it down on the desk. "You're lucky you didn't spill wine on my sweatshirt," I teased, pressing my hands down on the arms of the chair as I leaned over her. "That's one I would have made you replace."

I watched as her mouth worked, the words she wanted to say trying to come up but getting stopped in their tracks. She looked flustered, adorably so, as she lifted her knees to her chest, her bare feet resting against the leather of the chair. "At least this one probably wouldn't have been expensive."

"Not monetarily, no," I laughed, leaning down just a little further, our faces too close for my own good. "But replacing the memories that go along with it? Immeasurable."

Confusion flickered across her face. "Did you go to Harvard?"

"I did." I took the strings of the hoodie in one hand, twisting them around my knuckles. "Lots of memories there. But I think seeing you wearing it might be my favorite."

The noise she made was halfway between a squeak and a gasp. I couldn't help but laugh at it. "Jamey will be up soon," she whispered, her lips a mere centimeter from my own, her heart pounding beneath where my hand rested against her chest.

"You're right."

But I tugged her closer with the hoodie's strings, closing the distance between us. My lips pressed against hers, the stress and upset from the day melting away as I tasted her again, felt her again. She kissed me back just as eagerly, her legs returning to the floor to let me in, her hands settling on the heat of my neck.

Already, I wanted more. It was risky with Jamey potentially awake in the house, but the thought went to the back of my mind, certain I'd be able to hear his quick little steps before we were caught.

Scooping one hand under the curve of Sophie's ass, I lifted her from the chair. Her lips parted in a gasp, granting me further access to her mouth as I sat her down on the desk, her legs open and my hips between them. My cock came to life in my scrubs, pressing against the thin cotton fabric. I needed more. I needed to be inside of her again, her naked body below mine, her skin against my own. She was too perfect, too much for me to handle, and as my hands searched beneath the hoodie, I nearly groaned as I found no trace of a bra.

"Were you hoping for this, angel?" I asked her, my lips trailing the length of her jaw now, my hands grasping at her bare breasts.

"My... my bra got juice on it, too," she breathed, a little laugh escaping her as I rolled her nipple between my thumb and middle finger.

"Did it?" I challenged, squeezing just a little harder, making her jump. "How about your panties? Those too?"

A breathy moan crawled up her throat as I playfully nipped at the skin there. "Yeah, those too."

Not only was she wearing my clothes, but she was wearing them with nothing underneath. No barrier between her pussy and my sweatpants, nothing to stop me from touching her fully.

My other hand wandered without thought, down the plane of her belly to the waistband of the sweatpants. I didn't waste a single second, placing my fingers beneath the hem, past the thin, sparse hairs of her mound and down between her already-soaked lips. *Fuck*. It was too much, how easily she folded for me.

Suddenly, her body stilled, frozen like a statue. "Hudson," she whispered, her voice almost frantic as I found her clit, my fingers flitting across it. "Hudson, Jamey. Jamey's coming."

I retreated immediately, letting go of her and taking a step back, my heart beating rapidly in my chest. The bulge in my scrub pants was far too noticeable, but as long as I stayed where I was, Jamey wouldn't see. A string of Sophie's wetness dripped from my fingers, and as the little feet raced down the stairs, I popped them into my mouth, sucking them dry. Christ, she tasted so fucking good.

Sophie's eyes went wide as she watched me, her mouth open just a bit, her hand up in her hair. Even as disheveled as she looked, I only wanted more of her.

Jamey appeared in the doorway, his eyes half closed and sleepy, his teddy bear clutched in one hand. *Too close.* We were way too close to getting caught. "Hi, Daddy."

I took a deep breath to steady myself as I looked at my son, half asleep from his nap, and made myself switch into dad mode. "Hey, bud," I smiled, pushing my hair back from where it had fallen in my face. "Sophie and I are just having a private chat. Why don't you go watch something while we finish up, okay?"

He nodded as he rubbed his eyes. "Okay. I'm hungry."

"I'll make you something to eat in a few."

"Okie dokie."

I watched as he walked away, my ears trained on the sound of his steps until I could hear the television turning on. I took a step toward Sophie as I let out a sigh of relief, but her hands went up, a silent request to keep my distance.

"I don't feel comfortable continuing that while he's awake," she whispered.

"Neither do I. Don't worry," I chuckled, plopping down into the leather chair. Even sitting down I was taller than her. "I just need a minute to uh, calm down."

Sophie nodded, the blush on her cheeks not going away. "Actually, I do need to talk to you about something. My parents invited us over Friday night." In her lap, she wrapped her fingers around the base of her wrist, wringing the skin there. "Can you make it?"

Friday night. I'd have to bring Jamey. The idea of it was appealing, but I couldn't help but wonder if it would confuse him. Surely, he was too young to really understand, and if we kept him occupied with games or a show, he wouldn't pay too much attention.

"Sure," I nodded. "I'll have to bring Jamey, though. My parents are still out of town and I don't have a babysitter on call anymore."

Her brows furrowed as she looked at me. "Okay. That, uh, that should be fine."

"You know Jamey is part of the package with me. I can't just pretend he doesn't exist."

"I know. I'd never ask you to do that. It's fine. It'll be fine." She gave me a half-hearted smile as she hopped down from the desk. "I think it's best I go home now. I'll, um, wash your clothes and bring them back tomorrow."

I almost wanted to ask her to stay, to have dinner with us again, to stick around until Jamey fell back asleep and I could have my way with her. Almost. I didn't, though, and as I watched her leave in my sweatpants and hoodie, her makeup smudged and bun askew, I wished I had.

Chapter 14

Sophie

Wednesday

Jamey's tiny hands clutched his ice cream cone, the green mint chocolate chip leaking out of the bottom and coating his hands and arms. He grinned up at me as I snapped a photo, quickly texting it to Hudson before sliding my phone back into my pocket.

"Sophie?"

I turned, one hand on Jamey's shoulder, and blinked in confusion as Lisa walked up to us. "Hey," I smiled, my arm nearly twisting as Jamey tucked himself behind my legs. "What are you doing here?"

"Just got a trim," she chirped. Her thumb jutted out behind her, toward the hair salon next door to the ice cream shop. "I think they went too short though."

"It looks great." I looked down at Jamey, his mouth hovering over the minty ice cream, his big green eyes staring up at me. "Jamey, this is my friend, Lisa. Lisa, this is Jamey, Hudson's son."

Lisa grinned at him as she squatted down in front of him, placing herself at his height. "Hi, Jamey. Aren't you adorable." She glanced up at me, her smile a little forced. Lisa had never been great with kids, and she didn't want any of her own, so it made sense. I'd never judged her for it.

"He's a little shy," I explained, taking a step to the side so Jamey couldn't hide behind me any longer.

"What kind of ice cream is that?"

"Mint chocolate chip," he mumbled, holding it out a little toward her. "You can try it if you want."

Lisa's lower lip poked out, her eyes going soft. "That is so sweet, Jamey, but I don't like ice cream. Thank you, though."

Jamey glanced at me in confusion before returning to licking at his ice cream. I laughed awkwardly, holding out a hand to Lisa to help her stand back up, and she gladly took it.

"Are you free tonight? Maybe we could meet up for drinks or something." Lisa looked at me hopefully, her gaze only occasionally glancing down at Jamey with a *what the fuck* expression. "I need a catch up."

"Sure," I smiled. "Is seven okay?"

Lisa rolled her eyes as she adjusted the purse on her shoulder. "Bit early, but I guess it's fine."

———

PAW Patrol pencil in hand, it was the only one I could find, and sketchbook on the counter, I found it shockingly easy to design with cartoons playing in the background. Mom had been right when she told me that tuning it out became easy when I was a kid, and I wondered if it was becoming the same for me, if it *would* be the same for me when I had one of my own.

By the time the front door opened, I'd drawn roughly six designs, all perfect for hiding a baby bump or complementing it. I'd even adjusted the little models to have one.

"Daddy!"

Jamey ran past me, his socks sliding on the slick floor. "Jamey! Slow down!"

He slammed into his father at light speed, nearly knocking Hudson over. "Hey, bud," Hudson smiled, tight-lipped and almost fake, but not enough for Jamey to notice. *Odd.*

I hopped down from the high-top seat, closed my sketchbook, and returned the pencil to the everything-lives-in-here drawer. I watched as Hudson picked up his son, giving him a tight hug and holding him to his chest, as I made my way over. "Jamey had some ice cream this afternoon so he might be a bit rambunctious."

"That's fine."

I stared up at Hudson, his face unreadable, his response too quick, too short. "He was very brave today, though. He met one of my friends and even offered her some of his ice cream."

"That's great." Hudson passed me, his mind elsewhere as he walked toward the kitchen, setting Jamey down in the seat I'd just been sitting in.

Jamey didn't seem to notice the change in demeanor as his father opened up the fridge and plucked out a bottle of wine. I took a step toward them, and Hudson's gaze landed directly on me, stopping me in my tracks.

"Thanks for watching him today."

Oh.

"I'll see you tomorrow."

Oh.

I took a step back toward the door, the awkwardness that was hanging in the air so thick I could slice it with a knife.

"Okay," I said quietly, showing a little too much disappointment for my own good. I slid my feet into my slippers and picked up my bag, watching as Hudson turned away from me, picking out a wine glass from the cupboard. "Bye, Jamey."

"Bye, Sophie!" He shouted, his little hand waving furiously, his grin wide enough to split my heart in two.

I tried not to think about how much it hurt as I walked out the door, back toward my condo and away from the two of them. I had two hours to kill until meeting up with Lisa, two hours I'd thought I would be spending with Hudson and Jamey. But it was fine. Totally fine. I could work on my sketches and take my time getting ready for the night ahead.

It was fine.

Totally, completely fine.

———

"You're doing *what*?" I asked.

Lisa cackled as she leaned back in her seat, the blues

and pinks of her cocktail nearly spilling out of her hand. "You don't have to react like that."

"You're sleeping with a professor."

"It's not like I'm still in school!"

"Yeah, but you were up until, what, a year ago?"

She stifled her laugh as she took a gulp through her straw, careful not to let it explode out of her nostrils. "He was never *my* professor. Well, I guess he is now. But he wasn't before. Besides, he teaches at Harvard. I wouldn't have ever crossed paths with him at Northeastern."

"What does he teach?" I asked, narrowing my gaze at her. I took a hefty sip from my glass of wine.

"I..." Lisa looked down at her drink, wracking her mind for the answer, but came up short. She snorted. "I have no idea."

"Oh my god."

"What?"

"This has been going on for months and you don't even know what he teaches?"

She contained her giggles as she looked across the table at me, her perfectly manicured nails tapping against the vinyl coating. "Nope."

"And why didn't you tell me sooner?"

"I wanted to wait until I knew it was... serious. I really like him." She smiled as she fished out her phone, flicking across the screen until she found what she was looking for, sliding it across the table toward me. A very handsome man looked back at me, taking up the majority of the screen, with Lisa's blonde hair poking up from the side. She'd never been good at taking selfies. "Look how cute he is."

I laughed as I flicked to the next picture, immediately regretting it as the horrible selfie was replaced with what was practically a nude, Lisa's toned body covered in red lingerie as she laid back on plush sheets. I turned off the screen and slid it back across the table.

"How are things with your fertility doctor?" She asked, not even mentioning the nude she'd seen me flick to.

"Uh, yeah, good, I think."

"Have you fucked him again or are you keeping those walls up?" She smirked at me as she sipped from her straw.

"I haven't slept with him again, no," I laughed, my cheeks heating at the thought of it. "We came close, though. Thankfully, Jamey woke up and we had to stop."

"Sophie!" She exclaimed, her eyes wide and her mouth split in a massive grin.

"Dinner with my parents on Friday will be interesting."

"Oh my god, you're going to blow it. I can already tell," she giggled, keeping her straw between her teeth. "Or maybe you'll actually be able to sell it, based on how easily you fall into him."

"Oh shut up. If you were constantly around him, you'd want him too," I joked, sending her a wink. "He's bringing Jamey, though, so we need to keep our distance. I don't want to confuse him. And I haven't even told my parents about Jamey yet, so that's going to be hellish. Fingers crossed they don't condemn him as a Satanist or something."

Lisa chuckled, but the idea wasn't all that insane. They could very well react badly to all of it, telling me I was setting myself up for failure for 'marrying' someone with a child already. They would see through all of it when they asked him what his profession was. It made me nauseous to imagine. What if it was real? Would they react the same way?

It's not real, so it doesn't matter.

"At least the ring is supposed to be delivered tomorrow," I said, giving her a half smile, but I was too full of worry to mean it. What if Hudson stood me up? He didn't seem happy to see me earlier. Sure, he could have had a particularly horrible day at work, but he'd never acted like that before. It hurt, and it shouldn't have, but it pierced me just the same. I desperately wanted it not to bother me.

I knew though, deep down, that it wouldn't stop until he was normal with me again. That was all I wanted. Just, normalcy.

Right?

Chapter 15

Hudson

Friday

"Impressive ring."

Sophie looked over at me from the passenger seat of my Mercedes. I'd picked the least flashy of my cars, hoping that no one would ask questions, but I knew from experience it was inevitable. She was wearing a yellow summer dress, a little less fancy than I'd gone, but we complemented one another nonetheless. "Thanks," she said, spinning it around on her finger. "It was only fifty bucks. My friend Lisa picked it out."

Jamey's tablet played the sounds of that damn pig show from the backseat, his mind entirely wrapped up in it. I didn't need to worry whether or not he'd be confused when I spoke about the ring. "It's definitely an authentic-looking engagement ring. I don't think they'll ask questions."

Sophie grinned as she held out her hand in front of her,

watching the way the setting sun glinted off the cubic zirconia. "You don't think it's too, I don't know, gaudy?"

I laughed as I turned into the neighborhood where her parents lived, the houses far larger than I expected. Not quite as large as my own or my parents, but what would most likely be considered upper middle-class. I had to physically restrain myself from putting my hand on her knee and moving it farther up. I clutched the steering wheel to keep my boundaries in place. "No, I don't think it's gaudy. If I *had* to buy an engagement ring again, I'd probably go for something similar."

She rolled her eyes, her chuckle coming quick and short. "You say that like it would be a massive chore."

I shrugged, following the GPS instructions through the maze of houses until we arrived. In the driveway, two BMWs were parked; a sedan and a mid-sized SUV. Along the curb, there was a third car parked, a Lexus RX..

"That's my brother's car," she said, a hint of confusion in her voice. "I'm sorry, I didn't realize they'd invited him too."

"It's fine," I replied, flashing a half-hearted grin at her. "They have a kid, right?"

"Yeah, but she's like, four months old."

"That's fine. Jamey loves babies." I pushed open my door and hopped out, heading to Sophie's side to help Jamey out of the car, but she was already on it. She smirked at me.

"So there *are* differences between you two." Jamey's feet hit the grass, one hand in Sophie's and the other holding his tablet.

I scoffed at her. "I don't dislike babies, Sophie. I had one. I actively work to make women pregnant."

She motioned to her stomach, her brows furrowing as

she looked up at me. "Really? Because I don't see anything happening here."

I shut the door behind them both, rolling my eyes at her joke. "Come in for your appointment on Monday and maybe you'll get lucky."

Blush spread across her cheeks as she stopped in her tracks.

"Jesus, Sophia, not like that. Get your mind out of the gutter."

"Yeah, Sophie, get your mind out of the gutter," Jamey echoed, and I swear my eye twitched.

"Don't say that" I muttered. "Those are adult words."

Sophie's dad opened the door for us as we approached, his eyes going wide as his gaze landed on my son and Sophie holding his hand. "Well, hello," he said, looking between Sophie and Jamey. "Who's this?"

She hadn't told them. Why? Was it something she didn't think they'd approve of or was she ashamed herself to 'be with' a single father? "Hi, Martin. Nice to see you again. This is my son, Jamey."

Martin looked down at Jamey as he took his place behind Sophie's legs, his tablet clutched to his chest. Sophie's father seemed confused, surprised, but not angry.

Did she know they'd be okay with it and hadn't said anything? Still, the idea that she was ashamed sat heavily on my shoulders, and I tried to bat it away.

"Well, hello, Jamey. I'm Martin," he said, a little smile lifting his lips. "I suppose you can call me Pops."

Jamey looked up at me, his lip between his teeth, and I already knew what was going to come out of his mouth.

"Why?"

Sophie answered him before I could. "Because this is my dad, and he likes being called Pops."

"But I already know a Pop-pop," Jamey said quietly, his little hand tightening in Sophie's grip.

"Lots of people can be called the same thing," I explained, following Sophie and Martin inside, ushering Jamey along. Already, the whole thing felt like a horrible idea, but we'd committed to it. Couldn't turn back now.

"Sophie!"

Sophie's mom, Leslie, appeared behind a corner, oven mitts on her hands and a flour-covered apron covering her clothes. She, too, stopped dead in her tracks when she saw Jamey, and my stomach twisted just a little bit more.

"Who's this?"

"This is Jamey," Martin answered. "Hudson's son."

"Oh," Leslie said, studying the three of us as if we were aliens before her face leveled out. "Hi, Jamey. I'm Sophie's mom."

"Hi," he whispered, his gaze traveling the room, taking in the surprisingly grand aesthetic of it. It wasn't anything like ours but more like my parents, just scaled back. Decorated by people in their fifties who loved cats and chickens.

"It's lovely to see you guys again," Leslie smiled as she walked up to us, giving her daughter a peck on the cheek.

"Hi, Mom."

Leslie removed an oven mitt and extended her hand to me. I took it, gave her a firm shake, and plastered my best smile on my face even though I felt a little like I was dying. This was a lot for me, and likely more so for Jamey, but I told myself it would be fine, that the evening would pass by quickly and we'd be able to sell them on the idea of our engagement. I needed things to go smoothly, for my sake and Sophie's.

"Oh! The ring! Let me see, let me see," Leslie babbled, grabbing for Sophie's left hand with her mitt-less one. The worry on Sophie's face complimented the blush spreading across it, and I crossed my fingers in the hopes that they didn't realize it was fake. "Oh my goodness, this is gorgeous."

Sophie laughed awkwardly as she glanced up at me. "Yeah, Hudson has good taste."

I breathed out a sigh of relief. "It better be gorgeous. Spent a little too much on it if I'm honest."

Martin chuckled as he slapped a hand against my shoulder. "Good man."

"Nothing is too much for our Sophie," Leslie grinned, leading Sophie into the living room by her hand, dragging along Jamey by default.

———

"So, Hudson, what do you do?" Aaron, Sophie's brother, asked me around a mouthful of green bean casserole.

Clearing my throat, I wiped my mouth on my cloth napkin before returning it to my lap. "I'm a doctor," I said. I lifted my glass of wine, holding it in front of me. "I work in a clinic near our side of town."

"Like a general practitioner?" Leslie queried.

"Yeah, kind of," I laughed. "I work in the family planning field."

Sophie went rigid next to me, her fork halting its movement against her plate. She recovered fairly quickly, returning to eating before anyone could notice.

Leslie stared at me, her head tilting. "What's your last name, Hudson?"

"Brady," Sophie answered for me.

"Oh my goodness. Are you Betty's son?"

How the fuck...? "Yeah," I answered slowly, a little confused. "How do you know my mom?"

Leslie's face lit up, her smile spreading so far it was almost comical. "I met your mother at the country club down in Brookline," she said. "It was a few years ago, I think. She's one of my closest friends. She talks about you all the time."

Fuck. If she knew my mom... well shit, this was going to get bigger than either of us originally planned. "Oh, what a coincidence," I said, desperately trying not to show how much it had rattled me. I wondered if Sophie was thinking the same thing I was, if she was coming to the same realization.

"Funny, your mom never mentioned you seeing anyone."

"We haven't told them yet," Sophie answered far too quickly, but thankfully, no one seemed to bat an eye. "They're next on the list."

"Wow, keeping it a secret from everyone." Aaron laughed. His wife, Michelle, chuckled along with him.

"We just wanted to make sure it was, you know, real. And then we realized how nice it was to keep everyone out of the loop, and it just sort of stayed that way," I explained.

"How long have you two been together, then?" Martin asked.

"Just over a year—"

"Two years—"

Sophie and I stared at each other in horror as we realized we'd given different answers at the same time. *Fuck, we should have thought of this. We should have planned for this. Play it off, play it off.* "Has it really been two years already?"

I asked, leaning a little closer to her and tucking a strand of her deep brown hair behind her ear.

She chuckled nervously as her cheeks turned rosy. "Yeah, it has."

I closed the distance briefly, pressing a quick peck against her lips. Thank god Jamey was in the other room watching cartoons. "I'm sorry, angel. I didn't even realize."

———

"So, this one is from fifth grade. Sophie performed a Cher song for the talent show, she insisted on dressing up like her and everything. What song was it, honey?" Leslie asked Martin, the photo album spread out on the table in front of us.

"Oh my god, Mom, please don't."

"I think it was Dark Lady," Martin laughed, crossing the room and taking a look at the photo Leslie pointed to. "She got in trouble for singing about killing people."

I laughed as I looked at it, the sunglasses on her face and the sparkly dress so very Sophie. I turned the page, desperate to see more, and Sophie glared at her mother from the kitchen. "Mom, please."

"What? You look adorable."

The next page featured a younger version of Sophie with a reddened face and puffy eyes, tears halfway down her cheeks, as she clutched a baseball bat in her hands. Leslie cackled as she noticed me looking at it. "You'll never believe the story behind that one. She had this great idea when she was at a friend's party that they could play a game —what did you call it Sophie?"

Sophie's face paled as she buried her head in her hands. "Catch Grandma With a Baseball Bat."

Martin started laughing, clearly recalling more of the story. "That's right. One of you decided to be the baseball bat wielder, and the rest were 'grandmas,' right?"

She nodded into her hands.

"And you went first," Leslie continued for Martin, her laughter barely contained. "And you hit your best friend in the face with the bat."

Sophie groaned. "Yeah."

I pressed my lips together as I tried not to laugh, little Sophie's crying face staring up at me from the page.

"She felt so bad about it. Broke Sandra's nose, do you remember?" Martin asked her.

"Obviously."

I chuckled as I looked at her, her bright blue eyes trained on me from between her fingers. "I'll make a mental note to never let Jamey play that."

———

The car ride home was quieter than I expected. Jamey had already fallen asleep in the backseat as I weaved through the Boston traffic, the excitement of meeting new people and playing with Aaron and Michelle's baby, Brynn, too much for him. Sophie spent the majority of it on her phone or staring out the window, silently watching the world pass by.

Despite the initial awkwardness and having to think on my feet most of the evening, I'd had a good time. Martin and I had bonded over the fact that he teaches psychology at Harvard, we'd never crossed paths, but he loved that I was an alumnus. Sophie's mom didn't need to work. She came from old oil money, which explained their decently lavish home and cars, and likely how Sophie managed to purchase a condo at her age with a startup business.

I'd found myself actually enjoying being around her family. They were entertaining, to say the least, and seemed to buy everything we told them, even the hiccup about how long we'd been together. It had gone better than I expected, even with Sophie not telling them about Jamey.

I wanted to ask her about it. It had sat in my head like a stone all evening, but I wanted to wait until Jamey wasn't in earshot, until he couldn't potentially wake up and overhear us. I didn't want to confuse him further, he had already begun asking questions before we'd left.

I carried Jamey up to his bedroom once we got home. Sophie had left some of her things at the house, so she'd insisted on coming in, even though I knew how horrible of an idea that was. By the time I'd made my way back downstairs, not bothering to change out of my slacks and button-up shirt, she was sitting where I'd found her before on the couch. In her hands, she held two glasses of red wine, and I seriously considered going back upstairs to change my shirt.

"Hey," I said, slowly crossing the room that separated us. In the low light, she looked ethereal—her long brown hair hanging around her face, the yellow of her dress complimenting the freckles on her skin, the blue of her eyes. I already salivated for her, but I tried to tamp it down.

"Hi," she breathed. "You didn't change."

"I was hoping we wouldn't have another spilled wine

scenario," I chuckled, pressing my palms into the back of the sofa and leaning over the edge. "Oh." She said with a weak smile.

She passed the glass over the couch and sipped on her own as I took it. I'd only had one drink earlier since I was driving, but she'd downed at least two with dinner and a third after the whole grandma-with-a-bat situation. I watched her, studying her. *Why do you need another glass of wine, Sophie?*

"Do you... uh, would you like me to go?" She asked, her voice quiet.

Every part of me screamed to say no, to tell her to stay, to drag her upstairs. "Only if you want to."

She set her half-empty glass on the coffee table and stood, smoothing out her dress. Fuck, I'd said the wrong thing. *Ask her to stay, ask her to stay, ask her to fucking stay.*

Sophie rounded the couch, her dress swaying around her knees, and stopped in front of me. "I don't want to go home yet."

The relief that washed through me was far more than what I should have felt. Quickly, I downed the entirety of my wine in one gulp before tossing the empty glass on the couch. "Perfect," I mumbled, grabbing her face in my hands as I took a step toward her, and then another, forcing her backward until her spine was flush with the wall, her wide eyes staring up at me.

I couldn't hold back for another second. Every inch of me needed to touch her, to feel her, to finish what we'd started the other day. My questions could wait.

I pressed my lips against her mouth, separating hers with my tongue. I wrapped an arm around her waist, forcing her back to arch, and gripped at the fabric as I shoved one knee between her own. She was too much, too dangerous, too tempting for me to restrain myself. I could hardly think with her around, could hardly pay attention to anything besides the shape of her lips, the curves of her body, the way she fell apart in my hands.

Here I was again giving in to her temptation, and I didn't think twice about it.

Chapter 16

Sophie

Friday Night

I could hear my heartbeat in my ears, the steady, quick drum of it the only sound other than our muffled breaths and the shifting of fabric. Hudson's hand gripped the upper hem of the back of my dress, right between my shoulder blades. The feel of his skin against mine was otherworldly, the body heat emanating from his fingers alone enough to warm me so thoroughly I thought I'd never need the sun again.

"I'll buy you a new dress," he said through gritted teeth, his lips moving against my own.

"What?"

One swift tug and the fabric tore along the center seam, the back of it splitting open in two almost perfect halves. The rush of chilled air did nothing to calm the rising heat within me, and as he wrestled the cotton sundress from my arms and removed it entirely, the look on his face as he pulled back made me want to curl inside myself and die.

"Planning for this, were we?" He smirked, his gaze raking down my body.

I'd done the most ridiculous thing I could have thought of when I'd gotten ready earlier. I'd worn a white, skin tight teddy, lacy and frilly and strappy with all the bells and whistles. *Lingerie.*

"Did you want me to fuck you tonight, Sophia?" He asked in a raspy whisper, leaning back into me as he tossed my ruined dress onto the couch. "Were you hoping for it?"

I blinked up at him, my head foggy and needy, and uttered the only thing I could think of. "Yes."

His laugh surprised me, dark and heavy as it was, and before I could react to it, his hands gripped my thighs. He lifted me up, forcing my legs around his waist, his fingers digging into the meat of my flesh. "You could have just asked," he muttered, shifting me until he was holding my weight with one arm, his free hand wrapped in my hair. "Do you know what I would have said?"

"I imagine it would have been a yes—ah..." I grunted as he tugged my hair to the side, forcing my head in that direction and opening up my neck to him. His lips latched on, kissing and nipping at the sensitive flesh beneath my ear as he turned us.

"You clearly don't know me very well, angel," he mumbled against my skin, the air chilling the damp patches he left behind as he began to walk. "I would have said get on your fucking knees."

A chill ran up my spine as we ascended the stairs, his footing solid despite my weight. I knew we were going straight to his bedroom, having done this dance with him before, and the excitement went straight to my core and down between my legs, dampening the patch of fabric that sat between me and his dress shirt. I hoped it didn't leak through and ruin another one.

The smallest rush of sense hit me as he pushed open his bedroom doors. "Hudson," I breathed, my nails digging into the skin of his back as I held on for dear life. "If we do this again, that has to be crossing some sort of line."

"Don't care," he mumbled, his grip tightening. "Do you?"

Do I? I knew I wasn't necessarily in my best frame of mind, it was hard to be when I was around him. But despite that, the pit in my stomach knew what it wanted. It wanted Hudson, it wanted this, and if I was being entirely truthful to myself, it wanted a hell of a lot more.

Slowly, Hudson released his grasp enough for me to slide down his form, my feet hitting the plush carpet in front of his bed.

I shook my head. "No," I said, my voice too quiet. "I don't care."

My fingers found the buckle of his belt at the same moment that his lips found mine. He gripped the back of my head, his fingers knotted in my hair, and held me to him as he kissed me with enough force to sway my balance. His teeth nibbled at my lip, his kiss soothing the little ache it left behind, his breath mixing with my own, the taste of wine on our tongues delicious and sweet. I released the belt, tugging it through the loops as quickly as I could manage before starting on the button and fly.

Below my palm, I could feel how hard he was already. I slipped my hand between his slacks and boxers, his tucked-in shirt hanging loose, and wrapped my fingers around the length of him. I'd been yearning for him all week and I couldn't wait to touch him.

Hudson groaned his pleasure as I squeezed gently, the tip of his cock pressing hard against his boxers, the smallest bit of sticky dampness deepening the gray of the fabric. I wanted to taste it. "Fuck, Sophia," he grunted, his erection only growing from the small amount of friction.

I held the side of his hip with one hand as I slowly lowered myself to the floor, my knees settling into the soft carpet. His eyes went wide as he watched me, one hand working on his shirt buttons and the other still holding tightly to my hair. I tugged the hem of his boxers down, freeing the length of him, and wrapped my fingers around the base.

"You don't have to—"

"I want to," I drawled, dragging my fingers down his shaft and back up with featherlight movements. "You got to taste me last time. You think I haven't wanted the same?"

His cock twitched in my hand, excited for the attention, and he nodded once as he freed the last button of his shirt, exposing his chest for me. I pressed my lips to the tip of him, the little bead of precum coating them, and I licked it away. He tasted sweet, a hint of saltiness.

Slowly, I moved my head forward as I closed my lips around him, my hand meeting me halfway along the shaft. He kept his hand in place against the back of my head, guiding me gently, hesitant to thrust his hips. I pulled back to the tip, dragging my tongue across the soft, slick skin of him.

"Fucking hell, Sophie," he grunted, the soft lines of his face contorting in pleasure as I looked up at him.

I retreated, just enough that a sticky strand of my saliva connected my lips to his cock, and grinned. "What?" I asked, my hand taking the place of my mouth and stroking him gently, a little twist at the tip and right back down.

His fingers twitched with restraint as he stroked my cheek, his jaw hard set, those deep green eyes staring straight into my soul. "You are perfect. Just fucking perfect."

Butterflies stirred in my gut and I had to swallow the lump forming at the back of my throat. "Thank you," I breathed, feeling that familiar sense of warmth as it flooded my cheekbones. Hudson was far, *far* too good at making me feel flustered.

"But even as perfect as you are, he started, his knees bending as he lowered himself to my level, "I don't have the patience to wait." His hands wrapped around the backs of my thighs, lifting me before pushing me back down, my lace-covered spine hitting the mattress with a soft thud.

"Hudson," I breathed.

"Did you make this?" He asked, his knees hitting the floor, his head between my thighs. His lips slid against the thick, fleshy skin there, his hands ghosting over the fabric that covered my most intimate parts.

"No," I whispered.

"Then it's getting ruined, too." He fisted the flimsy fabric at my waist, tugging swiftly downward until the little fibers holding the lace together snapped, tearing a hole in it. He kept pulling, kept destroying, snapping apart the lace until it could barely be called scraps, the loose strings dangling across my skin. The entire lower part of my abdomen was exposed, my parted legs bearing all, the bias tape along the edges the only thing still attached to my body.

My pulse quickened as he kissed his way closer to my center, his lips brushing little pieces of lace away, and as his tongue and lips met flesh, I nearly cried out. I held my breath to keep it in as he began to devour me, to eat me alive.

I wished I hadn't worn the damn lingerie in the first place, but I'd be lying if I said it didn't make me feel sexy to have the shredded pieces of it lying across my skin, if I said it didn't turn me on even more as I watched him pull at it again, exposing little parts of my breasts and nipples to the air. He seemed to enjoy it too based on his playful humming as he flicked his tongue across my clit, the fingers of his free hand teasing my entrance and coating themselves in my juices.

"Do you want me to make you come, Sophie?" He murmured, the little vibrations of his voice across my bundle of nerves making my back arch off the bed.

"I don't... I've never come like this," I breathed. I sunk my fingers into his hair, not wanting to admit that but trusting him to be the one to do it.

"You make it sound like it's difficult," he muttered. Slowly, two fingers slipped past my entrance, sinking into me. He curled them up at the tip, stroking that spot inside of me that made me feel like I was melting with annoyingly accurate precision. I clasped my hand over my mouth to contain the sounds that wanted to escape. "I guarantee you, it's not."

His tongue moved faster, matching the rhythm of his fingers, and holy shit it nearly felt as good as when his cock was inside of me. It had always felt nice—a good warm-up— but good god with him it felt like the main act. It was almost *too* good.

He worked me as his free hand slid across skin and silk, touching me just the right way to ignite my senses and make me squirm. Already, I could feel my orgasm building low in my stomach, threatening to pull me under with one perfect move. "Oh my fucking god," I moaned, struggling to keep my breathing in check.

"I can feel you tightening around me." He started moving a little faster, but his pressure stayed consistent, something I was thankful for. "Come for me, angel."

My fingers tightened their grip on his hair, holding him fiercely against me as that dam began to burst, as my body flooded with pleasure so intense it rivaled the two orgasms he'd given me last time. I bit my tongue to hold back the scream that desperately wanted to crawl from my throat, the smallest taste of copper invading my mouth.

Slowly, he stilled, waiting until the waves had passed and my body had calmed to remove his fingers from me. "You taste so fucking good, Sophie," he said, standing at his full height. His chin dripped, his lips soaked with a combination of his own saliva and me. He climbed on top of me, my body too loose to stop him if I wanted to. "Let me show you."

He leaned down and kissed me, forcing my lips apart with a swipe of his tongue. The familiar taste of him was there, but there was also a lingering sweetness, not overwhelming like sugar but pleasant. *Me.*

The warmth of his arm beneath my shaking legs was welcome, and he suddenly shoved them up, pressing them against my chest as he lined himself up against my center. He broke the kiss, coming up for air, and with one quick push, he sunk himself so deeply inside of me I may have briefly forgotten my name.

This time I was ready for his girth, he'd stretched me enough from our previous romp. He slowly began to move. With each thrust, his hips met mine, the tip of his cock rubbing against that traitorous, blissful spot inside of me. His lips moved against my skin, over my thighs, calves, the spots on my chest he could reach with my legs up between us. He touched me like he couldn't get enough of me, like I was a drug he was drawn to and couldn't quit, and as his fingers found the spot between my thighs that made me feel like heaven, I could feel myself begin to build again.

"God, you feel so good when you squeeze me like that," he breathed, slick hair stuck to the sides of his face from sweat and saliva. His fingers kept their pace, little circles over my too-sensitive clit, not daring to change in pressure or speed even as his thrusts became a little harder, a little faster.

My nails dug into the sides of his biceps as my body began to go rigid, my orgasm nearing its peak. I shakily let go with one hand and stuffed the side of my palm between my teeth, silencing the cry that I knew was going to come, that I knew I wouldn't be able to control. Sure enough, as I began to break, the muffled scream seeped out around my hand, dulled and quiet enough so as not to wake Jamey.

"Fuck," I squeaked, removing my hand when I was sure my voice was controllable. He slowed down enough for me to catch my breath, the touch of his fingers becoming lighter, and each little wave of pleasure that rolled through me felt coaxed out by him. "It's too much. *You're* too much."

He laughed as his hips stuttered, his fingers retreating from between us. Before I could tell what he was doing, he pulled his cock from inside of me, wrapped his arms around my waist, and flipped me flat on my face. "Seems like I'm the perfect amount, Sophie," he grunted, grabbing my hips and lifting them to his waist.

With another quick push, he was back inside, filling me to the brim.

"I don't... I don't know how much more I can take," I whimpered, arching my back for him to get a better angle, my body still twitching and limp.

"You can take it," he said, his voice more soothing than

140

instructional. His hands splayed out across my ass, his fingers gripping in, and slowly, he rocked me back and forth in time with his hips. "One more time for me, angel. Come for me one more time."

I nodded, a soft whine falling from my lips and onto the plush sheets.

Chapter 17

Hudson

Sunday

The shimmer of light reflecting off the early morning's calm waters was almost blinding. I'd ensured Jamey had on his child-sized sunglasses, still comically large for his face but they got the job done and slathered him in an ungodly amount of sunscreen despite his protests. Although his skin was slightly tanned already, the kid still burned bright pink like a peach.

Nathan had come by before the sun had even risen, declaring it the perfect day for going out into the bays. He'd done the hard work for me—setting up the Land Rover with the trailer hitch, getting the boat loaded and the wires hooked up, packing snacks and fishing supplies. Meanwhile, I'd staggered around the house in my boxers, getting Jamey up and ready in my half-asleep haze, still drunk off of Sophie from Friday night. I'd walked her home after we finished, her legs shaking and hair a mess. I'd let her wear my Harvard hoodie home since she seemed to like it so much, and fuck, she'd looked so good walking up the steps on her front porch with nothing underneath. It was all I'd been able to think about for the last twenty-four hours, save for her not telling her parents about Jamey.

We'd driven the thirty minutes down to Quincy to my favorite launching spot, idled the boat through the no-wake zones of Quincy Bay and the Boston Harbor Islands, and out into the Massachusetts Bay. Despite the countless warnings I gave him every time we went out on my boat, I still found myself having to keep one hand on Jamey's lifejacket to keep him from flinging himself overboard, accidentally or not.

"What's that, Uncle Nathan?" A little tug from Jamey as he tried to step forward toward my oldest friend, and I nearly had a heart attack. As much as I loved taking him out, it was a constant battle for relaxation.

"Shrimp." Nathan held up his line, the gray, pallid corpse of a shrimp thrust through his hook. He grinned as Jamey's eyes lit up. "They're good bait, Jim-Jam. If your dad bought you a rod like I keep telling him to, I could teach you how to thread one."

Their nicknames for each other had always hit a soft spot in me. Ever since he could talk, Jamey called him Uncle Nathan, and Nathan had called him some variation of his name. James, Jimmy, Jim-Jam, Jammy. It was as absurd as it was adorable.

"Daddy?"

"What's up, bud?" I asked, reaching for the anchor and dragging him with me.

"I wanna learn Uncle Nathan's thing." He tugged on my shorts, pulling them down just a hair as I lowered the line into the water, foot by foot until it thudded against the bottom. I hated anchoring my boat, it wasn't what it was made for. It was meant to go fast, to crest the waves with ease, to speed past the buoys and slower boats.

But Nathan wanted to fish. He always wanted to fish.

"I'll get you a fishing rod, then."

"Oh, so when *he* asks for it, you'll buy one?" Nathan quipped, a laugh behind his tone. He cast his line, sending it farther than I thought it would go, and as it sunk the little floater rose to the surface.

"Well, he's my son," I chuckled. "I'm not going to buy him something he might not want just 'cause you think it's a good idea, Nate."

"So frugal with your money."

"I just don't see a point in spending it like crazy."

"Nah, just on your cars and house, huh?" Nathan laughed. He pulled Jamey into his lap, the rod between both of their legs. "Keep an eye on the floater for me, Jim-Jam."

"The what?" He asked.

"The floater. The white and red thing on the surface, there." Nathan pointed with one hand. "Tell me if it goes under the water."

"Okie dokie."

Nathan's eyes turned to me then, his hands on either side of Jamey's legs, keeping them in place. I still felt on edge, though. "So how's it going with the whole, uh... ?"

"The fake?" I motioned with my hand as if I were putting a ring on my third finger. Nathan nodded. "Yeah, it's alright. We went to meet her family the other night. They're really nice, I think we sold it to them actually."

"And are you still..." Nathan scratched his chin as he thought of a way to disguise his question so Jamey wouldn't understand, but ultimately ended up just covering his ears. "You still thinking about her?"

I sucked my teeth, glancing out at the horizon so I wouldn't have to meet his gaze. "Bit more than that, now."

Nathan's eyes went wide, his hands still firmly on either side of Jamey's head. He lowered his voice just in case. "Don't tell me you've slept with her."

"Twice."

Fuck, he mouthed. "Why don't you seem happy about that?"

"I am," I sighed, my back straightening as I watched Jamey's legs kick against the painted white side of my boat. "It's just... when we had dinner with her family, she didn't tell them about Jamey. I had to bring him along because my parents were still out of town, and she didn't warn them. We showed up and it was so awkward, man. They looked at him like he was an alien before they managed to pull themselves together."

Nathan's hands left Jamey's ears, one wrapping around his tiny abdomen and the other taking its place next to his leg, keeping him from squirming out of his lap and into the ocean. "I wouldn't overthink it, she probably just forgot. Or maybe she was nervous about how they'd react."

"She should have at least warned me, then."

"You don't know what was going through her head. Her parents are mega religious, right? Maybe that played into it. I wouldn't worry too much about it, Huds, but if it's bothering you this much then you should ask her about it. Talk to her."

"It's probably not even worth that." I pushed the hair from my face, tilting back to get a good blast of sun. Nathan was right when he'd shown up this morning, it was the perfect day to be out on the boat.

"If you like her, it is."

"I don't even know if I like her, Nate." It wasn't a lie exactly. I knew she wasn't good for me, and I was far too attracted to her for my own good, but that didn't necessarily mean I liked her. That didn't mean that I was falling for her. I motioned for Nathan to cover Jamey's ears again, and he did. "Just because the sex is fucking phenomenal and she's amazing doesn't mean I have feelings for her. We can mess around and still be casual."

"In all honesty, I've met your flings in the past, heard you talk about them, complain about them... this doesn't feel like the same thing. This is, fuck, you're going to hate this when I say it, but you seem more into this girl than you were with Becks when you first met her."

I winced at the sound of my ex-wife's name, the way it felt entering my ear and the way it crawled down my back like a snake. "I did hate that. You're right."

I could have told him that Sophie was coming in for her next appointment tomorrow. I could have told him how excited I was to see her after not having seen her for forty-eight hours, but I didn't. It was caught somewhere inside of me, desperate not to see the light of day, hiding beneath the surface. Maybe I could keep it down there. Maybe I could hide it away forever.

I should have told him, though.

"Uncle Nathan, it's moving!"

Chapter 18

Sophie

Monday

To say that I was nervous would be an understatement. My legs wouldn't stop bouncing, I couldn't stop twisting the skin of my wrists, my jaw locked and eyes forward as I waited for my name to be called. I wanted to get started on the drugs, desperately, and I knew my nerves stemmed directly from having to discuss that. Not from inevitably seeing Hudson. No, I was far too used to that by now.

"Sophia Mitchell?"

The nurse across the room wore a plain white set of scrubs and held a clipboard to her chest, her small smile trained on me. I rose, grabbing my purse from the chair beside me, and followed her back to what I now knew was Hudson's—Dr. Brady's—office.

As she opened the door, an almost calm relief washed

over me when we found it empty. That dissipated as she shut the door behind us.

"So, we've had a look at your file," she started, stepping around me and dropping into Hudson's chair. "Based on the report that you gave us when you first came in, you should be due to start your period this Friday. You track it, yes?"

I nodded. Slowly, I sank into the seat I'd sat in last time, the one I'd nearly tripped over when I tried to storm out.

"We should be able to start the drugs then in approximately two weeks' time. It's important that we time it with your cycle. It's regular, correct?"

I sighed as I leaned back, the realization hitting me. I'd been far too caught up in all the shit going on in my personal life to consider my period and how it would affect my treatment. *Stupid.* "Yeah, pretty much bang-on twenty-eight days."

She wrote something down on the clipboard, occasionally glancing up at me. "But you have polycystic ovarian syndrome?"

I nodded. "Yeah. My cycles are regular, though. I just have the cysts and the... you know. The reason I'm here."

Her tight-lipped smile nearly made me want to cry. I hated having to watch strangers feel pity for me, I'd seen it far too often on the faces of the women in the sperm bank. "Alright. We'll have Dr. Brady come in to double check your vitals and have a look at your bloodwork."

As quickly as we'd arrived, she left, leaving me in the silence of my own breathing and winding thoughts. Hudson would be coming in soon, he would look at my file, notice that my period was starting on Friday. I tried to stop my mind from telling me that he'd stay far away for an entire week, that he wouldn't want to sleep with me again until my period was definitely done.

Stupid of me to forget it even mattered. Stupid of me to want him to fuck me again.

The door cracked open, and as I turned, I caught sight of Hudson's back as he shut it behind him. "Hey, Soph," he said, so casually that my spine stiffened, my body already on edge. He walked around the back of my chair, placing his hand on my shoulder as he went, slightly too close to my neck to be nonchalant.

I watched him with bated breath as he took his seat across from me, the rigid cotton of his scrubs tightening around his thighs. "Hey."

"I heard they're making you wait because of your cycle. I'm sorry about that." He gave me a half-hearted smile, the same as the nurse that spoke to me moments ago, and it made my gut twist from the sympathy.

"It's fine."

"I just need to go over a few things with you for the interim," he continued, turning toward his computer and clicking away at the keyboard. "Are you on any medications currently that we should be aware of?"

"I used to take spironolactone for my PCOS, but that's it. Stopped it nine months ago when I first started trying to get pregnant." My leg started tapping again, my nerves getting the best of me. I had to separate Hudson and Dr. Brady in my mind—I could tell Dr. Brady all the gruesome, sad details of my journey so far, but then it had to leave my head when I saw him at home. *His* home.

The clicking stopped for a moment as he glanced at me, that annoying, obvious pity making me want to throw up. "And you were using the sperm bank over in Milton Hill, right?" I nodded. "And you've opted for a donation for insemination?"

"Obviously," I said, my gaze fixed on his, my expression

straight. What, did he think I wanted someone I know to impregnate me? The joke was on him; I don't know enough people to even consider that as an option.

The side of his lips twitched before he spoke again. "And when was the last time you had unprotected sex?"

Was he actually asking me this? My lips parted, my tongue poking the inside of my cheek in annoyance. "This morning," I lied, happy for the quick distraction as I finally relaxed in my chair a little.

His answering glare told me he didn't care for my joke. "I'm putting down last Friday."

"Odd for a doctor to make assumptions," I mumbled. I found a particularly sharp bit of my filed-down nail and picked at it. "Don't you think?"

"Don't bait me into being jealous, Sophia." He clicked a few more times on his mouse, his eyes darting across the page. "Based on your file, you shouldn't need to do a pregnancy test between now and your next appointment. We can do one when you come back in to double check, but you should be good to go."

Ouch. I didn't think he'd intended for his words to hurt but based on his time in his line of work, he had to know on some level that they would. His sigh was enough to tell me he'd at least realized what he'd said.

"Sorry, I should have worded that better—"

"It's fine." I pushed my lips into a flat line as I fisted the fabric of my bag. "I guess I'll see you tomorrow unless your mom is taking Jamey again." I made a move to stand, but Hudson's chair rolled over, his hand wrapping firmly around my wrist and pulling me gently back into my seat.

As much as I loved it when he touched me, it just felt forced in his office, surrounded by the images of smiling moms and the guilt-ridden look on his face. "Wait. I wanted to talk to you."

I narrowed my gaze at him as I sat back once again, his hand still firmly wrapped around my wrist. *Does he just like to hold it?* "Is that not what we were doing just now?"

"I mean, me to you. Hudson to Sophie. Not Dr. Brady to his patient."

"O... kay?"

I watched as his tongue glided along the ridges of his teeth, his gaze somewhere past me, through me. "Why didn't you tell your parents about Jamey?"

Well, I wasn't expecting that. "Uh." I bit my lip, sighing as I folded forward, bringing us just a little too close for comfort. "I'm sorry about that. I was just so spaced out, you know? With everything going on. It's been a lot. Between watching Jamey and my work being spread out all day, and then... whatever this is." I couldn't tell him that I was scared of my parent's reaction. I couldn't form the words, couldn't breathe them into existence. Shame settled in my stomach as it hit me that I'd royally fucked up. "I'm sorry. I should have told them."

His jaw worked as he looked at me, too many thoughts hidden behind the forest of his eyes. "I understand," he sighed, nodding more to himself than to me. "It's just that Jamey is everything to me. I know you know that, but he's an unmovable part of my life. No Jamey, no fake fiancé."

"I know. I'd never ask for him to not be in the picture, ever. It just completely slipped my mind and I only realized when my dad opened the door with that fucking look on his face."

Hudson chuckled, slicing through the tension and making me feel slightly better about my lie. "He looked at him as if he had three heads," he laughed, "and your mom—"

"Oh my god, my mom." My eyes went wide as realization struck again. I buried my head in my free hand, the other still held in place by Hudson's. "Fuck, Hudson. She's going to tell your mom. She can't keep a secret to save her life."

His smile dropped, his mouth parting. "Well, shit."

"You're going to have to tell your mom before she does."

His grip tightened on the thin skin of my wrist, the only hint that he was a little frustrated. "That's going to make this a little bigger than I was expecting." He turned my hand over, running his thumb across the fake ring I still had on my finger, the little green band forming on my flesh beneath it.

"I'm sorry," I whispered, watching his fingers out of the corner of my eye. "I know it's a lot. You can tell her it's fake if she can keep the secret, we just need my mom to buy it."

"Unfortunately," he said through gritted teeth, "she's never been good with secrets either. Maybe that's why she and your mother get along so well." He sighed as he turned my hand back over, finally releasing it as he scooted his chair back, away from me and the brief comfort he'd brought. "I'll tell her."

"Thank you," I breathed.

"Take that ring off, though. Wear it for appearances only. It'll raise suspicion if people see the oxidation from it on your finger."

Chapter 19

Hudson

Wednesday

The rain came in sheets, drenching everything from one side of Boston to the other. Just hopping out of my car to run into my favorite Chinese takeout restaurant had left me soaked. Instead of leaving my Mercedes in the driveway as I often did, I parked in the garage, hopping out of my car still dripping with a bag full of food in my hand.

For a moment, a single, solitary moment, I stood next to my car. I looked out at my driveway, watching the grays and blues melt with each other as the droplets formed a wall of water between me and the slope of cement. It was calming despite the chill I felt. For a moment, I was me, not Hudson-the-dad or Hudson-the-doctor or Hudson-the-friend-with-benefits. Just me. Alone.

With a steaming bag of Chinese food.

Eventually, the cold began to seep into my bones, and I

had to go inside. I entered through the garage door, taking Jamey and Sophie by surprise as they turned from their spot in the kitchen. "I come bearing egg rolls and chow mein," I grinned, lifting the bag for them to see.

"Daddy!" Jamey shouted, nearly tripping over the mat by the sink as he rushed for me. "You're late."

I laughed as he slammed into my thigh, nearly knocking the food from my hand. Sophie gave me a half-hearted grin from across the room, her hands wet and a towel between them. Her black leggings had something colorful smeared across them, the cardigan she wore matching. "I'm sorry. There was a crash out near Columbus Avenue, the roads were all backed up. Didn't mean to get home so late."

"It's okay," she said, drying her hands quickly before crossing the space and plucking the bag of food from my hands. "I'll get some out for Jamey and then head home."

"Stay." It came out before I could think about it, before I could consider the ramifications of asking her to stick around *again*. "I got enough for all of us."

"Stay! Stay! Stay!" Jamey shouted, the grin on his face matching the sheer amount of excitement contained in his little body. He grabbed onto the side of her shirt, tugging it just a little for emphasis. "Please stay, Sophie. Pleeeeease."

Her smile was tight, but she nodded. "Okay," she chuckled, "I'm not one to pass up free food."

I quickly set out napkins, eating utensils and placemats, then poured a glass of wine for Sophie not because I wanted her to get tipsy but because she deserved it for staying so late. I decided to pour one for myself as well. She and Jamey took their seats at the dining table as I brought the plates and food over, setting down our glasses of wine last and a cup of grape juice for Jamey so he wouldn't get jealous.

The table fell silent as Sophie helped herself and I filled

Jamey's plate. I paid close attention to what she grabbed the most of, what she grabbed the least of, making little notes in my mind of what her favorites were and what I should order next time. *Next time. Stop fucking thinking about next time, you idiot.* Jamey filled the silence as we ate, talking around mouthfuls of chow mein about everything they had done during the day, from reading a book to playing with clay.

I knew why Sophie was quiet. I knew what she was worrying about, what was holding her on edge, but I couldn't quell her worries with Jamey in the room. I could have texted her, sure, but I was selfish. I wanted her reaction for myself, in person.

As I stood in front of the sink rinsing dishes and placing them into the dishwasher, Sophie got Jamey set up in the living room with that stupid pig show that was quickly becoming his favorite. I waited until she appeared in the doorway, an exhausted look on her face and her keys in hand.

"Soph," I said, craning my head to get a better view of her.

"This was really nice, but I'm exhausted and I haven't done much work today."

"I told my mom about the engagement."

Her tired eyes widened as she looked at me, her bones frozen in place. She blinked a couple of times, the words sinking in, and then she moved toward me quickly, wrapping her arms around my waist from behind, and pressing her head against my spine. "Thank God." The feel of her body against mine, in a nonsexual situation, made my chest ache in a way I tried to ignore. It felt far too nice.

I laughed, turning in her arms so I was facing her, but she didn't budge. Instead, she pressed her face into the front of my damp scrubs. "She was... well, she was happy for me, unsurprisingly. But she was angry that I hadn't said anything. I just went with what you've been saying to your parents."

"She wasn't suspicious?"

"She was a little since I'd mentioned you to her as the new nanny. But I explained it away." I placed my hand on her back, rubbing little circles between her shoulder blades. "I know you've been worrying about that since last Friday. I'm sorry I hadn't gotten the chance until now. I saw her on Monday when she watched Jamey but I couldn't exactly say we were engaged in front of him," I laughed.

"Engaged?"

My hand stilled as my gaze snapped toward the living room. *Fuck.* Jamey stood, his mouth dropped open, his little green eyes lit with so much disbelief that I hated how much of myself I saw in them.

Sophie pushed away from my chest, taking a little shard of ice from it with her. "Jamey—"

"What does that mean?" Jamey asked, taking a hesitant step toward us and erasing the instant anxiety I'd felt. *Of course he wouldn't know what that means. He's four, for Christ's sake.*

Sophie looked at me, her brows knit and body rigid, unsure how to answer the question. I didn't know how to either. On the one hand, I didn't want to explain it to him, to confuse him and make him think Sophie and I were together. On the other, he'd probably be hearing it quite a lot in the coming weeks to months, and his questioning would only get worse. Better for us to explain it to him than someone else.

"It's... a game we're playing," I explained, crossing the kitchen and dropping down to his height, my knees pressing against the hardwood floor. "Engaged means that two people are getting married. But in this case, Sophie and I are *pretending—*"

"You're getting married?" He asked, the excitement only growing as I watched him begin to bounce on his feet.

"No, no, we're pretending to—"

"Is Sophie going to be my mommy?" The words came out more as a screech than anything else, and I winced at how they bounced around in my eardrum.

I looked back at Sophie, and dammit, she looked flustered beyond belief. Neither of us knew how to handle the situation. "Jamey, listen to me," I said, turning back to him and grabbing his little bouncing body in my hands. "Sophie and I aren't getting married. We're just playing a game. Other people, like your grandma and pops, are playing too. We're *all* pretending like Sophie and I are going to get married, okay?"

Jamey wiggled from my grasp, ducking under my arms and making a beeline for Sophie. He slammed into her with too much force, nearly knocking her over as he wrapped his arms around her legs. "I always wanted a mommy. Can I call you that now?"

Sophie stared down at him, her hands shaking, and even from where I stood across the room I could see the tears welling in her eyes. God fucking dammit, this wasn't going well, and now he was hitting her in the most vulnerable spot she had. Seeing her like that threw me into action and released a bout of adrenaline I didn't even know I had. "Jamey, stop." I lifted myself from the floor and pried him off of Sophie's legs, heaving him up so I could sit him down on the counter. "You've misunderstood, bud. We're not actually getting married, okay? We just... we need you to play along."

He looked between me and Sophie with a blank expression on his face, literally nothing clicking in his head. "I don't get it."

———

"I don't know where to go from here," I sighed, clutching a half-empty glass of whiskey in my palm as I sat back down on the couch. Sophie sat on the other end, her knees to her chest, her eyes focused wholly on the wine in her hands. That little moment of relief had come crashing down, and now neither of us could relax even though Jamey was in bed, asleep.

"Me either," she breathed. She'd hardly taken a sip, the glass in her hands still the one from dinner she'd barely touched. "I don't want to confuse him."

"He's already confused." I leaned forward, resting my elbows on my knees and holding my glass between them. The irritation was already bubbling inside of me, the stress hitting me of having to deal with this miscommunication and how our fake engagement was seeming to affect every part of my life now. "I can't do this, Sophie. I can't get his hopes up and break his heart."

"I know." Her voice was small, too small, and she set her glass down before wrapping her arms around her knees. Her eyes were everywhere but on me. "I'm so sorry, Hudson. I don't want to hurt him either."

"I can't be involved with you. We can't do this anymore. All of this, every single part, it's fake. It has to be fake. I'm not going to do that to him."

The silence that fell was thick, heavy. I glanced at her,

my grip nearly hard enough to crush the glass in my hand, and I swear for just a moment her lip quivered. "It's fake," she nodded, the words barely more than a whisper. She sniffled as she wiped her eyes with the back of her hand. "I don't want this to get any worse. I just want a baby, Hudson, that's it. Nothing else."

I steeled my jaw as I forced myself to look away from her. I knew deep down, if I watched her cry, if I watched her suffer the guilt she obviously felt about confusing my son, I'd want to take that away. I'd want to fix it, to make her feel better, to tell her it was fine. But it couldn't be fine. I had to put Jamey first, always. "I think the best way forward is to cut everything off."

"What do you mean?"

"No more sex. No more sneaking around when he could stumble in on us. That day in my office was too close, your moans are too risky. We can't keep doing that," I said, already hating every word of it but knowing it was the right thing to do.

I could feel her eyes on me. It made my skin crawl, but not in a bad way. It was everything I wanted. "Yeah," she breathed. "You're right. We have to stop."

"Are you okay with that?" *Why are you asking? It shouldn't matter. None of this should matter.*

"Yeah. Like I said, I just want a baby. It's fine."

She moved, and I watched from the corner of my eye as she stood from the couch, smoothing out her cardigan where it fell around her hips. "Sophie—"

"It's fine. Really."

I looked up at her, hating the way it made me feel to see the hard line of her jaw, her lips straight, her eyes glassy. "You don't have to go yet."

She turned from me, getting up from the sofa and

standing in place. When she spoke, she didn't look at me, didn't pause. "I think it's best I go home now."

I didn't watch her as she gathered her things. I listened as I heard the familiar jingle of her keys, the little keychains she kept on it clanging together, and headed toward the door. The silence in the house was nearly deafening, but I could hear as she slid on her slippers, as she opened the door and went out into the rain, closing it softly behind her so she didn't wake Jamey.

Chapter 20

Sophie

Friday

I stared down at the piece of toilet paper in my hand.

I'd woken to an alert on my phone from my period tracking app, a handy little reminder that my cycle should start today. *It's fine. It'll probably just start later, or in a day or two.* It wasn't the most unusual thing in the world for me to be a day or so late. I would be able to track when I'd be ovulating once I eventually started and would reschedule my next appointment based on that.

I flushed the paper down the toilet as I stood. Yesterday had been awkward, to say the least. I'd gotten to Hudson's a few minutes before I knew he needed to leave, trying to minimize the amount of time we had to spend in each other's presence, and then spent the majority of my day trying to correct Jamey when he asked questions about our engagement. It was exhausting, and the few times I'd had to hide in the bathroom to cry were because of my PMS. I'd been far too emotional around my period since I started trying to get pregnant, and I didn't want to think about why that was and how it connected to the disappointment I felt every time I looked at the blood-smeared toilet paper.

I threw my hair up into a messy bun as I got dressed. In the hamper across from my bed, Hudson's Harvard hoodie glared at me, daring me to do my laundry and bring it back to him. I ignored it and pulled on my comfiest trousers and a black T-shirt from my closet.

I got to Hudson's as he was grabbing his keys to leave, a look of relief washing over him as I stepped through the door.

"I thought you weren't coming," he sighed.

"I would have texted you," I mumbled, shutting the door behind me and throwing my keys onto the entryway table. "Sorry."

"It's fine." He looked down at me, his green eyes hiding far too much behind them as he studied me. "Jamey's still upstairs. He was up and down all night, kept having nightmares. He should be up soon."

"Okay."

His gaze flicked between me and the door. Knowing that Jamey was still upstairs put me on edge. Yesterday, even during the most awkward few moments when Hudson and I were together, Jamey had been a buffer. But without him it just felt all too real, too emotionally taxing. "I'll see you when I get home."

I nodded, taking that as my signal that I was allowed to move, to get comfortable in a house that wasn't my own, without a fiancé that wasn't real. I walked toward the kitchen, aiming to get Jamey something for breakfast, and listened as the door opened then slammed shut.

162

———

"So, you're not my new mommy?"

I sighed for the thousandth time as I placed a red Lego on top of all the other red Legos. He'd insisted on making a red-only Lego tower. "No, Jamey, I'm not."

He pouted as he looked down at the bricks in his hand. "All of my friends have a mommy."

His words hit me like a bullet to the chest. I inhaled, lifting my head to the ceiling so the burning behind my eyes would dissipate, and lowered it only when I felt in control. "You know, Jamey, not everyone has a mommy. Maybe one day your daddy will find a mommy for you, but it's okay if he doesn't. Some people just don't have one. Some people have two daddies, some people lose their mommy when they're little. Some mommies don't get to have babies." I fought the quivering in my lip as he looked up at me, his eyes wide. "Your daddy does what's best for you even if it doesn't feel like it. If he decides to get you a mommy, it'll be someone even better than me, the best of the best. He wouldn't settle for less for you."

"But you're the best of the best."

I laughed as I pulled him into my lap. "I'm hardly the best, you little squirt," I joked as he wrapped his little arms around my neck.

He really was such a sweet kid, even though he had so much of his father in him. If and when I eventually got pregnant, I hoped that whoever popped out would be at least half as funny, half as cute as Jamey. I could easily play with him forever, even when he asked me the same questions over and over, even when he got annoyed because I made him something he didn't love for lunch, and even when he played the same episode of Peppa Pig three times in a row.

I was ready to be a parent. More than ready. It was almost crazy how much I wanted it, how much the need for it floated around inside me, always in the background no matter what I did or to whom I spoke. It was always there. A constant want, a constant need.

I took solace in the fact that once I became pregnant, Hudson and I could call off our fake engagement. We could pretend that we had broken up—the death idea had gone out the window once I realized our moms were friends—and that I was left with the baby, free to raise it on my own because it wouldn't be his. We could part ways and never see each other again if that's what we wanted.

That was the part that hurt. I wanted to say it was because I would lose out on hanging out with Jamey and watching him grow, but I knew that wasn't the only reason. Annoyingly, I knew that Lisa was at least partly right; I'd gotten attached. Not massively, not like before, but a part of me liked being with Hudson, even though he didn't want more kids and even though he wasn't interested in anything more with me.

I pushed back the disappointment I knew would eventually hit me when we parted ways as Jamey wiggled out of our hug, Legos still in hand, and returned to his massive red-only Lego tower.

Chapter 21

Hudson

Saturday

I glanced at the time on my dashboard as I sat in the thick traffic of central Boston, the sound of Jamey's tablet playing one of his shows and the ringing coming from my phone the only things on which I could focus. I stared at the screen as it continued to ring, Sophie's name front and center on the top as the seconds ticked by. *Pick up. Please pick up.*

"What's wrong?"

I couldn't stop myself from laughing. "What? Why do you think something's wrong?"

"Because it's a Saturday and I'm off duty," she said monotonously through my car speakers, almost as if she were annoyed that she picked up in the first place.

"Did you only answer because you thought it was an emergency?"

"Yes."

"Are you busy?"

"Yes."

"What are you doing?"

"Oh my god, Hudson, are you fu—"

I reached out, turning the volume right down before the word could come out. "Jamey is in earshot," I said, turning the volume back up and moving half an inch forward in the stop-and-go traffic.

"Hi, Sophie!" He called from the backseat.

"Oh. Hi, Jamey," she replied, her voice friendlier for him. "What do you want, Hudson? I'm trying to get some work done today."

"We have a bit of a problem," I sighed, flexing my fingers against the steering wheel. "My mom has decided that she wants to have dinner with us tonight to get to know you. She's already annoyed that I haven't introduced her to you yet so I kind of had to say yes."

She groaned, and in the background, I heard the solid *thud* of what I could only assume was her head against her desk. "I'm really busy."

"I know. I'm sorry. I'll make it up to you." From the backseat, I heard the unmistakable sound of a virtual payment going through. I really needed to take that feature away from him before he drained my fortune dry with his purchases of in-game money. "I've ordered caterers. I'll have them make anything you want."

"Anything?"

"Anything."

She sighed in frustration. "Fine. I want crab legs. I've been craving seafood."

"Done. Be at my place before seven so she doesn't ask questions," I said, reaching for the little red button on my phone but stopping short. "Oh, and wear something you've made. She'll like that. She's very crafty."

"Oh my god, goodbye, Hudson."

———

I was convinced Sophie was actively trying to taunt me as she walked through my door, a scowl on her perfect face. Her makeup was flawless; her freckles shining through, her blue eyes popping from the muted colors on her lids, her lips a deep maroon, reminding me far too much of the wine stain from the first night I took her.

The ring on her finger shone brightly in the dim light, grabbing my attention and forcing it down Sophie's body. The dress she wore was figure-hugging, showing off every flawless curve of her body. The top was corseted, structured in all the right ways, and the see-through fabric of the puffed long sleeves brought her entire look together. It was a maddening outfit—one my mother would love when she found out Sophie had made it, and one that would keep my eyes glued to her all goddamn night long.

"Don't stare at me like that," she grumbled.

"Like what?"

"Like I'm a piece of meat." Her eyes met mine, her lined lips going flat.

My phone buzzed in the pocket of my neatly pressed slacks. I fished it out, a text from my mom filling the screen. She was five minutes away. "Shit, she's close. Okay, uh, Jamey?"

He rounded the corner of the living room quickly, his

shoes clacking against the floor with each little stomp. "What? Oh, hi Sophie!"

"Hi, Jamey."

"Listen to me," I said, lowering myself to his level. I'd dressed him up enough to set the mood, but not too much that he would complain all evening. He was wearing a nice set of black pants with a white button-up top and his nicest shoes, which he'd already fussed about because he had to wear them in the house. *Dammit, what is that red spot on his shirt? How did he already stain it?* "Grandma is coming over. We're going to have dinner."

"I know," he groaned, flopping around dramatically as if I were boring him to death.

"We're playing the game tonight. The one where Sophie and I are engaged. You have to play along, okay? And you have to remember that it's just a game."

He nodded. "Engaged means getting married."

Sophie sighed as she glanced out the window, her heeled foot tapping nervously against the wood floor. "Hudson, there's headlights in the driveway."

"Yes, engaged means getting married. But it's a game. It's not real. Got it?"

"Got it, Daddy."

We can do this.

———

"So, Sophie, you're a designer?"

Sophie sat upright, her mouth full of the inside of a crab

leg. She covered her lips as she swallowed, nodding. "Yeah. I made this dress, actually."

My mom grinned as she cracked a leg over her plate. She'd worn one of her nicer dresses, one I'd seen once before at the funeral of one of her coworkers. Her unnaturally blonde hair was tucked neatly up in a bun, her makeup sitting heavily over her Botox-filled face. A man in a suit and tie filled her glass of wine from behind her, and she turned and thanked him before looking back over at Sophie. "That's amazing. I've heard bits and pieces from your mom, but I had no idea how good you were."

She chuckled awkwardly. "Yeah, you know how she is."

Sophie had been fairly quiet thus far, and although I figured it was because of the nerves and the worry that Jamey would say something to ruin it all, it seemed like it was more than that. We'd been short with each other for days now, hardly having any kind of meaningful conversation, and I wondered if she was finding this difficult to navigate because of our conversation the other night. In fairness, I'd been off because of it, too.

"I just can't believe Hudson didn't tell me about you," my mom laughed. She dipped a solid chunk of crab into a bowl of melted butter before shoving it in her mouth. "Though, to be fair, the last woman he told me about was Rebecca, and we all know how that ended."

The crab leg in my hand shattered. "Can we please not talk about Becks?" *Not only is it fucking awkward to bring up in front of Jamey, but it's also rude as shit in front of Sophie.*

But it isn't real.

"Of course, honey. I'm sorry." My mom turned to Jamey as she cracked another leg, fishing out the flesh with a tiny fork. "How do you feel about all this, Jamey?"

I bit my tongue, and when I glanced at Sophie, I could tell she was watching him like a hawk. "I love that my daddy is engaged." He chirped as he picked at his chicken nuggets. "I think it's amazing that he's going to be married."

Jesus fucking Christ kid, this isn't a vocabulary test.

"Do you like Sophie?"

"I love Sophie," he grinned. "But she's not going to be my new mommy."

The chair beneath Sophie squeaked as she pushed herself back. She dabbed at her mouth with her napkin, standing on shaky legs. "I'm sorry, I'll be right back."

———

"I like her."

I sighed as I poured out a fourth glass of wine for my mother, more than a little relieved that her driver would be the one taking her home. The catering team had packed up and left, leaving the four of us alone, and thankfully, Sophie was more than happy to play with Jamey in the other room while I spoke to my mom. "I do too," I chuckled, hoping she didn't pick up on the tension.

"I think she's really good for you. She's obviously great with Jamey, too. I just don't understand why you didn't tell me, honey. You know I'd have supported you even if it went sour."

"I know," I sighed, holding out the glass of wine for her. She plucked it from my fingers within a second. "We just wanted to keep it quiet until we knew we were serious. We didn't even tell Jamey we were together until a few weeks ago. I just didn't want to get his hopes up."

I knew she'd come to terms with it. I also knew that when the time came that Sophie and I had to fake a breakup, she'd be okay with that, too. She'd been there through the thick and thin, the highs and lows of my relationship with Becks. She could handle this.

I just hated lying to her.

It made me happier than it should have to know that she liked Sophie, though. It shouldn't have mattered whether she did or not—it would become pointless when it eventually ended, but it felt good knowing that she'd approve if Sophie and I had met under different circumstances. If only I was capable of letting someone new in and she wanted to be with me. But she didn't. And that was fine. Totally fine.

———

Sophie stood in the doorway, her back to me as she waved at my mom's car backing down the driveway. She watched with eagle eyes trained on it until it disappeared around the corner, headlights far from view, then took one step off the frame and onto the porch.

I reached out instinctively, my hand wrapping around the small base of her wrist. She turned, the little ringlets of her hair flying about her face. "Hey," I said softly, pulling her back to the doorway and off of the front mat. "Are you okay? You seem... distant."

"I'm fine, Hudson," she sighed, turning her head back toward her condo. She didn't want to look at me, but fuck, all I wanted to do was look at her in that dress. "I don't know what you're talking about."

"You don't seem fine."

"Well, I am. And I'd like to go home." She tugged once on my hold, and I released her, but I didn't want to let her leave. I'd had two glasses of wine, I was more than loose enough to have a decent conversation with her, and if I was being truly honest, I wanted to keep looking at her.

"Jamey asked me if you'd read him a bedtime story," I lied. "Will you stay? Just for a few?"

She looked at me again, some sense of inner conflict thinly veiled on her features. "Okay," she sighed, taking a step back inside. "I'll read him a story. Then I'm going home."

The time passed way too quickly. Although Jamey hadn't actually requested it, he was more than happy to have Sophie helping with bedtime. I stood in the doorway of his room, the little glow-in-the-dark stars lighting the space so perfectly as Sophie sat on his bed, his favorite book tucked neatly in her hands. It only took him a few pages to fall asleep, and I prayed she wouldn't notice, that she'd keep reading, extending this stupid fucking lie of a moment as long as possible.

But of course, I can't have everything I want.

Sophie closed the door behind her as she walked out of his room, and instead of focusing on the way my son took to her so easily or how quickly he'd fallen asleep to the sound of her voice, all I could do was think about how much I wanted her beneath me. That little part of me that was animalistic, that wanted to take, take, take and fuck the consequences, was nibbling a little too hard at my mind. Her dress and her lips weren't helping.

I walked with her down the hall as she aimed for the

stairs, my mind swimming, and before I could take a moment to think about it, I sprung.

She gasped as I placed myself between her and the stairs, forcing her backward, further and further until her spine hit the wall. "What the fuck—"

"I was wrong," I said. Placing my hands on either side of her head, I caged her in. The perfume she wore flooded my senses, scrambling my brain even more, the thoughts of being close enough to her that I could smell it on every inch of her bare skin flooding my mind. "We can make it work."

"What?" She breathed, the little wave of hair that had fallen in her face jumping from the puff of air.

"It was a bad idea, breaking it off like that. Clearly, neither of us is happy with it. Am I right?" I challenged, leaning in just an inch further, her parted lips within reaching distance.

She hesitated before she answered me, her eyes searching mine for answers, her chest rising and falling too quickly, too unevenly. "Just because we're not happy with it doesn't mean it's a bad idea."

I took her face in my hand, stroking across the streak of freckles beneath her eye, and she turned her head into it. "Let me make you think it is, Sophie," I whispered, and the distance between my lips and hers felt too far. I couldn't fucking help myself—I needed to taste her, to have her, to take her again. I knew it was a bad idea. I knew I'd just keep coming back for more and more. I just didn't fucking care.

I pressed my lips to the corner of her mouth, just enough to satiate me for the moment she needed to make a decision. I'd honor her choice, whatever it was, but I'd be fucking disappointed if she made the wrong one.

"Let's keep the game going," I continued. "I'll pretend

to be yours. You pretend to be mine. Let me fuck you with that ring on, angel."

Her breath faltered as I moved my hand to the back of her neck, my fingers splaying out into her hair. Goddammit, Hudson," she whimpered, her head turning just a fraction, her lips pressing firmly against mine.

Chapter 22

Sophie

Saturday Night

This was dangerous, *more* than dangerous, and we both knew it. We'd agreed to no more of this, and although I was more upset about that than I should have been, it was the right thing to do, the best thing to do. But if we were going to throw all caution to the wind, being as far away from Jamey as possible was the only solution.

I grasped the black, thick cotton of his shirt in my hand, putting that little bit of space between us. My back rested solidly against the curve of the kitchen counter, pressing firmly into my spine. "Hudson," I gasped, pulling my mouth from his. "There's a chance he could still hear us here." I pushed back against his chest, my knuckles meeting solid muscle. His answering growl vibrated against them.

"Then where do you propose we go?" He asked, shifting the attention of his lips to my neck, to the soft spot beneath my ear that made me pant. "Or are you capable of being quiet?"

I almost laughed. "Not when I'm with you."

His hand dragged down my side, resting at the point where fabric met flesh, and slowly, he began to shift it upward. "You have about ten seconds before I fuck you over the counter, so if you want to go somewhere else, you'd better pick now."

Where? I glanced around frantically, trying to come up with a better idea that wouldn't potentially end with him regretting it entirely because of our proximity to Jamey. Everything was too close in this massive house, too much of a risk. My options were dwindling, his roaming fingers against my thigh an indication that the clock was ticking. *Garage? No, it reeks of motor oil.* "Backyard," I breathed, my heart leaping in my chest at the thought. "Jamey's room looks toward your neighbors, right? He won't be able to see anything."

I could feel his erection against my hip, throbbing in time with my heartbeat. He was impatient. "Great. Perfect. Now *go*."

———

With my back to one of the many columns of his back porch, Hudson's lips found mine again. With one hand, he cushioned my head from the hard concrete. With the other, he searched the back of my dress for the zipper, all of the patience he possessed located solely within those fingers. It made those butterflies take flight in my gut again, though he hadn't been so gentle with the last dress I'd worn.

But I'd *made* this one, and he knew that. He didn't want to ruin it.

He tugged the zipper down as far as it would go, the rigid fabric and boning of the corseted bodice falling forward between our bodies. I pulled the sleeves down my arms quickly, releasing the entirety of my upper body to the elements. Thank God it wasn't a cold night.

"No bra?" He asked, his words a whisper against my lips.

My cheeks warmed. *Think, Sophie.* "The corset acts as one." I quickly fumbled with the buttons of his shirt, tempted to break them like he had the first time, the promise that I would sew them back on resting on the tip of my tongue, but he took over for me. Within seconds, his shirt was on the cold ground, my hands now pressed to the warmth of his skin instead.

As if on instinct, my senses rushed back in, banging against that locked little box I'd shoved them in and screaming *this is a bad idea.* I turned my head, separating our mouths just so I could breathe properly, fully. I needed a minute. I needed time to think, time to decide if this was something that would end with an ache in my chest and too many tears shed against my pillow, if it was worth the potential upset. "Let's swim." *That's the best you can come up with? Seriously?*

Hudson stilled, his eyes trained on me. "You suggest we go outside, and now you want to swim?"

I nodded.

"Are you just using me for my pool?"

"Maybe," I mocked. I winked at him as I slid down the column and out from the cage of his arms, kicking off my heels toward the door. "All this time you thought I was looking out my window at *you* that day. Jokes on you, Dr. Brady. I was just taken with your pool."

Hudson laughed, taking a step toward me as I retreated, my back to the water. "So you're saying my little voyeur is actually just a pool enthusiast?"

"That's exactly what I'm saying." I stopped where I was, just an inch from the steps that lead down into the water. Slowly, I lowered my dress further, pushing it past where it hugged my hips and down until it pooled like liquid around my feet.

Hudson's gaze hovered over my body, taking in every inch. "You didn't wear panties either, Sophia?" He asked, his voice guttural, deep, that lust creeping back in. I tried not to think about what he would assume that meant, the correct answer he would come to.

"No," I breathed. "I didn't. Join me?"

I watched as he unbuckled his belt from across the concrete patio, naked as the day I was born. I stole a glance at his neighbor's house—the one on the other side that wasn't mine—and felt the goosebumps creep across my skin as I wondered if they were watching us. By the time I'd brought myself to look at him again, he was pulling his trousers from his ankles, throwing the fabric back toward the house as he closed the distance between us.

His mouth met mine again as he forced us back, and I gasped, instinctually reaching for the railing along the stairs but finding nothing but air. My foot hit the first step, striking true, the warm water rippling around it and beckoning me further. He guided me down, one arm around my bare waist, as if he'd gotten in blind a million times.

By the time we were up to our chests in the water, I was using it to my advantage. I wrapped my legs around his hips, his rigid cock firmly between us and slipping against my clit, and had the water hold my weight as I reached up to kiss him again. I couldn't help myself. Even though this was meant to be a breather, a moment to calm down, I needed him close. I needed him on me or I was going to lose my goddamn mind.

Maybe I would either way.

He pressed my back against the edge of the pool, the tiled edges sliding against my skin, and held my face between his hands as his lips moved against mine. He went deeper into my mouth, exploring with his tongue, memorizing. My peaked nipples rubbed against the solid muscles of his chest, sending little waves of pleasure right down between my legs. "Why didn't you wear underwear?" He mumbled, lifting me higher on his body so he could access my breasts. He moved the damp strands of my hair out of the way, and before I could stop him, his mouth was already there, taking one between his lips and dragging his tongue across the sensitive skin.

"Fuck," I groaned, wrapping my fingers around the back of his neck for stability. "You know why."

"Naughty," he chuckled. "You're lucky I have a shred of patience. Otherwise, I'd fuck you right here."

I bit my lip as I looked down at him, his teeth around my nipple, his green eyes cast up at me. I'd hardly had a full glass of wine yet somehow, someway, I felt comfortable enough to speak freely. "Do you think I don't want that?" I breathed.

"Do you?"

I chuckled as I pushed my fingers into his hair, the wet strands thick and full around them. "Obviously."

I gasped as he lifted me higher, fully out of the water until my ass hit the cold ledge of the pool. Wet pieces of hair clung to my skin, sticking around my waist and breasts, clinging to me the way I wanted to with him. He lifted himself onto a step under the water, the upper half of his body rising from the pool and water sluicing down his frame. The moonlight reflected off of him, shimmering against his hardened chest in all its stupid, perfect glory. He looked like a Greek god emerging from the lakes of Hell itself, here to damn me for eternity.

"Jesus," I breathed, leaning back on my hands to get a better look at him. He nudged himself between my thighs, pushing them outward. "It's not fair that you look like that."

He pushed the loose strands of wet hair back from his face as he loomed over me. "I'm sorry. Should I just let myself get out of shape purely so you won't be tempted?"

"Fuck, no."

"Then don't complain." He leaned into me, pushing me back, guiding me with one arm around my waist. The more I pitched back, the more the moonlight reflected on me, not him. "Lift your legs, Sophia."

Sophia. The amount of times he'd referred to me by my full name now was getting out of hand. Still, I obeyed, lifting my calves from the water and higher, toward my chest.

He hummed his approval as his gaze raked over my damp body, down over my breasts and abdomen and lower, between my thighs. "That... god, what I'd give to keep you like this forever, spread open for me, waiting for me. Greatest sight I'll ever fucking see."

I laughed, lifting my left hand to his face, showing off the fake ring that was starting to turn my skin green from the water. "Well, lucky for you, *fiancé*, you can."

His face shifted, contorting into something I wasn't quite sure what to make of. His eyes narrowed, his jaw hardened. He took my hand from in front of his face, pushing me back and pinning it above my head on the cold concrete. "Don't tempt me, angel."

Pressure bloomed against my entrance, the head of his cock pressing firmly against it. Slowly, achingly, he pushed forward, sinking himself between my soaked lips. I groaned as the little shocks of my walls spreading turned to pleasure, as he reached his depth, as his hips met my ass. "Fuck, yes."

"Tell me what you want," he grunted, the sound of the water moving about his legs going silent as he held himself still. "Tell me how badly you want it."

Jesus, he had to stop saying things like that.

I lifted myself onto my elbow, the rough concrete cutting into the thin skin and wrapped one hand around the back of his neck. "I want you to fuck me," I drawled, that confidence coming from somewhere deep within me. "No, scratch that. I *need* you to fuck me, Hudson."

Wild, blazing green eyes met mine for a fraction of a second before his hips began to move, less gentle than he'd been before, more animalistic, more untamed. I dropped back onto the pavement, taking every hit he gave, water sloshing up the sides of the pool as he moved inside of me. It felt too good, too powerful.

I glanced up toward the house next to his, the one owned by the couple I'd come to know as Mary and Jeff Traeger. I hoped they weren't watching through the windows, hoped we wouldn't send their frail old bodies into cardiac arrest. *What would they think of me, to see me like this? Probably the same thing my parents would think if I were pregnant without a future husband.*

"Look at me when I'm inside of you, Sophie," Hudson ordered, his fingers grasping my cheeks and turning my head back to him. His other hand snaked between us, reaching the slick folds between my legs and pinpointing my clit with ease. My eyes widened as my back arched, his digits beginning to move in just the way he knew I liked.

I could've lived like that, died like that, with him above me, inside of me. I'd welcome every second of it. "Fucking hell," I breathed, staring up at him, at the drops of sweat and pool water that dripped from his face. "This is... *a lot*."

"You like being fucked outdoors?" He chuckled darkly, his hips moving faster, harder, his fingers sliding through the growing dampness. "Exhibitionist *and* a voyeur."

I moaned from the intensity of his movements, my pleasure building and beginning to peak. "Pool enthusiast," I bit out.

"Right, sorry. Exhibitionist and pool enthusiast."

I reached up, placing my hand on his cheek, my thumb on his lips. Slowly, I dragged it across them, pulling the skin along, dipping it between his lips. I was getting close, too close, and I needed more. "Hudson," I moaned, and suddenly the air around me ceased, the water sloshing faded into the background, the stars above disappeared and there was only him and me and the concrete beneath my skin. "Shut the fuck up and kiss me."

His eyes widened for a fraction of a second before he was leaning down, swift and eager, his lips firmly pressing against my own. I opened for him like a flower, welcoming anything he wanted to give me. The good, the bad, the ugly. Richer or poorer. Sickness and health. All that shit, I'd take it, and not because of the fake ring on my finger.

The warmth in my chest bloomed further down, and within seconds, I was breaking harder than I'd ever broken before. The wave of pleasure tore through me, replacing every cell in my body with bliss, every thought with him. I cried out into his mouth, the sound silent through my clouded ears, my throat feeling hoarse. His hips stuttered, his breathing increased, and before I knew it he was falling with me, deep into the abyss and away from anything and everything else.

Hudson's heavy breaths against my lips and his stagnant cock slowly brought me back to reality, back to the pool, back to his backyard. Slowly, I opened my eyes, his own an inch from my face. His heart was hammering against his chest and beating against my own, the effort to stay upright clearly showing in the veins popping from his arms.

"Shit," he sighed, his head dropping, his forehead resting against my lips. "This... this was a mistake."

Mistake.

Mistake.

Mistake mistake mistake mistake mistake mistake.

"What?" The word was barely a whisper, my lips hardly moving.

"This shouldn't have happened."

I scrambled back, my elbows and heels scraping against the rough cement, out of his embrace. His cock slid out and warmth seeped from my entrance, and instead of giggling with him about it, all I wanted to do was get the hell away from him, away from what had just happened.

Mistake.

"Sophia—"

"Don't. Don't fucking call me that," I snapped as I lifted myself to my feet. The skin on my elbows stung, and I focused on the feeling of that instead of the ache that was growing intensely within my chest. "I need a towel."

"I'm sorry—"

"Towel," I spat, turning to face him. Slowly, he lifted himself from the pool, water dripping down his calves.

"I'll get you one," he said quietly, shuffling past me and

toward the house. Instantly, the cold I hadn't felt before sunk into my skin, my bones, and I wrapped my arms around myself to keep from shivering.

Mistake.

I snatched the towel from his hands when he reappeared through the sliding glass door, wrapping it around me tightly as I wrung the water from my hair. I couldn't look at him, couldn't meet his eyes. I desperately didn't want to acknowledge what I'd feel if I did.

"I... I'll do better from now on. I'm sorry. I'll keep my hands off you. This can't happen again," he sighed, dragging a towel along his perfectly warm, naked body.

"It *won't* happen again," I corrected him. "Fuck you, Hudson. Maybe with the next girl you inevitably drag into your life, you won't let your fucking dick make all of the decisions." I grabbed my dress and heels from the ground, holding them to my chest, and shoved past him. I just wanted to go home. I needed to be alone, to process this in my own way, to not scream and wake the four-year-old upstairs. *Mistake.*

"Sophie, I'm sorry. I didn't mean it like that." His hand caught my wrist, and I was tempted to break it just to get away. *Stop grabbing my fucking wrist.*

I laughed, a physical, full-bodied laugh. "Is this a joke to you? Am *I*?" The backs of my eyes burned, the threat of tears imminent, and god fucking dammit I didn't want him seeing me cry. I didn't want to cry in the first place, but it seemed there was no helping that. "Do you think it's okay to say that having sex with me was a mistake when your cock was still inside of me, Hudson?"

"It's not that," he insisted, taking a quick step toward me as I took one back. "It's just... it's Jamey. It's always Jamey, okay? I don't get to do what I want because I have someone else I have to constantly be thinking about. You think you want this—"

"Don't," I warned, lifting one hand to shut him up before he could say something worse. "You have no right to say what I should and shouldn't want. I'm not even a mother yet and even I know that you can still have a damn life and a child at the same time."

He fell silent as his grip on my wrist loosened. The wind whistled through the trees of the subdivision, lifting the strands of his too-perfect hair away from his too-symmetrical face. It was more than I could bear, all of it. The air made my face feel damp, and when I pressed my fingers against it, I realized it wasn't wet from the pool. I'd shown too much of myself. *Mistake.*

"Goodnight, Hudson." I stepped through the doors, thankful that he seemed to stay put, and gathered the rest of my things before heading straight out the front door. Wrapped only in a towel, with my thoughts spiraling and my chest aching, I walked across the lawn to my home, to my safety net.

I need to get out of all of this.

Chapter 23

Hudson

Tuesday

The temptation to apologize sat heavy in me as I went about my life. I'd only seen Sophie briefly yesterday and this morning, she'd arrived right as I was leaving, not saying a word.

I hadn't been able to stop thinking about Saturday night. Seeing her like that—wild, free, easygoing with me—was too much. It had chipped away at the ice in my chest, had made me want more than I should have. But, god, the sex had been insane. I'd never stepped so far out of my comfort zone, and seeing her naked, glistening, sprawled out on my pool deck had been far too tempting. The image was still burned into my mind, still taunting me as I worked, as I cooked, as I drove. I couldn't do a damned thing without it lingering in the background.

I needed to make up with her. I knew that. I needed to apologize, to make it right, to tell her that I'd fucked up. *You told her it was a mistake with your dick still inside of her, you idiot.*

I stood from my desk, deciding that the least I could do was set up the appointment she was desperately awaiting. Quickly, I made my way to reception, interrupting the nurses and staff chatting behind the counter.

"Can you make an appointment for one of my patients, Sophia Mitchell? Should be approximately two weeks from now if she's called to update us on her cycle," I said, pointing my pen lazily toward the computer for bookings.

Janice came around the corner, her clipboard clung to her chest. "Didn't you hear? She called this morning saying she no longer needed our services."

The pen in my hand nearly snapped as I turned to her. *What the fuck?* "What do you mean she no longer needs our services? Is she going to a different clinic?"

"No, Dr. Brady. She said she's pregnant."

Pregnant.

My vision blurred as my mind spun. *It's mine. It's mine. It's mine.* I felt like I was going to faint, like the world was going to slip out from under me and I'd fall, fall, fall, out the other end and deep into the milky way, gone. *How did this happen? How could I let things go this far?*

"Dr. Brady?"

"Cancel my appointments," I mumbled, my shaky fingers already fumbling with my white coat. "I need to go home."

"But you still have three—"

"Cancel them," I snapped. "Shove them off on someone else if you have to."

———

. . .

I pushed the front door open with too much power behind it, making Sophie and Jamey jump from where they stood in the kitchen. Jamey was wearing his little apron and a small chef's hat, a whisk in one hand, standing proudly on his stool as he turned to face me.

"Daddy!"

"What are you doing home?" Sophie asked, but midway through her sentence, she seemed to realize. Whether it was the look on my face or the sheer idiocy one must have to call my workplace telling them she was pregnant, she knew I knew. "Hudson, I—"

"Garage. Now," I barked, and bless him, Jamey hopped down from his stool. "Not you, bud. You stay in here. Play on your tablet or something."

Slowly, Sophie removed her apron, lying it flat on the counter beside Jamey before tentatively taking a step toward me. "I'll be right back, Jamey."

It felt as though we were moving in slow motion as we walked through the house together. I needed to be away from my son, away from the possibility of him overhearing the conversation we clearly needed to have, away from what would inevitably come out as anger. It could only be anger.

I shut the door behind us as we entered the garage, the heavy scent of motor oil settling around us. "How dare you—"

"I'm sorry. I'm so sorry. I wanted to tell you but I didn't know how," she rambled, her shaky hands pushing into the strands of her hair, tugging at the base. "I only found out yesterday."

"Yesterday?" I breathed, the shock hitting me once

again. She'd waited an entire day, told my *staff*, yet failed to inform me. "Is it mine?"

"Obviously," she croaked, her voice breaking in the middle of the word. I could see the tears welling in her eyes the way they had the other night and come to think of it, she absolutely should have been on her period Saturday night, but as far as I could tell, there'd been no blood on my cock. "I don't know how it happened."

"We had sex, Sophia. That's how it happened."

"I shouldn't have been able to get pregnant, though," she insisted, pushing the hair back from her face. She quickly wiped the tears away that threatened to fall, but more formed before she could stop them. "I've been trying for almost a year. Every goddamn week I went to the sperm bank, kept trying, trying. Hell, I even slept with a few random guys to see if maybe it was the way they inserted it that wasn't working, but no. Nothing. Nothing until now. This shouldn't have happened. It wasn't supposed to."

"Well, it has!" I slammed my fist down onto my work table, making her jump from the sound, and despite my anger, I felt guilty. "Why didn't you tell me the moment you found out? Why did you call my office and tell them? You had to know that they'd tell me. Did you want them to, Sophie? Did you not want to have to be the one to do it?"

"No, I—"

"Then tell me! I canceled my appointments. I have all fucking day."

She sniffed, the sound of her stuffy nose filling the quiet space, and anxiously wiped at her eyes again. "I can't do this," she whimpered, taking a step back. "I can't. I need to go home."

"Sophie—"

"Can you take care of Jamey, please? I just... I have a lot

of work to do and I can't, I can't do this." She stepped back again, her shoulders colliding with the wooden door, and I watched as she fumbled with the handle. I moved toward her, wanting to stop her even through the anger, but her twist held true and the door unlatched, setting her free.

I followed as she quickly made her way through the house. Desperately, she tried to hide the tears from Jamey, the sniffles, the wipes.

"Sophie, I put the eggs into the soupy thing, but they're not mixing—"

"Daddy's going to help you finish the brownies," she said, her feet planted firmly by the front door.

"Oh, okay. Daddy, how do I break the eggs open?"

Oh my god, I do not need this right now. "Stay," I said quietly to her. "Let's talk about this. Please."

Quickly, she shook her head, letting herself out through the front door before I could talk myself into stopping her. God, I was angry, but fuck if I didn't feel bad for the way I'd reacted, for Saturday night, for all of it.

"I got the eggs to break, Daddy!"

Great. Now I had to fish egg shells out of brownie batter.

Chapter 24

Sophie

Wednesday

P*regnant.*

When I took the test Monday morning, two vertical lines were the last things I was expecting to see. I was so used to negatives, to that gut punch in my chest every time I had to look at a used test. I'd taken another, and then another, and after I'd gotten home from watching Jamey I'd run to Target, buying as many tests as I could fit in my arms. I'd only taken half before the realization settled.

Pregnant, actually pregnant, confirmed by every single midstream early pregnancy test I could find. From the most expensive down to the cheapest, most basic, most unreliable. *Pregnant, pregnant, pregnant, pregnant.* The test said two to three weeks, and if I wasn't mistaken, that would mean I got pregnant either the first or the second time we'd had sex.

If only I hadn't been lying that day in Hudson's office when I joked I'd slept with someone else.

Hudson didn't want another child. That was fine, I could understand his reasons, and in all honesty, I felt bad for my own idiocy in thinking we didn't need protection. He didn't have to be involved and I would be absolutely fine with that, but I couldn't help but worry over how he would feel about having another kid out there that he didn't know, didn't see grow up. I'd always planned on being a single mom, to raise my kid happy and healthy and alone, but that had always rested on the idea that I wouldn't know who fathered it. Surely, I could look past that. I could make this work even though I knew the father, even though we'd slept together, even though I'd taken care of his kid for weeks now.

Right?

I groaned in frustration as I leaned my head against the tile wall of my shower, the hot water streaming across my body. I was happy. So genuinely happy, ecstatic even, to be pregnant. But the weight of the situation still sat heavily on my shoulders, my chest, making it hard to breathe, hard to feel more than just anxiety. Not to mention the sheer amount of confusion because I hadn't needed the IVF after all.

I turned the shower off, letting the steam dissipate and the warm air turn frigid on my damp skin. I could do this alone. I'd planned for it. My business was successful, I had two spare rooms, I had family and friends that would be there for me and help in whatever way they could. I didn't have time for a man in my life, whatever that relationship may be.

I'd be fine.

I had to be fine.

I wrapped a towel around my body and stepped out of the shower, checking the time on my phone. Just past five. Hudson would be home soon, and normally, the idea of that would send butterflies into flight in my stomach. But I wasn't at his house today. He'd texted me this morning insisting that I stay home, saying he'd already asked his mother to come watch Jamey. I didn't know if he wanted to cut ties and whether or not he wanted me to stop watching Jamey altogether. I hadn't responded. I hadn't had the guts.

I couldn't avoid him forever, and I knew that. We were neighbors for Christ's sake. I'd see him eventually.

I pulled on my favorite sweatpants, hesitating when I glanced at the Harvard hoodie still sitting in my laundry basket, yet to be washed, yet to be worn again. I grabbed it without giving myself a moment to wonder why, pulling it over my damp head of hair and sinking into the warmth and the little bit of comfort it gave me.

I had a shit ton of work to do. I had at least twenty backed-up orders for custom pieces that I'd yet to even start on, and as I made my way down the stairs with one hand on my nonexistent bump, I didn't let my thoughts turn to Hudson and the stress that was piling up inside of me. I wanted an evening of peace, an evening where I could do the work I loved while just being happy about the life growing inside of me.

But of course I wasn't going to get that. A knock at the door made me physically jump, the scissors in my hand cutting wrong across the too-expensive fabric. "Shit," I mumbled, already knowing how horribly I'd messed up the delicate lace.

Another knock and I was on my feet. I already knew who it was, already knew that my evening was about to get much more stressful.

I pulled open the door, hoping that maybe, just maybe, I'd find a smiling delivery person making their last-minute stop. But no. Instead I was greeted by bright green eyes, scrubs, and a mop of dark hair.

"What do you—"

"Can we talk?" He asked, cutting me off and taking a step toward the open door. "Please?"

"I'm really busy right now."

"I get that. But you can't avoid this forever, Sophie." He pushed past me, letting himself in, and all I wanted to do was scream in frustration. Couldn't he just give me a day?

"I don't want to avoid this forever," I mumbled as I shut the door behind him. "I just need time to come to terms with everything."

"I get that." He pushed his fingers through his hair as he crossed the room, his eyes wandering over the patterns laid out and the fabric that was draped across my dress form, pinned in place. "I'm sorry for yesterday. I shouldn't have reacted that way."

I wasn't expecting an apology.

"And I'm also sorry for how I acted Saturday night. That was... it was really shitty of me. I know that."

I leaned back against the front door, watching him as he took the too-expensive lace in his hand, feeling the fabric that he'd startled me into ruining. "Thank you for apologizing."

"I wish you'd told me," he muttered, his gaze turning far too slowly toward me, looking me up and down, realizing I was wearing his Harvard hoodie. "Why didn't you talk to me first? You had to know that I'd find out if you called the office. It's been gnawing at my brain since yesterday and I just can't figure it out."

I pursed my lips as I twirled one damp strand of wavy

hair around my finger. I knew why I'd done it. Deep down, I knew, and looking back on it now, it felt ridiculous. It was stupid, childish. "I thought it would be best to keep it professional," I sighed, slipping my other hand into the pocket of the hoodie and placing it flat against my stomach. "I know you don't want another kid. So I thought, I guess, that it would be better for you to find out as my doctor instead of as... whatever the hell this is."

He blinked at me, confusion contorting his features. "Did you think that because I'm not actively pursuing having another child I wouldn't want to be involved?"

I hated this. I hated this conversation, the tension, the heaviness in the air between us. "You said you were happy with Jamey and that you didn't want another."

"That doesn't mean—" He cut himself off, his grip on the lace tightening. "If you're having this child, Sophie, *my* child, I want to be involved."

"If?" I scoffed, pushing off from the door and standing up straight. "Of course I'm having this kid. It's a goddamn miracle I'm pregnant in the first place. Why would you even say that?"

He sighed exasperatedly, his eyes rolling. "I didn't mean it like that and you know it."

"Do I?" I pressed, taking another step toward him. "You said you didn't want another kid. You made it clear that Jamey was enough, that you didn't see a need to change that. Am I supposed to just blindly believe that you're entirely fine with this? That you want to see this through?"

"Yes," he deadpanned, his green eyes narrowing. "Do you think I'm some sort of heartless monster that would ask you—someone who has had a horrible time trying to conceive, someone who desperately wants a child—to terminate it just because I wasn't planning on having another kid?"

"No. I don't," I admitted. "But I do think that you aren't exactly thrilled. I do think that you don't necessarily want it, and that the only reason you want to be involved is because you think it's the right thing to do, among maybe a few others."

"That's not—"

"I wasn't planning on sharing this child with anyone anyway." I shoved past him, my shoulder bumping his arm, and tried not to think about how nice it was to even touch him like that. Opening the fridge, I scanned the shelves for something I could use to make dinner, deciding I was well and truly done with this conversation and that I needed to get on with my evening.

"What do you mean?"

Chicken. Broccoli. Camembert—shit, can't eat that anymore. "I mean that I'll be fine on my own, Hudson. I don't need your help with raising it. You can live your life and I can live mine."

"But I want to be there."

I slammed the refrigerator door shut as I turned to face him. "Do you? Or do you just want to be around me so that you can fuck me?"

His eyes widened as he took a step back. "Jesus, how much of an asshole do you think I am?" He snapped, dropping the fisted fabric back onto the table.

"I don't know, why don't you ask your cock? It seems to be the only brain you have."

His jaw hardened as he turned his gaze from me, toward the door. "Why are you shutting me out like this? Why do you desperately want to believe that I don't want to be there through this?"

"I don't."

"You do, Sophia," he snarled, whipping his head back toward me. "You know damn well that I'm a good father, at least as good as I can be. Why would I abandon a child that I helped create?"

I nibbled my lower lip as I stared at him. Words became stuck in my throat, too harsh, too scared to crawl out. This was all too much for me to even try to comprehend right now, not when I had so much to be happy about and focused on. For all the times I wanted him around me, I wanted him gone ten times more at this moment.

I wished we'd never had sex. I wished I'd never ended up at his clinic, as his neighbor, as his nanny. I wished we'd never crossed paths.

"I need you to leave." I leaned forward onto the counter, dropping my head so I wouldn't need to look at him. "Go be that stellar father to the child you already have, Hudson. I need to be alone."

The silence fell heavy around us. I heard him breathing, the rustling of his scrubs as his chest rose and fell, the slight whistle as the air blew from his nostrils. Then, the shuffling of feet, hard footsteps against tile turning soft as they landed on the mat in front of my door, the sound of the handle turning and the door latching shut as he left. Then, the sound of my tears hitting the pale white countertop, of my nails scratching against it as I curled my hands into fists.

I should be happy. I should be ecstatic. But all I felt was dread and resentment, fear and anger, so palpable I could feel it boiling in my veins.

Why did it have to be him?

Chapter 25

Hudson

Friday

"I don't want to go to Grandma's all weekend!" Jamey whined, his little voice carrying from the back seat of my Land Rover. "I want to see Sophie."

He'd been upset ever since I told him Wednesday morning that my mom was going to be watching him instead for the foreseeable future. I didn't know when Sophie would want to come back to work, if at all. I didn't have the heart to tell him that, though.

"I'm sorry, bud. Uncle Nathan and I have errands to run."

"Errands?" Nathan chuckled from the passenger seat. "That's a funny way of saying—"

I shot him a glance that said *do not say another word*. If Jamey found out we were going to an MMA match today, especially to see our favorite, Dylan Mitchell, he'd be furious. He also wouldn't shut up about it for the next few days and I desperately didn't want to deal with that.

I'd taken the day off work specifically for this. I had a lot of money on Dylan—it was his last fight—plus I'd bought us the best seats in the house. I couldn't miss it just because Jamey was angry about going to my mom's.

"Daddy?"

"Yeah?" I replied, pushing my arm back between the seats and grabbing his foot where it dangled from his car seat. He giggled.

"Can you just let me out here? I'll walk to Sophie's."

I laughed as I shook his foot, the idea absolutely ludicrous. We were already deep into my mom's neighborhood, at least a fifteen minute drive from my house. Oh, and he was *four.* "Absolutely not."

———

"I'm sorry, back up. How the fuck is she pregnant, Hudson?"

I sighed as I pulled into the VIP parking spot at the Agganis Arena. People were already filtering through the lot heading toward the stadium, decked out in merchandise and sweatbands to support their favorite fighters. "We didn't exactly use protection."

Nathan's mouth gaped, his expression trapped somewhere between surprise and disbelief, either with me or my stupidity. "Well, why the fuck not?"

"She hadn't started treatment yet and her file suggested that the likelihood of her becoming pregnant was one in a goddamn million. I didn't think for a second that this would happen, but here we are." I pressed my forehead to the steering wheel, reminding myself to breathe and that everything was going to work out. I'd been on edge since Sophie and I had talked the other night. "She didn't even tell me herself. I had to find out from the nurses in the office. She'd called them to let them know she no longer needed treatment."

Nathan leaned back in his seat, his head tilted back, gaze locked on the roof of my car. "Well, what are you going to do?"

"I don't know. I have no fucking clue. I want to be involved in the kid's life, obviously, but Sophie seems to want to keep me as far away as possible."

"Have you told Jamey?"

"Fuck no." I cracked my knuckles, watching each one as it popped. "I love being Jamey's dad. I didn't plan on being a dad to another kid, but now that this has happened, I want to. I want to be there. I haven't been able to stop thinking about it. But where Sophie and I stand... it's rocky. It's really fucking rocky, man."

"Do you genuinely think she'd cut you out of the kid's life?" He asked, turning his head toward me.

I sat up straight as I took a deep breath, combing through my thoughts and the memories of our argument the other night. "Honestly? No, I don't think she would. I know she feels she can do it alone but I don't believe she's the kind of person to keep my child from me."

"Then you just have to give her time to calm down, Huds."

"Time?" I scoffed. "I don't have time, Nathan. What the fuck am I supposed to do about the rest of it? I don't even know if we're still engaged. What am I supposed to say to my parents?"

Nathan blinked at me, one brow raised above the other. "You know you just referred to it as an engagement, right? Not a fake engagement?"

"Shut up."

"I'm serious. How do you truly feel about her? I've never seen you like this over anyone, man. I mean, I know there's a kid involved now, but this is different."

I had no idea how I felt about Sophie. On the one hand, I knew there was a lot between us, a lot of unspoken lust and desire, but on the other... I didn't want to go down that path. "I don't know," I admitted, rolling my shoulders, my neck, anything to let out the tension I felt inside of me. None of it worked. "She's a great neighbor. A great nanny. The sex is fucking incredible. But I don't know."

I watched as Nathan plucked at a loose thread on his shorts, the fabric unraveling. "Maybe you should give it some serious thought."

I bit down on the inside of my cheek. I knew exactly what would come from giving it too much thought. "There's nothing to think about," I snapped. I pulled the handle on my door, swung it open, and hopped out. "I'll be the father to my new child. No doubt there. But there's no room in my life for a relationship."

Nathan shuffled out his side, grabbing his bag from the back, and looked at me through the open car door. "Hudson—"

"No. Don't. I'm not making that mistake again, Nate, and you're not going to talk me into it."

———

. . .

We sat in near silence as the fight played out. The crowd cheered around us, Nathan and I occasionally joining in, but there was a heaviness between us, the same heaviness that felt like a crushing weight against the ice in my chest. I didn't want to think of Sophie, but there she was, as always, tucked neatly into the back of my mind.

I cheered as Dylan won round after round, my winnings piling up, but I couldn't find the energy to actually be excited. I didn't want to be there. I wanted to be with Sophie, I wanted to work out whatever the fuck was going on between us, and the more I sat there and thought about what I absolutely shouldn't have been thinking about, the more I wanted to see her. Feel her. Taste her. Fuck her.

I hated when Nathan was right.

Chapter 26

Sophie

Saturday

Even though I knew exactly who was walking up to my house, I didn't dread seeing him. I'd spent the entirety of the last couple of days hating myself for what I'd said, what I'd implied.

I was on my feet and away from my laptop before the doorbell even rang.

Hudson's face was stern as I opened the door, all hard, flexed muscles. But I could tell by his eyes that he wasn't upset with me. There was something else there, something more like regret, remorse. "Hey," I said.

"Hey."

"You can come in." I stepped to the side, opening the door wider for him to come through, and watched every piece of him as he entered my house for the second time this week.

"I know you're still mad at me, but—"

"I'm not," I said, closing the door behind him. He stood a little too close, a little too tall. I must have looked tiny in my pajama shorts and tank top next to him. "I'm sorry about the other day. I was just so frustrated with everything and I took it out on you. I've calmed down considerably since."

His brows raised as he looked down at me. "I'm sorry too. Can we have a real talk this time instead of getting mad at each other?"

I chuckled. "Yeah, we can try." I stepped around him, crossing the open plan space into the living room and plopping down on the sofa. "There's some wine in the fridge if you want it. Someone should drink it before it goes bad."

I watched as he made himself at home, opening and closing cupboards until he found my stash of wine glasses before pouring himself a full glass worth. He glanced at my laptop, at the designs I had loaded up and the patterns I was digitally designing, nonchalantly sipping his wine.

"Please don't spill wine on my computer," I joked, hoping to cut the small amount of awkward tension.

"If I did it would only be payback for you spilling wine on my shirt and my couch." He leaned forward over the screen, using two fingers to scroll along the trackpad. "These are amazing. Your designs. I should have told you sooner."

I felt the heat warm my cheeks as I looked away from him, the little balls of lint on my sofa suddenly far more interesting. "Thanks." I didn't want to admit that it made my stomach twist to get a compliment from him, and it definitely wasn't just because of the bout of nausea I was currently wading through thanks to the little one inside of me.

I felt the vibrations of his feet against the floor, only spotting him once he came into my peripheral vision. His buttoned-up white shirt and the casual slacks he wore made that twisting in my gut a little bit worse. "Right." He came around the couch, the glass of wine in his hand steady as he sat down on the opposite end. "I'm willing to go all in if you're prepared for that."

All in? What the fuck did that mean? "I'm already all in."

"I mean I'm ready to be a parent again. I'm all in on this. I want to be in my, I mean, *our* child's life if you're okay with that."

I watched as he sipped his wine, his eyes tentatively glancing between me and the glass in his hand. I wasn't used to seeing him like this—vulnerable, hesitant. Despite our argument the other night, he didn't need to be worried. I hadn't been able to stop thinking about it, about what my life was going to look like now, about how stressful but how much easier it would be raising this child with someone else. Hudson was a good dad. I knew that.

"Sophie? Can you say something?"

"Sorry," I mumbled. I pulled my legs up to my chest, my lip caught between my teeth. "I want you to be involved. I didn't mean what I said the other day, and I'm sorry about it." I glanced at him, noting the sigh of relief that flooded from his chest. "I want to figure this out. All of it."

His head leaned back, settling on the hardwood of the back of my couch, his eyes closed and Adam's apple bobbing. It made that spot in my chest ache again, the fire in my gut spread.

"Are you okay?"

"I'm fine," he mumbled as he peeked at me out of the corner of his eye. "Just relieved. Not that I thought you meant all of it, but there was a chance you did. And that chance honestly had me terrified."

I didn't know what to say to that. I'd done wrong, I knew that. I knew I'd lashed out. I still felt bad about it, no matter how many times I would inevitably apologize. But still, from the way he looked at me, the way he sat, the way he nearly choked on relief made it feel like there was more. And that 'more,' if it existed, could be dangerous.

"I'm happy to continue with the fake engagement if you are," he said, rolling his head to the side and resting it against the soft cushion.

I nodded. "Yeah, that would be ideal. I don't think my parents would be too pleased if I told them I was continuing with a pregnancy when my fiancé and I broke up just after conception," I chuckled.

"How very secular of them," he sneered, and I glared in response.

"Be nice. It wouldn't end well for you either, not with my mom knowing yours."

He cracked a smile, a small one, but I caught it, nonetheless. "I think mine would kill me if she found out I wasn't helping raise a child that I helped create, so you're not wrong. Really, I should be thanking you for saving my life."

"You should."

He lifted his head, draining his wine before placing the empty glass onto the coffee table. "Thank you." He leaned toward me, just an inch, his posture relaxing further. "What do we do after the baby is born, though?"

I bit my lip, averting my gaze to hide the sudden uneasiness in my gut. I'd tried not to think that far ahead—every time my mind had wandered in that direction, it seemed to spiral, to sink below the depths and make me fully fucking panic. We couldn't get married, I knew that much. I didn't want an eventual divorce, not when I'd be doing damage to the child growing inside me and Jamey as well. We could put off the wedding, blaming the stress of pregnancy and then the stress of the baby, but I didn't want to be in a perpetual, endless fake relationship. At least not with someone I didn't have feelings for.

And I definitely did not have feelings for Hudson. I couldn't, I wouldn't. I was attracted to him, sure, and the sex was incredible. But I wasn't about to go having feelings for someone who wasn't willing nor appeared even capable of having feelings for me in return. I'd been down that road too many times. I knew how it ended.

"I don't know," I admitted. "I've tried not to think that far ahead."

He nodded in response to my answer. "Got it. Well, I'll do some thinking, see if I can come up with any solutions. Okay?"

"Okay."

I watched the way his pupils dilated as he stared at me, the way his eyes glanced across my features, the way his mouth parted as if he had more to say. There was a part of me that wanted to believe that somewhere inside of him, Hudson cared for me at least a little bit. I knew I was fond of him, maybe a little too much. But I was being cautious in allowing myself to feel anything in the first place. I definitely wasn't going to put myself out there expecting to hear words I knew didn't really exist.

This was far too complicated for my pregnancy-brain.

"Do you want to go get dinner?" He asked, the veil of stoicism falling back over him, extinguishing any lingering hope that remained. "I'll buy."

I smiled lightly at him as I tugged at the side of my shorts. "Not really dressed for it."

"I can wait. Jamey's with my mom tonight, so I have all evening."

"That's really nice of you, but honestly, I'm exhausted. I was going to get a bit more work done and then hit the hay. A rain check maybe?"

The edges of his lips drew down, the hallmark of disappointment, but he blinked it away. "That's fine, no worries. You really should eat something though," he insisted, pushing himself up from the sofa and grabbing his empty glass. "I'll order you takeout. Pizza okay?"

"Hudson—"

"It's fine, I don't mind. I'm going home anyway so you won't have to deal with me," he chuckled.

"I..."

"You like pepperoni, right? I'll order from the place I got it last time. Shouldn't be too long."

I watched him like a hawk as he walked toward the kitchen, placing his glass directly into the dishwasher. God fucking dammit, why did he have to have such good manners, too? *Other than barging into my house uninvited.* "Okay," I relented.

He grinned at me from across the room, the kitchen counter dividing us. "Do you want to watch Jamey again? I could really use your help this week."

Now *that* was something I could be enthusiastically happy about. "Absolutely. I missed the little squirt."

Chapter 27

Hudson

Sunday

Although Jamey loved going to his grandparents ninety-nine percent of the time, the excitement he showed every time I walked through the door to pick him up always tugged at my heartstrings.

"Daddy!" The sound of his little feet padding across the tile floor in their obnoxiously grand entryway accompanied his ecstatic voice, and as he ran toward me, that smile a mile long across his cheeks, I couldn't help but think that soon he'd joined by another little set of feet.

"Hey, bud," I grinned, kneeling down so I could scoop him up into my waiting arms. His legs wrapped around my waist, his arms around my neck. "Did you have a good time with Grandma and Pop-pop?"

He nodded excitedly before placing a little kiss on my cheek. "Grandma taught me how to make a... um... adult drink? The juice stuff I'm not allowed to have."

For fucks sake, she taught him how to make a cocktail? "Of course she did." I rolled my eyes as I set my keys down on the table, carrying Jamey through the entryway and toward the main sitting room. My dad was laying on the sofa, his legs kicked up on the recliner, golf playing on the large screen that sat above the imposing stone fireplace. It was one of those televisions that were meant to be placed slightly farther away due to its size, but it was a status symbol for them. "Hey, Dad."

He grunted his response. He'd never much been one for talking—he was always pretty passive. The most personality I'd seen from him growing up was during our time on the golf course.

"Where's Mom?"

"Kitchen."

"Great. Good talk." I carried Jamey through the expanse of the living room, over the plush, Indian carpets and through the second living room, the main dining room, and finally, into the kitchen. Their house was like a damn maze, and I was glad they'd moved into it after I'd moved out on my own. I wouldn't want to live in something so massive and flashy, even though I could easily afford it. It was just a hassle.

"Honey! You're here," Mom smiled, turning from her stand mixer, her apron covered in flour and what I hoped was some kind of red-colored jam.

"Yeah, just picking up Jamey. Figured I'd say hello so you didn't think he'd run off." His little legs kicked against my waist, so I plopped him down on the countertop next to his Grandma. "Was anyone watching him?"

"Oh don't be ridiculous, Hudson. Julia was looking after him."

Julia. One of their many hired-in maids that practically

lived on site, Julia was at least one of the nicest, but I still didn't love the idea of a cleaning professional watching my son instead of someone with experience. Like my parents. "Great," I deadpanned. "I heard you taught him to make a cocktail?"

"Oh, *that's* what Grandma called it!" Jamey chimed in.

My mom chuckled as she flipped the switch on her stand mixer, turning it off and lifting the whisk attachment out of the beige-colored batter. "I taught him how to make a Mai-Tai. Should be useful for both of us, sweetheart."

I groaned as I lifted Jamey from the counter, plopping him back down on the floor. "Why don't you go grab your stuff and pack it up so we can get going, okay?"

"Okay, Daddy," he chirped, his legs kicking into action and carrying him off to god-knows-where.

"Can you maybe not teach my son how to make mixed drinks? It's a little inappropriate, don't you think?" I leveled my eyes at her as I leaned forward on the counter. I stuck a finger into her batter then popped it in my mouth, savoring the taste of what was unmistakably my mom's famous cinnamon-swirl muffins. *So where did the jam come from?*

"Oh, honey, don't be so strict with him. You were making your father and me cocktails when you were his age," she laughed, swatting my hand away as I went back for another dip.

"Yeah, and you guys would get drunk and forget I existed. Did you *forget* about that part?"

She rolled her eyes at me as she moved the bowl a foot away from my meddling hands. "No, I didn't forget that part. But we don't drink that heavily anymore... at least not often."

"Mmm."

"So how are things with Sophie? How's the wedding planning going?"

"Great," I lied, because things were honestly more confusing than ever right now even though we were back on good terms. "Though the wedding planning is a little tricky at the moment."

She didn't seem to be fully paying attention, and I thanked my lucky stars because had she been, she would have questioned it. "Are you guys living together now?"

"Oh, no. She lives next door, actually. That's how we met."

"But you're engaged. Shouldn't you be actively getting her more involved in Jamey's life?" She pulled out an ice cream scooper from one of the drawers and began filling a prepared muffin tray.

"We just don't want to get too ahead of ourselves for the time being, and she spends enough time with Jamey as it is. We'll move her in after the wedding."

"Wait, hold on, rewind," she faltered, turning quickly. She faced me with her brows knit, her eyes narrowed. "If the wedding planning is tricky at the moment, why would you wait to move her in? And for that matter, why is it tricky?"

I bit my lip as I watched her. I'd have to tell her eventually; I couldn't hide it eternally. And if I was being honest, I wanted to tell her. I was excited to be a dad again, more than I thought I would have been if this situation ever occurred, and it was because of that excitement that I let it slip. "Sophie's pregnant."

The scoop in her hand slipped from her grip, clanging to the floor and spilling batter down the front of her apron. Slowly, a smile as wide as Jamey's when I'd come through the door spread across her cheeks. "She's pregnant?"

I nodded.

"Oh my god, Hudson, that's amazing!" She reached for the towel hanging from the stove and wiped her hands and the batter from her chest. "How far along is she? Do you know the sex yet? Does Jamey know?"

"Only a few weeks. No, we don't know the sex, and no, Jamey doesn't know," I chuckled, reaching down and picking up the scooper for her before chucking it in the sink. "We're still in the danger zone so we haven't really told anybody yet. We only just found out earlier this week. And as far as Jamey goes, we'll tell him when we think the time is right."

"Oh, honey. I'm so excited for you. I wish we'd have had more, but we just... we didn't have the time, you know? And you were so perfect."

Jamey rounded the corner, his backpack in hand and as many toys as he could carry tucked under his arm. I glanced at my mom, sending her a stern *don't say a word* look. "Ready to go, bud?"

"Ready!"

"Thanks for taking him, Mom. I might need you to watch him a little more often for the next, uh, nine months or so," I chuckled, ruffling Jamey's hair as he dragged his bag toward me.

"No worries, honey. I'll take him whenever I can if Sophie needs it."

"But I like hanging out with Sophie," Jamey complained, his voice a little smaller.

"I know, bud." I picked up his backpack for him, throwing the comically small bag over my shoulder. "I do, too."

Chapter 28

Sophie

Monday

Looking after Jamey while pregnant was an entirely new experience. It put a lot of things into perspective and made me consider how I'd parent a child in the situations we got into, more so than it had when I'd just been trying. It felt more natural, more motherly, and I hoped he didn't notice the shift.

"So, I was thinking after we finish lunch, maybe you could watch some TV while I get some work done?" I plopped his plate of food down in front of him, the dinosaur-shaped chicken nuggets and raw baby carrots rolling around on the plate. I was already having cravings, and nuggets weren't going to cut it for me.

Jamey's little smile turned into a pouty face. "But I wanted to play spaceships with you."

"We can play spaceships later on this afternoon, okay?" I offered, sliding him his little dipping bowl of ranch. "I've

214

got some designs I need to make. You can always draw some up for me if you'd like. I'm sure my clients would love them." It was a lie, but it would at least interest him.

"Okay!"

A knock at the door had me spinning around from where I stood. I glanced at the clock, it was only twelve-thirty. Hudson definitely wasn't back yet, he'd have texted me if he was leaving early.

Jamey didn't seem concerned in the slightest as I walked across the house, his attention fully focused on his nuggets and carrots, and I wished right about then that Hudson had given me access to his doorbell camera.

Peeking through the glass at the top of the door, I could see a mop of bright blonde hair, tied up neatly in a high bun. Feeling slightly less worried that it wasn't a man coming to murder us both, I opened the door, surprised to find Hudson's mother on the other side.

"Oh, hi, Mrs. Brady." I smiled at her, taking a step back and letting her through. I suddenly wished I'd dressed nicer —I was in lounging clothes, my go-to for work and watching Jamey. My leggings and Hudson's Harvard sweatshirt weren't exactly the high-brow attire she went for.

"Oh, please, call me Angela," she smiled, her eyes glancing down at my outfit and only briefly showing a flicker of disapproval. She stepped inside, closing the door behind her, and Jamey grinned at her with food in his mouth. "Hi, honey! You left your bear at my house so I thought I'd bring it back to you."

"Oh, how sweet of you." I lead her toward the kitchen, feeling far more awkward than I should have. At least when I met her the first time, Hudson was there as a buffer. "Do you want something to eat? I was about to cook something for myself but I can make you something too."

"Oh, I'm alright, thank you." She sat down next to Jamey on one of the high-top seats of the breakfast bar, plucking a carrot off his plate and popping it into her mouth. "I'm surprised you're hungry," she said, her gaze landing on me.

The fuck does that mean? I haven't put on any weight since I saw her last. It's way too early to show. "Oh, uh, I haven't had breakfast yet so..."

She nodded, ruffling Jamey's hair as he finished off his carrots and started eating the last of his nuggets. "Congratulations, by the way."

"Thank you," I grinned, shoving my bare hand devoid of any ring into the pocket of the hoodie. I hadn't been expecting her and the ring was tucked away at home in my jewelry case upstairs. But she had seen me since we'd gotten 'engaged' and already congratulated me so what was she congratulating me for now?

"How are you feeling?"

I blinked at her. *Did Hudson tell her I was sick or something last week? So that's why she'd been watching Jamey?* "I'm fine," I said. "A, uh, bit better now." *Just play along.* I threw in a cough for good measure.

"No morning sickness or anything?"

Fuck.

He'd told her. He'd fucking told her. Heat spread in my cheeks out of annoyance, but I played it off, covering with a light laugh as I glanced at Jamey. I hoped he didn't know what morning sickness meant. "I've had a bit, but not too badly. I'm sure it'll hit me eventually."

"Probably. I'm so excited for you two, though. I hope you know that."

I gave her a tight smile, my stomach already swirling,

but not from nausea. No, this was irritation. "Thank you. I'm excited too."

———

After Angela left, I'd had plenty of time to stew in my own annoyance. I didn't want to be angry at Hudson again, not right after we'd come out of an argument and made peace but *come on.* I hadn't even told my parents yet. This was *my* pregnancy, not his. I got to decide when and how we would tell people, not him, and now that his mother knew, I would inevitably have to tell my parents sooner rather than later before the two of them talked. If I knew one thing for certain, I knew my mother would have my head if she found out from a friend rather than her own daughter. Hudson was interfering in my life, making this far more difficult than I needed it to be just because he, like our mothers, couldn't keep his goddamn mouth shut.

I was on my feet the moment I heard the door open.

The look on Hudson's face as I rounded the corner of the living room told me he knew just how annoyed I was. "Outside," I snapped, pointing behind him at the open front door. Jamey was well and truly engrossed in his show, he'd be fine for a few minutes.

Hudson didn't say a word as he turned around, his scrubs pulling annoyingly at the back of his thighs and showing far too much of the muscle beneath them. I followed him out, shutting the door a little too aggressively behind me, but fuck it, I was annoyed.

"Your mom stopped by today." I crossed my arms over

my chest as he turned to face me, all of that confidence and bravado disappearing.

"Shit."

"Shit, indeed, Hudson. Want to explain to me how she knows I'm pregnant?"

He sighed as he leaned against one of the pillars of his front porch. "I'm sorry. I picked up Jamey yesterday from their house and it just... came out."

"It just 'came out'? Are you fucking for real?" I stepped toward him, getting into his personal space, and he didn't flinch. "You didn't even tell me. You didn't even ask. This is my pregnancy, Hudson, not yours. You don't get to decide when it's okay to tell people."

He glared down at me, his expression shifting from sheepishness and more towards irritation. He didn't get to be fucking annoyed. That was all *mine*. "It's my baby too, Sophie. You don't get to make every single decision. I admit I should have told you and that I should have asked, but surely we should have discussed this already."

"When have we had the time?" I challenged. "You found out last, what, Tuesday? And then we spent our time arguing. We've barely had a moment to even decide how we're going to do this, let alone talk about when we're going to tell people. You realize I have to tell my parents now, right?"

"You can tell them on your own time—"

"No, I can't," I spat, jabbing one finger into his too-toned chest. "Your mother will tell mine. I don't get to make that decision now because *you* took it away from me."

His eyes went wide as he realized his mistake. "Fuck, I'm sorry, I didn't even think—"

"No, you didn't. If you can't let me do this on my terms then I don't know if this is going to work."

The little bit of remorse vanished from his face at my words, and immediately, I wanted to take them back. I knew I couldn't. "Don't fucking threaten me with that shit. I messed up, I know that, but you can't be throwing that around every time as if it's some trump card. I helped create that child growing inside of you, Sophie. I want to be involved. I want to be a father to it. I want to be in both of your lives. What more do you want from me? I can't be perfect every moment of the day."

"I want you to keep your fucking mouth shut until I say it's okay to tell people. We're still in the time frame where something could go wrong. I could lose it, or something could occur to where I'd have to terminate it. We don't know yet. And all of this goddamn stress you're filling me with is certainly not helping." I took a step back, needing space again. I had to watch my words, I couldn't let myself spit the venom that was bubbling in me. But the space wasn't enough.

"I'm sorry about that. We need to sit down and talk all of this out, start to finish," he offered. "I can order us takeout tonight, we can chat after Jamey goes to bed. Okay?"

I shook my head, taking another step back. "No, I need to go home. I need space."

He sighed, his jaw hardening as he looked at me with pure exhaustion. "Sophie."

"I need to go home," I repeated. One more step back, and then another, and I was off the porch and closer to my own house. "I need time."

Chapter 29

Hudson

Tuesday

I glanced at the time on my phone, the clock creeping far too quickly for comfort. "Jamey!" I shouted. "Get dressed!"

I watched as he ran up the stairs at lightning speed, his pajama pants swishing about his ankles. I didn't have time to take him to my mom's, he was going to have to come to work with me. I'd only had to do it once before and thankfully my coworkers took him in shifts, but I hated the idea of putting that on them without warning. If Sophie wasn't going to come, it was my last resort.

"Daddy! Can I wear my superhero suit?" Jamey called from the top of the stairs.

"No, bud, come on. Just put on some shorts and a shirt. We gotta go."

He pouted as he turned, and I realized at that moment that trying to get a four-year-old to respect the idea of being late was just impossible. I stepped toward the stairs, fully anticipating a showdown while just simply trying to get him dressed, but the moment my hand touched the banister, the doorbell rang out. My saving grace. My green light.

I yanked the door open, relief washing over me as Sophie blinked at me. "I thought you weren't coming," I said, moving to the side to let her through. "I was going to take him to the office."

She rolled her eyes as she stepped into the house, kicking off her slippers by the mat. "Just because you and I are arguing doesn't mean I'm going to punish Jamey. It's not his fault that his dad's an ass."

Ouch. I deserved that. "That's fair. I'm sorry—"

She held up one hand, silencing me. "I don't want to hear it. Go to work. You're going to be late."

"Sophie, come on. I know I fucked up. Just let me apologize."

"Nope," she said, popping the *p.* "Go."

I bit my lip as I checked the time again. Fine. If she wasn't going to hear me out then I might as well leave it, even though she was being annoyingly stubborn. I'd try again this evening. I'd try again tomorrow. I'd keep trying until she finally fucking believed that I wanted to be involved without messing up her life.

———

Work was slow and tiresome. Not enough to keep me busy, not enough to keep my mind away from Sophie, the argument, and the baby. I just wanted to apologize. Why wouldn't she let me? Why did she have to be so damn stubborn?

The door to my office opened, stealing my attention away from my racing mind. I clicked out of whatever I'd absentmindedly opened on my computer as I looked toward the door. *Shit.* Jannie and Steven. I hadn't even checked my calendar to see who was coming in; I really should have been more prepared for the couple who had been coming to me the longest.

"Hi, Dr. Brady," Jannie said, sidestepping her husband and plopping down into one of the chairs. "Today's the day."

"One second." I flashed her a quick smile as I clicked through my documents on the computer, pulling up the notes for her appointment on my screen. *Final appointment,* I'd written. *No more rounds of IVF after this. Last pregnancy test.* I swiveled back around to her. "Indeed it is, Jannie. Nice to see you, Steven."

I pulled open a drawer, fishing around inside of it for a pregnancy test instead of sending her off with the nurses to have one done. If it was going to be her last one, I wanted it to not have all the horrible connotations that had gone along with each one she'd had previously. The likelihood was sure to be the same, but I wanted her to be comfortable, to ideally not be expecting the worst.

"Here," I said, offering the plastic-wrapped test to her as well as a clear cup for her urine. "Why don't you go test in the bathroom and bring it back here to develop?"

She bit her lip, her eyes latched onto my outstretched hand, and slowly, her mouth spread into a smile. "I don't need to," she said calmly as she leaned back in the chair, one hand coming to rest on her stomach. "I tested myself this morning. I'm pregnant."

Steven grinned as he looked at his wife, his eyes practically shining, and as I watched him I couldn't help but wish that was the reaction I'd had when I'd found out that Sophie was pregnant. Maybe things wouldn't be where they are now if I hadn't come home guns-a-blazing. "That's... amazing. I'm so happy for you guys." *Lie.* Well, it wasn't a lie exactly, it was more that I couldn't fucking focus enough to actually be genuinely happy for them. Every time I tried, my thoughts drifted back to Sophie, to the mystery of what our future held, to our current argument. And every time that happened, the sinking feeling in my gut that I was beginning to potentially be falling for her became more intense, more overwhelming. There was no other reason that I'd care this much that she was upset with me.

I needed to make things right once and for all.

"I'm really sorry to have to ask you this, but is there any chance you can watch Jamey for an extra hour today?" I said to Sophie's name brightly lit on my car's display. Traffic wasn't horrible despite the rain, but I needed extra time. I needed to think, and I needed advice.

"That's fine," she said, her voice sounding tinny through the speakers of my Mercedes. "I'll make Jamey dinner."

"No, don't worry about that. I'll grab something to bring home for both of you. You can take it back to your house if you want. Just hang out with him or something, okay? I'll be home soon."

"Okay."

"Bye, Sophie."

"Bye, Hudson."

I hung up the call as I turned into Nathan's neighborhood, the slender, tall townhouses taking up the majority of the land. It was a nice area of Boston. We'd gotten into a lot of spats back in college about who would become wealthier once our careers were established but we were such close friends that those silly bets became a moot point.

Pulling into his driveway, I placed the car in park and pushed the door open, not caring if I got wet from the absolute torrential downpour. I raced up the curved walkway toward his front door, thinking to myself that I should have called first, probably should have warned him. *Oh well.* Hopefully, I wouldn't get trapped here all night catching up with the whole family.

I rang the bell. My anxiety released its hold on me as Nathan opened the door, and before he could call out to his wife or kids, I grabbed him by the shirt and pulled him out under the covered awning of his front porch, shutting the door behind him.

"What the fuck—?"

"Listen," I said, my voice a little loud over the sound of the rain. "You were right. You were fucking right, okay? I think there's something there between me and Sophie."

"Well, obviously," he drawled, and I dropped my hold on his shirt.

"What do I do?"

He raised one comical eyebrow at me. "What do you mean?"

"How do I make it go away?" I pressed, taking a step closer to him. My heart was already racing from the admission, hammering so hard in my chest that I could hear it in my ears. "I don't need this, Nathan. What do I do?"

He opened his mouth as if he were about to say something, but closed it a second later, his eyes looking me up and down. I was damp, my scrubs almost soaked through, my hair a soggy mess. I wasn't looking forward to seeing Sophie like this. "You can't do anything about it, man," Nathan mumbled, so quietly I almost didn't hear him over the pouring rain and the thumping in my head. "You have to feel it or get her out of your life."

"You know I can't do either of those."

"Those are your only options, Huds. I'm sorry."

"Fuck," I groaned, pushing one hand through my hair to get the dripping strands off of my face. "I can't deal with this. It's going to drive me insane. But I can't let her go, either. Not when I have these feelings, not when she's carrying my child."

"Tell her, then," he said, the words falling so easily from his lips as if telling her was the easiest thing in the world. "What are you afraid of? If she's going to be in your life, you're going to have to tell her eventually. You can't run from it forever, and you can't keep it bottled up."

"Absolutely not," I scoffed. "What if she doesn't feel the same? Or worse, what if she *does*? I can't go through it all again, Nate. I can't do what I did with Becks. I can't."

Nathan shrugged, the sleeve of his dress shirt clinging to his arm from where it stuck out into the rain. "This is something you have to figure out yourself. I can't do it for you. I'm not in your head, man, but I think you should tell her. The benefits outweigh the risks."

"I can't just—"

"Huds, respectfully, I'm in the middle of cooking dinner and my roux is certainly burned now. I need to go back in. You're welcome to join us for dinner, but I can't promise you'll get out of here very quickly."

. . .

———

I parked my car in the garage again. My leather seat was soaked and soggy, my ass collecting the majority of the water that slid down my skin as I drove home, leaving me sitting in a horribly warm puddle.

I didn't want to tell her. I didn't want to make things even harder between us, not when they were already so difficult, but fuck, what else could I do? It seemed the more time I spent with her, the harder things got. And the amount of time spent with her was only going to increase.

I pushed the car door open and grabbed the bag of Chinese I'd picked up, hopped out into the oil-fumed garage, and made my way inside.

"Hey," Sophie called from the kitchen, her head poking around the corner. "I got the table set for you guys. Jamey's upstairs changing into his pajamas."

"Thanks," I sighed, kicking off my damp shoes and socks and padding across the wood floor, each step making a wet *thwap*. "I got you chow mein and some egg-drop soup. Hope that's okay."

She nodded. "Yeah, that's fine. Thanks, Hudson."

I met her gaze as I started pulling out the boxes of food. Her blue eyes shone far too brightly, her freckled skin so perfect that I just wanted to plant my lips on it. Her brown hair was swooped up and away from her face, sitting high on her head in a messy bun. No Harvard hoodie today. Just leggings and a tight-fitting shirt, showing off every inch of her curves.

Suddenly, it was as if a switch flipped in my mind—the thought of not telling her how I felt hurt more. I didn't want to keep it in, I wanted to let it fall from my tongue, I wanted to explain everything.

But the words just wouldn't come out. So I watched her leave, out into the rain, her chow mein and soup clutched to her chest, leaving me alone in my house with my son and my far too warm heart.

Chapter 30

Sophie

Wednesday

The events of last night sat heavy in my mind for the remainder of the evening, continuing to linger into the morning, taking up every waking moment of my thoughts. Hudson had that look about him again, that one where he seemed like he desperately wanted to say something but couldn't quite get the words out, and at this point, it was beginning to become frustrating. If he had something to say, I'd rather he just say it.

The sound of the door opening pulled me away from the Lego set Jamey and I were building. "Just a sec, bud," I said to him, lifting myself to my feet and feeling the tightness in my lower back. As I stepped around the corner, Hudson shut the door behind him, his scrubs dry and crisp in comparison to last night. I didn't know how much longer we were going to be awkward around each other, sidestepping the problem until both of us forgot. I was already tired of it.

"Hey," he sighed. I watched as he placed his keys on the entryway table, the way his hand opened and closed, the ligature that sprung to life beneath his skin. I hated looking at him. He was too perfect, too handsome, too well-built that it was infuriating rather than intoxicating. In another situation it would have been exhilarating.

"Hi." I bit my lip as my gaze wandered lower, along the ridges of his abdomen and past the way his pants were a little too tight around his hips and the *why* between them. "How was work?"

"Fine." He looked around me, toward the living room. "Where's my little guy?"

I chuckled. "He's very invested in his Lego set right now. Honestly, I'm thankful you're home. My back was starting to kill me from being on the floor for so long."

He smiled lightly as he stepped around me. "Take some acetaminophen. Lower back pain is quite common in the first trimester."

I shoved him lightly with my shoulder, knocking him slightly off course, liking the calm that had overtaken the awkwardness. "Thanks, Dr. Brady."

———

"I'm pregnant."

The glass of wine in her hand nearly dropped, and I reached out to steady her fingers around the stem. "What?"

"I'm pregnant," I repeated, unable to contain the little

smile forming on my lips. It felt so good to say it properly to someone who didn't know.

"I..." Lisa's mouth opened and closed like a fish, entirely lost for words. "I'm... happy for you. I just didn't expect it to be this quick."

"Well, I haven't even started IVF," I admitted, watching the way her shoulders shifted beneath the fabric of her white blouse, wondering if she'd catch on or if it would go right over her head. "So it's a surprise to me, too."

She nodded as she sipped her wine, her eyes lost in a daze somewhere behind my head, off toward her kitchen. The couch we sat on was one she'd gotten from a thrift store three years ago, and no matter how many times I'd offered to buy her a new one because the springs were going, she resisted. "How far along are you?"

"Four, five weeks maybe. It's early. There's still a chance things can go wrong, so don't go off telling everyone."

"Wait a minute." Her gaze found me again, her eyes narrowing. "I thought you weren't going to the sperm bank anymore."

"I'm not." The glass of water in my hand was suddenly incredibly interesting, and I watched the way the ripples moved across the surface, blotting out as they reached the edges.

"So..."

"Yeah."

"No," she gasped, her eyes going wide. "No way. Tell me it isn't your sexy neighbor's."

I nodded, lifting the glass to my lips and taking a sip. Fuck, I was going to miss wine. I already did. "It's Hudson's, yeah."

"Oh my god, Sophie. Are you okay with that? Have you told him?"

"Yeah, of course he knows. I think he's excited about it, actually. He said he wants to be involved through all of it," I explained, my finger scrubbing the side of the glass and leaving a trail devoid of condensation. "As for how I'm feeling about it, I honestly don't know. It's a lot, and it's not what I'd envisioned when I started all this."

"What do you mean?"

"I mean that I'd planned on being a single mother, not knowing who the father was. I planned on doing it all myself, and now I have this man involved, this man who is a wonderful father, a stable provider, a genuinely nice person, and I still don't know how I feel about it. I should be more excited, right? I mean, I am about the baby of course, but having it with Hudson has made things so different from what I originally planned."

She shifted herself, turning toward me on the couch, and part of me wanted to just burst into tears when she took my hand in hers. "Sophie. I am so happy for you, honestly, and I don't want you to think that what I'm going to say means that I'm not. But I think a lot of this might be because deep down, you *do* have feelings for him. Feelings you maybe can't admit to yourself yet. I think that scares you because he's cemented in your life now."

I fucking hated when she was right.

She hit the nail on the damn head, explaining every bit of frustration and stress that had surrounded my worry about Hudson being involved. It explained why I wanted to push him away at every opportunity, why I had to fight myself to not tell him he couldn't be a father to this baby. Why did she have to be right?

"You're right," I sighed, leaning back onto the sofa as I watched her eyes turn softer, more sympathetic. "But I highly doubt he feels the same. He's said multiple times that he's not interested in anything serious, not after what happened with his ex. It's pointless. I don't want to have to be around him, feeling the way I do. It's just constant disappointment."

She nodded as she squeezed my hand, nearly crunching my bones. "You should talk to him. What's the worst that could happen? He shoots you down? At least then you know and you're not left wondering 'what if' forever."

I chuckled as I tried not to bury myself in thoughts of what could happen if I told him how I felt. "I don't think I can do that."

"I know you don't. But you'll never get anywhere with him if you don't at least try, whether it's platonic or more than that. You owe it to yourself," she pressed, leaning a little bit closer to me. "You owe it to your kid."

Well, shit.

Chapter 31

Hudson

Friday

Most days in the office, the beeping of machines faded into the background like one of Jamey's cartoons. Today, however, I couldn't help but notice it, beeping incessantly from the next room and pulling me out of every possible thought I tried to hold on to. Normally I'd be thankful for that, especially when my thoughts veered too close to Sophie, to her body, to our child growing inside of her and the reason for that. But I'd rather wade through those mental pictures than hear the incessant beeping.

I clicked through the files on my computer, each click in time with the beeping and checked my schedule for the day: Elizabeth, ten-thirty; Pamela, eleven; Sangah, twelve; Molly, one-thirty.

I had some time before my first appointment of the day.

I tapped through my phone, the temptation to message Sophie and ask how she and Jamey were doing gnawing at the back of my mind then being driven away with each stupid fucking beep and opened my emails.

Fuck.

Staring straight back at me was a flight reminder, a forwarded email from Nathan, and a confirmation for my hotel in New York City.

I'd completely fucking forgotten.

All at once, Sophie forgetting to tell her parents about Jamey felt far more believable considering that I'd forgotten about a four-day long conference I was meant to be attending next week. I hadn't even sorted out childcare. Although I liked to think of myself as a good father, it was times like this that made me reconsider.

I couldn't ask Sophie. That was far too much to put on her plate, especially with the baby. No, I'd have to ask my mom. Jamey would be upset and Mom might teach him how to make a goddamn mojito or something and would probably leave the maids to watch him like she used to do to me.

I groaned in frustration as I sat forward, resting my head on my hands. I didn't have the willpower to deal with this. I didn't want to deal with it, didn't want to be gone for four days away from Sophie and Jamey. But I needed to go. I'd made a commitment, and I had to stick to it.

———

"I know, I'm sorry," I sighed, my hands clutched around the leather of my steering wheel. The late afternoon sun beat down on the hood of the Mercedes, nearly blinding me with the reflection as I moved at a snail's pace down I-93. "I didn't mean to throw this on you last minute. It was an accident."

"I know, sweetheart, but I'm going to have to cancel some plans. Or maybe your father can watch Jamey for a little bit while I go out with the girls. Either way, I'll make it work, but some warning next time would be nice." I could hear the sounds of a knife on a cutting board, cutting through something hard, like an apple or celery.

"Thank you." I moved what felt like an inch forward in the thick traffic. "I'm going to give Sophie your number if that's okay. Can you keep an eye on her while I'm gone?"

"Of course, honey. No problem." The knife slipped, and I heard a sharp intake of air on her end of the call, followed by a little chuckle. "Jeez, I almost cut myself."

"Thanks, Mom. And be careful with the knife, you know Dad's much better at chopping."

———

As I stood outside my front door, I took a deep breath. Would she be upset with me for leaving? She was only in the first trimester, but if something went wrong, if she lost it, I wanted to be there. I wanted to help her through it. But would she even want me there if something happened?

I pushed the door open, the sounds of cartoons and

giggles invading my senses, and couldn't help but smile as I heard Sophie counting down from ten, likely playing a game of hide-and-seek with Jamey. I should have told her the other day. I should have.

"I'm home," I called out, and Sophie's counting ceased. Jamey's little body appeared from behind the curtains on the far side of the room, his eyes lit up with excitement, his smile wide.

"Daddy!"

God, that never got old. Would it still feel as good with two of them?

"Hey, Hudson," Sophie chimed, stepping around the corner of the living room. Jamey looked up at her with wide eyes.

"This doesn't count, okay? You haven't found me yet," he giggled, tucking himself behind my thighs as if he were still hiding.

"Of course it doesn't. You're still winning."

I ruffled Jamey's hair as I looked at Sophie. She wore her hair down, the Harvard hoodie back on, not a word said about it as if she'd decided it was well and truly hers now. She looked far too good to be true, and a part of me wished I could just cancel the trip and stay with her and Jamey, keeping her close. "Can I talk to you?" I asked, keeping my voice as soft as I could to keep her from getting worried. "Alone."

An expression of confusion spread across her face before evening back out. "Uh, sure. Jamey? Why don't you go back to your cartoons while your dad and I chat?"

Jamey groaned his frustration as he stepped out from around me. "Fine." His lower lip jutted out in a pout as he walked back to the living room, his hunched back and dangling arms showing just how dramatic he could be.

I reached for Sophie's hand without thinking, taking it firmly in my grasp and feeling the little jump my heart made at the contact. We hadn't had sex in a while, and even just the feeling of her skin on mine was enough to make my cock twitch. I led her to the office, putting enough space between us and Jamey that he wouldn't overhear. Best to leave him out of the loop until Sunday otherwise I'd hear him complaining for the next forty-eight hours.

Sophie leaned back against the oak desk, and the temptation to corner her, kiss her, feel her made my chest ache. "I have a conference next week," I sighed, my feet moving of their own accord and stepping just a little bit closer to her, a little too close. "I'll be out of town from Monday until Thursday."

Her eyes widened as she looked up at me, and damn if I wasn't desperate for it to have just been because of my proximity. "Oh. Do you need me to watch Jamey?"

"No, I've sorted it with my mom. She's going to take him," I explained. I shoved my hands in the pockets of my scrubs, needing to keep them contained so I wouldn't reach out and touch her. "You can call me if you need me. I'll text you my mom's number as well just in case. It's only a few days, so it should be fine, but if you need anything at all I can come home."

She pursed her lips, her gaze wandering away from me. Was there something behind her eyes that she didn't want me to see? "I should be fine, Hudson. It's just a few days. I don't need you to watch over me like a hawk."

"You know that's not what I mean," I said, taking another step toward her. I didn't have it in me to stop my feet. I knew now that it wasn't just an urge to fuck her, although that was lurking beneath the surface. It was more than that, it was deeper than that. "We both know you're still in the danger zone."

"Nothing should happen," she nodded, and I wondered if she was telling me that or herself. "It's fine. I can get a decent amount of work done, at least."

"Okay, but seriously, Sophie. If you need anything, if you have a question, no matter how silly you might think it is or if you just want to talk to me, you can call me. Don't feel like you can't." Her cheeks warmed as she looked up at me, the pinkish hue spreading beneath the smattering of freckles under her eyes. She looked so warm, so perfect. *Tell her. Tell her. Grow a fucking pair and tell her.*

"Thanks, I think?" The little chuckle that seeped from her lips made me want to touch them. "Didn't realize you were such a worrier, Hudson."

"I'm not a worrier," I smiled, taking one more step toward her, the heat from her body emanating onto mine. "Stay for dinner tonight. I'll order whatever you want."

Her breathing became a little uneven, her lips parting. *Does my closeness make you nervous?* "Do you ever cook for yourself?" She joked, her throat bobbing as she swallowed.

"Occasionally. I'm not a particularly good cook, though."

"Well, it's a very sweet offer, but I think I'm going to go home," she breathed, sidestepping my towering frame and escaping toward the door of the office. "Thank you. I'll see you next Friday?"

What? Why won't I see her until...? "Oh, uh, yeah. Okay. Next Friday."

She pushed the door open, heading out without another word. I didn't follow her, I couldn't get my feet to move an inch. Despite her need to keep her emotions under a veil, it seemed like she was a little bothered that I was leaving, and I wondered if it was just the worry of being in her first trimester or if it was something more. God, I wanted it to be more. I needed it, craved it, and that was the most terrifying part of all.

Chapter 32

Sophie

Sunday Night

I wished I'd stayed for dinner Friday night. The idea of not seeing him for a week sat heavy like a rock inside of my stomach, and not for a second did I think it was worry over the possibility of something going wrong. I was fairly confident in my body taking care of things, and now that I knew I could get pregnant, the idea of losing it was less daunting. Still a horrible feeling, and I'd mourn the loss every second of the rest of my life, but I knew now that I could try again.

I had to admit that part of me wanted 'again,' no matter what that looked like, to be with Hudson.

Trash television played from the screen in my living room as I fed fabric through my sewing machine, the pressure on the foot pedal so soft it was barely moving. I had to be careful with each stitch, and I should have hand-sewn it, but I was falling behind on orders. I had to finish it quickly.

A knock at the door nearly threw me out of rhythm, but I lifted my foot off the pedal before I fucked something up again. I was learning.

I hurried to the door, not bothering to check who was on the other side before opening it. It was either Lisa or a delivery man—no chance of it being Hudson, not when he'd mentioned over text that he was going to bed early to make his five-thirty a.m. flight. He had dropped Jamey off at his mom's earlier so it wasn't entirely impossible…

Needless to say, however, I was still taken aback when the aforementioned man stood on my doorstep, his dark hair pushed back from his face and his form clad in pajamas. I hated those gray sweatpants. They showed far too much, made me want to stare. "Uh, hi?" I muttered, dragging my gaze back up to a far more appropriate spot on his body.

He took a step toward me and I stepped back, letting him through. *What the fuck was going on?* "Couldn't sleep," he mumbled, and I glanced back at the time blinking at me on my stove. It was only nine.

"So you came here?" I asked, turning back to him as I shut the door. "You should just take some melatonin or something."

The way he looked down at me stopped me mid-sentence. There was a hunger there behind his eyes, painting every feature of his face with hard lines and sharp edges. If he had come over simply to get his fucking dick wet and call it a mistake again, he could leave the way he came in.

"Hudson," I said slowly, narrowing my gaze at him.

He moved too quickly for me to react, closing the distance between us. He placed one hand at the small of my back, planting his other hand firmly against my cheek, then pressed his lips against mine. I felt the swarm of stupid, mindless butterflies taking flight in my gut, the warmth spreading across my face, and this time, the way he held me was different. It wasn't that same greediness of before, the cock-brained zombie getting what he could. No. This was soft, gentle, almost desperate.

I hated how easily I melted for him.

I parted my lips, granting him access to far more than just my mouth. The hand around my waist fisted my shirt, gripping me to him, and slowly but surely he walked me backward, back toward the door, until my spine pressed firmly against it.

His lips left mine, gently grazing the edge of my mouth, and he rested his forehead against my own. "Tell me to stop," he whispered, the heat of his breath spreading across my cheeks. "Tell me to stop, Sophia."

"Why?" I breathed. My hands fell to his chest, the warmth of his skin seeping through his shirt, the thudding of his heart shaking my palms.

"Because I can't come back from this." The way he said it felt so final, so defeated, as if he'd been holding back far too much for far too long. I wanted to know what was beneath his words, what lurked in the depth of his mind. I needed to know. I needed it like I needed air, like I needed the life growing inside of me.

"You can," I said softly, not sure if those were the words he needed to hear. The fabric beneath my fingertips felt like far too much of a barrier.

He exhaled a quick breath, the warm air filling the space between us. "I can't." His hand slid down the small of my waist, over the crest of my ass then down further, along the outside edge of my thigh. He wrapped his fingers around it, lifting until my knee hooked around his hip. "I didn't even fucking come here for this," he muttered, the ghost of his lips pressing barely-there kisses along my cheek. "I thought maybe we could chat, that I could have a glass of wine and we could talk about appointments and telling your family. But this... I should have known I wouldn't be able to stop myself."

I inhaled a shaky breath as his lips moved against my skin, each word bringing him closer to my ear, to the soft spot beneath it that he knew damn well I liked him to kiss. "I don't... I don't want this if you're just going to tell me it's a mistake."

"It wouldn't be a mistake, angel," he breathed, his fingers pressing harder into my skin, unwilling to let me go. "Nothing with you has ever been a mistake."

His words felt like a punch in the gut. I knew damn well that he'd thought I was a mistake before, but the way he was touching me, the gentleness with which he was speaking to me was too much. I was too soft for this, too soft for him. I hated it. But I couldn't stop myself, either.

Before I could even form a response in my quickly fogging mind, Hudson's mouth crashed into mine again, igniting that stupidly easily influenced flame inside of me and pushing aside my better judgment. His lips moved as if they held silent words, filling my mouth with his tongue and the whispers of whatever he held inside.

This was a different Hudson.

In the span of a second, he lifted me, holding my weight with his arms as he stepped us away from the door. I wrapped my arms around his neck for stability, keeping our lips and our upper bodies firmly in contact. My nipples rubbed against the fabric of my white shirt, bra lost to the gods of discomfort last night and abandoned since, and I knew damn well if he looked down he'd see them poking through.

Hudson's knee hit the edge of the couch and he cursed under his breath. The cockiness he had in his own home was absent here—he didn't know the layout as well, didn't know where every little thing was, didn't keep a running tab of toys strewn across the floor so he wouldn't trip. Slowly, eagerly, he dropped my weight onto the large table where I cut my fabric. At the far end was my sewing machine, sitting still with thin, woolen fibers stuck beneath the needle.

"I need you," Hudson breathed, the words escaping between our lips in little gasps.

"You have me." The words felt too real as they slipped from my mouth, but there was no going back now. I had to own them.

He didn't say another word as his hands began to roam, gently lifting the hem of my shirt, fingers splaying out against the bare skin of my stomach. His other hand lazily dragged down along my thigh, over the smooth skin left exposed from my shorts and the curves of my muscle. Each movement felt like memorization, like a caress, not hasty and desperate but wanting and needing. He needed me, but he wanted to take his time. He needed me, but he wanted to savor every second of it. He needed me, but he needed me to need him more.

I was already starting to.

I turned my head to the side, giving myself room to breathe as he moved to my neck, devouring the softest spots that sent shivers up my spine. "We can move to the bedroom if you want," I breathed, gasping in air as his fingers moved gently across the curve of my breast.

"No," he rasped, and as I waited with bated breath for him to elaborate, he gave me nothing but warm touches and butterflies. Slowly, carefully, he lifted my shirt higher, bearing my chest to him but holding the fabric just above my collarbone as if he couldn't bear to part with the skin of my throat just yet to remove it.

I leaned back, forcing a little bit of distance, and lifted the bunched-up shirt over my head. The way he looked at me, his eyes heavy-lidded and his lips damp, told me he wasn't ready for that space. He didn't want to let go of me. He wanted to keep me as close as he could, and dear god, that made my heart jump.

"Come here," he mumbled, wrapping one hand around the base of the back of my neck and pulling me gently toward him. I followed his lead, pressing my lips against the slope of his jaw, the rounded edge of his chin. He heartily hummed his approval, the vibration in his neck tickling my lips, and as his hands began to explore every inch of my chest, I could feel myself warming to him. Every touch felt less like ice, less like anger. He couldn't possibly think it was a mistake this time.

He didn't seem bothered by his own clothing, but with every passing second, I was. I fisted the front of his shirt, tugging it upward, higher and higher until it was bunched beneath my lips. I understood how he felt just seconds ago —I didn't want to pull away, either.

Biting the bullet, I pulled back just an inch, lifting it up and over his head. In the small amount of space between us, I could see his cock pressing dangerously against the tightness of his sweatpants, threatening to rip the seams and take me down with it. I lowered my hand, planting kisses along his neck as I pulled him to me. My fingertips dragged against every ripple of muscle in his chest, making him shiver, his sharp intake of breath making me feel far more powerful than I had the right to feel.

I wrapped my fingers around his length over the cover

of fabric, feeling just how hard his pulse thrummed inside. He groaned, tightening his grip on me, and I could happily stay right where I was forever.

Unable to resist temptation, I shoved my hand beneath the elastic hem of his sweats. They hung so low on his hips that I could see the corded muscle, pointing down toward where I held him like an arrow. "I want to be gentle with you," he said, his hand wrapping around the base of my skull and pulling my head back. He met my gaze, his darkened eyes wild beneath lowered lashes. "You're making it incredibly difficult."

"You're making me impatient," I mumbled, heat rising in my cheeks. I squeezed his shaft and it twitched for me in response. I knew the moment he explored beneath my shorts, he'd find a similar measure of my enjoyment.

"Then lean back, Sophia."

I did as I was told on instinct, letting go of him and leaning back onto the table, resting on my elbows. He followed me, looming over top of me, his mouth closing around my freckled left nipple. His fingers hooked the waistband of my shorts, and using my knees around his waist as support, I lifted myself so he could pull them down.

Hudson's tongue began its magic against the sensitive bud of my breast, coaxing out a whimper as his fingers ghosted down my inner thigh, leaving a trail of goosebumps in their wake. The moment he made contact with my clit, it was as if my body had a mind of its own. I dropped all the way down, my head hitting the wood tabletop, cushioned by Hudson's other hand.

"So eager for me," he mumbled, his fingers sliding in little circles. I moaned as I buried my hands in his hair, my hips lifting to meet his strokes, my legs pulling him closer. "I could do this forever, Sophia."

I breathed in shakily. That cynical side of me knew it was just talk, just something he wanted to say in the moment, but the gullible side of me wanted to believe it. I wanted to take it and run, to put it in my pocket and keep it with me always. "Hudson," I whispered, not entirely sure what I wanted to say but knowing I had to say something.

"I mean that."

No, you don't.

His fingers slid down, two of them breaking past my entrance, curling up at the tips as he buried them inside of me. His thumb took over against my clit, rubbing so precisely that my mind fogged over once again. Head empty, no thoughts, just him and what he was doing to me and how he made me feel. At that moment, it felt like everything.

Another finger, and he bit down against my nipple before soothing the ache with his tongue. I could feel the orgasm building, could tell he wasn't going to let up, but I wasn't ready yet. I wanted more, I wanted all of him inside of me. I wanted him to kiss me again, to say he needed me again, to hold me while he fucked me as if he really meant it.

"God, look at you," he breathed, relinquishing my nipple as he pulled back, his eyes tracking every inch of me as I squirmed in his grip. "So fucking beautiful. I love that face you make."

I tipped my head back, pleasure spreading through my veins like wildfire as I got closer. He was making me rapidly approach the brink, and I didn't want to go over it yet. "What..." I breathed in, my breasts rising with my chest, and couldn't hold back the moan that ripped through me as he quickened his pace. "W-what face?"

"The face you make when you're about to come for me."

That was all it took. I did a swan dive over the ledge, my orgasm shattering through me. I didn't bother holding back my moans of pleasure—for once, I didn't have to. There wasn't a child in the next room that I could wake, there wasn't a single soul within these walls apart from us. His fingers dragged me through the rolling tide, and as my eyes closed from the sheer bliss of it, his mouth met mine far more gently than I thought him capable of. I kissed him back hungrily, far too caught up in my own ecstasy to be able to concentrate, and as he slowly dragged his fingers out of me and replaced them with what I really wanted, he took my face in both of his hands, lifting my back from the table.

I could feel my own dampness against my cheek. He deepened the kiss as the last shudders of the climax faded, and finally at least slightly in control of my own body, I kissed him back just as eagerly. How he swapped from rough to tender so easily was beyond me, but something about it made my chest ache, made me long for more of it.

Slowly, he began to shift his hips, and the stretching feeling that normally made me wince was nowhere to be found. Instead, it was only pleasure, only ripples as his hips met mine. He grunted into my mouth as he pushed my hair back from my cheeks and forehead, each restrained thrust more for me than for him. In the afterglow of my orgasm, it was too much, too real, too gentle. It had never been like this between us before, and I knew that after experiencing this, it would be all I ever wanted from him.

I broke the kiss, pulling back just a hair, blinking through the fog and searching for some hint of disingenu-ousness on his face. Anything, anything at all just to kill what I knew was blooming inside of me. If my feelings for him grew, all of this would be too hard, too heartbreaking, and I knew I couldn't do it.

Soft eyes met mine, and I knew I was done for.

His thumbs slid back and forth along my cheekbones, holding me so softly as if he thought I'd break into a million pieces. I felt like I might. Each thrust of his hips was swift, precise, and easy. He breathed through his mouth, his gaze searching mine for something, anything. "Sophie," he whispered.

I wanted to speak. Truly. But the lump building in my throat, the burning at the backs of my eyes prevented anything other than whimpers and moans. His hooks were sunk so deep within me I didn't think I'd ever surface.

"Fuck," he breathed, and in one quick motion, he pulled me toward him, burying my head in the crook of his neck. I could feel his breath in my hair, could feel the movement of one hand holding me to him as the other slid down between our bodies. I couldn't think, I could hardly breathe. All I could hear were the sounds of our grunts and moans and the steady, fast beating of his heart.

His fingers found my clit again, sinking me further into bliss, distracting me enough to pull me back into the moment.

"There we go," he said, the words feeling flat, the veil back on. "Fuck, the way you clench for me feels like heaven."

My head was swimming. This unexpected version of him, the back and forth, the hot and cold was like a match to gasoline within me. I dug my fingernails into the flesh of his chest, gripping on for dear life as his pace quickened. I knew I could come again, and he knew damn well how to get me there.

He just had to stop fucking with my head first.

I tilted my hips further, getting him to penetrate deeper. He moaned his thanks against the top of my head, pressing a little kiss against my hair before resting his chin on it. Every thrust, every circle of his fingers forced the buildup to begin again deep within my gut, making my muscles tense. "You're too much," he said, his voice breaking in the middle. He cleared his throat immediately after as if attempting to cover it, but there it was, clear as day.

Stop reading into things.

I couldn't fight back the sounds crawling out of my throat, the gasps for air as I got closer and closer. "That's it, angel," he cooed, his hand smoothing out the hair on the back of my head. "Come for me again. Come with me."

His thrusts grew reckless, desperate, less well-timed and more erratic. His hand kept its pace though, weathering the storm, and as I felt myself tipping over the edge and falling into that euphoric oblivion again, Hudson's hips stuttered. The sounds I was making were incomprehensible and I could hardly hear a thing over the thrum of his heartbeat, but I was sure I'd said his name, was sure I'd dug my nails so deep I might've drawn blood. I could feel his heat seeping out inside of me, could feel the trickle of it onto the table beneath me, and as we started to come down from the high I could feel his lips press a kiss to the top of my head.

The word that slipped from my mouth was muffled, eaten by the rigidity of his chest.

"Hmm?" He pulled my head back, soft eyes meeting mine, glassy in their crash back into reality. "What did you say?"

"Again," I breathed, forcing my way back to him, clawing my hands up his chest and wrapping them tightly around his neck. In the fog, I didn't care how obvious it was becoming that I craved him, that I wasn't done yet. I didn't want this to end, I needed it, lived off of it. "Again."

Effortlessly, he lifted me from the table, his cock sliding out of me as he kissed the side of my face multiple times. "Again," he mumbled, almost as if reassuring me. His hand held me firmly to his chest, my legs wrapped tightly around him, and wordlessly, he made his way up the stairs toward my room, following what I could only assume was the layout he imagined when he saw me looking through my window weeks ago.

———

The warmth on my face from the late morning sun was what eventually woke me. Every part of my body felt heavy, thick with sleep and the leftover heat from the night before, the intensity of our time together. I hadn't even closed my blinds—Hudson and I had fallen asleep moments after the action had ended, naked and sweaty beneath the covers, his arms around me and my back against his chest.

Hudson.

Hastily, I grabbed my phone, checking the time. Eleven-twenty a.m. "Shit, shit, shit, Hudson, your flight—"

I rolled, the clang of my phone hitting the floor only elevating the stress, but as I reached out to touch him, I found only cold sheets and fluffed pillows.

I blinked away the sleep from my eyes as I stared at the empty space next to me. "Hudson?" I called, pushing myself up on one elbow, looking toward the ensuite in case he'd woken just before me.

No answer. *Had he left when I'd fallen asleep?* The ache in my chest spread at the idea of being abandoned after everything last night, but as I looked back at the spot he'd occupied, I noticed a little piece of paper sticking out from under his, *my* pillow.

Sophie,

I'm sorry for not waking you up. You look so peaceful when you're sleeping, and I thought you deserved a little more rest after everything. I'm also sorry that you'll wake up without me. If I hadn't had to make my annoyingly early flight, I would have stayed. I mean that.

Please don't hesitate to call me if you need anything. No matter how small or insignificant, I'll answer.

I'll see you soon.

Hudson

I stared at the words in my hand, reading them over and over until they sunk in. *I would have stayed. I would have stayed. I would have stayed.*

It wasn't much, but it was enough to satiate me for the time being. And after everything that had happened last night, the words he'd said, the way he touched me as if he would lose his mind if he ever had to let go... I was beginning to think that maybe, just maybe, the idea of him actually having feelings for me wasn't so insane after all.

Chapter 33

Hudson

Monday

There was a reason I lived in Boston and not within the crowded, hectic streets of New York City, Manhattan, to be specific. My family had plenty of ties here, and a couple of my uncles lived amongst the high-rises overlooking Central Park. My parents had even suggested I move here after I'd finished up at Harvard.

But I fucking hated the big city life.

I loved the suburbs of Boston. It was calmer, close enough to still be connected to the hustle-and-bustle of the center but far enough away that I could pretend I wasn't near the city when I wanted to. Manhattan didn't really come with that option, and as I made my way through the crowds on Seventh Avenue, my shoulders bumping against strangers with cameras around their necks and maps in hand, that was never more obvious. I didn't want to be here.

I wanted to be back in Boston. I wanted to be with her.

I hadn't been able to stop thinking about Sophie since I left early this morning. I hadn't known what to write to her; I'd tried to piece something together in my mind as I frantically searched her condo for a scrap of paper and pen, settling for a sharpie and a page from her sketchbook. I didn't know how to write what was going through my mind, because none of it made sense. I knew I felt bad for having to leave. The idea of her waking up alone after last night had sat heavy in my gut as I stared at the empty page for too long in the dark of her kitchen. I wanted to tell her everything, wanted to have said it last night, but the words felt hollow every time I tried to write them down. It wouldn't have been enough.

The short four hours I'd slept had been some of the best sleep I'd had in years, since well before Jamey was born, and I didn't know exactly how to feel about that. I'd never felt that comfortable in someone else's bed. Not even Becks.

It wasn't just sex, either, and that became apparent when I was holding her face in my hands as I was buried inside of her, her wide eyes watching mine, a thousand words left unsaid between us hanging in the air. But it really sunk in as I was thirty-six-thousand feet above the ground, my phone no longer interesting enough to keep me distracted, my gaze fixed solely on the clouds stretching out of my first-class window. It definitely wasn't just sex anymore. It went beyond that, beyond anything I'd ever had with anyone before. We'd made love, formed a connection that seemed unbreakable.

And all I wanted to do as I walked through the doors of the AMA Conference Center in Times Square was turn right the fuck around.

———

As I stood at a high-top cocktail table, a martini glass of pale shrimp and red sauce serving as the centerpiece, I watched Nathan's mouth move a mile a minute but didn't hear a single word he said. The sound of everyone else talking, the noise filtering in from a speech in the next room, the low music playing in the background... it was too much. I was never a fan of this shit. I only came because I was expected to, because networking was important, because being invited in the first place was seen as a success within my field.

"Are you even listening?" The words were louder, and they cut straight through the muffled sounds that filled my ears.

"Oh, uh," I started, picking up a shrimp and dipping it into the sauce, "it's kind of hard to hear in here."

"It really isn't." Nathan glared at me, his deep brown eyes nearly boring a hole in my head. "What the fuck is going on with you, man?"

I bit off the body of the shrimp, dropping the tail in the receptacle behind me. "Nothing," I said, the word garbled from the food in my mouth. "Everything is just fine."

"We've been to, what, three speeches so far? And every single one of them, you've been staring at the back of the head of the person in front of you. You're not with it."

I rolled my eyes as I reached for another shrimp, but Nathan moved the cocktail glass away from my greedy hands. "Am I not allowed to find the back of someone's head interesting?" I drawled, rolling my eyes at him.

"More interesting than a new development in ultra-sound tech? No, you're not."

Shit, is that what the last one had been about? That would have been something I should have paid attention to. "What are you trying to say, Nate?"

"I'm saying you haven't told me what the fuck has happened between you and Sophie and... don't give me that look. It's so obvious, Hudson."

I steeled my jaw as I reached for the shrimp again, wrestling the glass out of his hand. "Nothing. Nothing's happened." I popped another into my mouth, desperately searching for a distraction.

"What happened when you told her how you felt?"

"I didn't," I grumbled. "We fucked last night. Are you happy now? You know you don't need to know every single thing that happens with my cock, right?"

Nathan blinked at me, his brows furrowed, his eyes wide. "Wait, what? You slept with her again and you still haven't told her?"

"No, I haven't."

Nathan scoffed as he took a step back from the table, his deep brown hair shifting about his face as he shook his head. "Jesus, Huds. You're a fucking idiot." He pursed his lips as he stared at me, opening and closing his mouth as if he had something he needed to say but couldn't quite find the words.

If he took much longer, I was going to go to the next speech without him.

"You realize you're going to ruin any chance you have with her, right?" He spat. "You can't just keep having sex with the poor thing and leading her on without giving her anything in return. You like her. You *know* there's some-thing between you two, and if she's put up with you for this long, she must have some kind of feelings for you too. You're dragging her along."

His words felt like an attack, highlighting every issue I was already aware of yet desperately trying to force to the back of my mind. "It's not like she's said anything to me about how she feels."

"That doesn't fucking matter anymore, man. That's not good enough. She's pregnant with your kid. You and I know better than most how much hormones can fuck you up in that first trimester. You can't rely on her to make that move."

I knew he was right, but every part of me wanted to tell him that he was wrong, that he was making assumptions he shouldn't be, but I couldn't do that. I couldn't give the words life, not when I knew deep down that I was the one being stupid.

I should have told her last night. I shouldn't have waited this long.

———

By the time I'd managed to get checked in to my penthouse and out of the hustle and bustle of the streets, I was exhausted. I needed a shower, I needed sleep. The four hours I'd had, although incredible, weren't enough to keep me going in a place like New York.

My suite at the Chatwal was more luxurious than I needed. The amenities, the butler, the living space... I didn't want any of it. What I wanted was to be at a certain condo in the suburbs of Boston.

I needed to call her. I hadn't been able to stop thinking

about her and what Nathan had said for the rest of the day. Instead of staring at the back of someone's head and imagining Sophie naked in my arms, Sophie kissing me, Sophie asleep against my chest, I'd been imagining Sophie leaving. Sophie turning me down when I eventually worked up the nerve. Sophie running away, just like Becks had.

Pulling my phone from my pocket, I opened the glass doors that lead out onto the balcony, regretting it the moment the door unlatched and the loud sounds of the city filled my ears. Honking car horns, blaring sirens, shouting, a plane overhead. It was too much, too loud, but I needed the somewhat-fresh air if I was going to do this.

My thumb hesitated as it lingered over Sophie's name. I didn't know what I was going to say, but I knew damn well that if I took ten minutes to try and come up with something rather than speaking organically, I'd lose the nerve.

I pressed her name.

It rang six times before the dreaded message: *The person you are trying to reach is unavailable. Please leave your message after the tone.*

I hung up.

Chapter 34

Sophie

Tuesday

I missed him more than I wanted to admit to myself.

I missed him more than I should have.

I missed him more than I knew how to handle.

I'd stared at my phone last night, watching as his name and a photo I'd taken of him and Jamey filled my screen, my ringtone playing loud enough to drown out the sounds of trash television and the humming from my sewing machine. I wanted to answer, to speak to him, to tell him that I missed him. But I knew I couldn't do that, and without that, I didn't know what else to say.

I couldn't bring myself to answer.

He'd called me again an hour later, and I couldn't answer then, either. All I could think about was how he'd looked down at me, how he'd held my face in his hands so softly as if I would shatter, how he moved inside of me so perfectly that it felt like we'd become one. How words had formed in my head that I couldn't bear to say out loud.

It replayed in my mind over and over, forcing a lump to form in my throat as I pulled into my parents' driveway. I didn't know what to do with all the extra time not watching Jamey; I'd gotten too good at doing my work quickly and efficiently that I'd finished up by noon. Hudson had already told his parents, so at least we'd be equal now.

I pushed open my door, shaking the thoughts of Hudson out of my head. Mom was already standing in the doorway, a massive smile on her paint-coated face, her clothes stained to high-heaven.

"Are you guys painting?" I asked sarcastically, throwing my bag over my shoulder as I made my way up the cobble-stone walkway.

"Obviously," Mom laughed, stepping back to let me through the open doorway. The house smelled of paint fumes and I briefly wondered if it would harm the baby. I made a mental note to look it up asap. "I'd hug you but I don't want to get paint on your pretty dress. Did you make that one?"

I nodded and gave her a little twirl, the yellow and white lace spinning. "What are you guys painting?"

"Your old room." She grinned as she shut the door behind me, placing her paint-free hand on my cheek. "We're not quite sure what we're going to do with it yet. We've moved the last of your stuff to the attic, so don't worry, it's not gone far. Just had to cover up that awful deep purple you insisted on."

I rolled my eyes at her as I plopped myself down on the sofa, the plush familiarity seeping into my bones. Some-times I missed living at home. Although the house was fairly grand, it was always homey, and the idea of my baby getting to spend so much time here was enough to make the backs of my eyes burn. "I uh... I might have an idea for it."

Mom furrowed her brows at me, one hand on her hip. "What's that supposed to mean?"

I chuckled as I leaned my head back onto the pillow. "Go get Dad and I'll explain."

"I don't under..." Slowly, as if wading through quicksand, Mom's eyes widened. Her mouth opened, words escaping her, and I watched as she glanced between my eyes and my stomach. "Are you pregnant?"

I bit my lip as I released the urge to place my hand on my not-yet-there bump. "Is it that obvious?"

Her eyes went glassy as a small smile tugged at her lips. "Oh, sweetheart. I'll get your father."

———

"I'm sorry, this is just a lot to take in considering we only properly met him a couple of weeks ago." Dad leaned back in his recliner, his gut taking up the majority of the space. "It's not that I'm not happy for you, sweetie, I am. I'm just a little blindsided."

Mom squeezed my hand. Her body was so close to mine, her legs brushing against my own. "We're so excited for you, but your father's right. We only just met your fiancé. It's a little worrying."

I sighed, searching my mind for the right words to say. "I get that," I started, squeezing my mom's hand in return. I didn't want to lie, but I needed to. "But I've known him a lot longer than you have. I wouldn't have agreed to marry him if I didn't want this with him as well."

"Were you guys doing IVF? I know you mentioned it..." Mom tapered off as she searched my eyes for answers.

"Nope," I said, popping the *p*. "I was going to, but it turns out we didn't need it. It was accidental, to be honest. But I'm happy nonetheless."

"Are you sure you're ready? Are you sure *he's* ready?" Dad asked, his glasses tipping down his nose before he pushed them back up. "You're not even married yet."

"Hudson's a great dad. Amazing, really. I know you didn't get to see much of that when Jamey was here, but he's the best man I could have asked for to be the father of my baby." I couldn't fight back my grin as I imagined what would be our child in Hudson's arms, him fast asleep on the couch with the baby tucked into his neck. I couldn't wait for that to become a reality. "I'm more than ready too. I've wanted this for a while. I'm just really lucky that it all fell into my lap."

"How far along are you?" Mom asked, searching for a bump where there was none.

"Five, six weeks maybe. We're still in the danger zone so we haven't really told anyone, just Hudson's parents, you guys, and Lisa knows, too."

Mom pursed her lips, letting out a sigh through her nostrils. "And you're sure he's the one? You know this isn't exactly by the book."

I laughed, squeezing her hand one more time for good measure. "I'm sure, Mom. I know it's a little sooner than expected, but it doesn't change anything. We love each other, and we're getting married. I'm honestly thrilled. I just want you guys to be happy for us, you know?"

"Oh, honey..." That glassiness returned to her eyes as

she wrapped her arms around me, pulling me into her paint-stained clothes anyway. "Of course we're happy for you. We love you and I'm sure once we get to know Hudson more, we'll love him too. And we'll absolutely love that baby. We just want the best for you, sweetie, that's all."

The lump in my throat returned with a vengeance as the backs of my eyes started to burn. I watched my dad crack a smile over Mom's shoulder, and for a moment, everything felt right. Everything I'd wanted was being handed to me on a silver platter. Approving parents, a baby, a successful business.

But as I pulled back, the weight of my words hit me like a freight train. *We love each other.* As much as I knew in my heart that I wanted that to be true, the heaviness returned, lashing me with one-sided fears and the idea that Hudson could never move on from the hurt he'd received. As much as I wanted him, as much as I knew it was becoming far too hard to hide, the likelihood of him returning those feeling seemed so small, so absolutely minuscule.

I had to remember that, even as my mind drifted back to the memories of the night before. Even as I thought about the note he'd written me, the one that hadn't been any kind of declaration of love or fondness, but had been written with care beneath it, more care than he'd shown me before.

I had to keep my guard up. But I also couldn't continue to pretend that was the right thing to do.

Chapter 35

Hudson

Thursday

Four days without her and three sleepless nights had left me feeling like a fucking zombie. If Nathan had thought I was distracted before, he hadn't mentioned how much worse it had gotten since.

I'd called her every day. I felt like an idiot, listening to her phone ring and ring and hoping she'd answer. After I'd tried Tuesday night I started to worry that something was wrong. I'd called my mom, asked her if she would drive over in the morning and check how she was doing. Wednesday morning brought calm once I learned Mom had checked on her, assuring me that she was fine. But she still didn't take my calls that evening.

As I sat in the back row barely listening to the woman that was speaking on the stage about the new catheter inventions, I couldn't help but feel like I was fucking up.

The conference had been extended by a day, and that was one more day without her. I wanted to see her this evening, to tell her everything, to do what Nathan said and just suck it up and tell her how I feel. But now I couldn't, at least not until tomorrow.

"I'll be right back," I whispered to Nathan, lifting myself from the fold-down chair. I squeezed down the aisle, my thighs and calves brushing against the knees of those sitting along the same row as me. It was almost sacrilegious to leave mid-speech, but I needed space, I needed air, and I needed Sophie. More than most things, it seemed.

As I made my way through the crowded hallways, one hand gripped my phone where it sat in the pocket of my slacks. As much as I hated this city, being outside was better than being in the godawful conference center filled with people who only cared about work and the money they could make from it.

I pushed the front doors open, my name tag swinging wildly from my neck, and pulled the phone from my pocket. I had to speak to her. I had to try, at least one more time. I had to know that I hadn't ruined everything.

Ring.

Ring.

Rin—

"Hi, Hudson."

I sighed in relief as I leaned back against the concrete wall of the AMA. Even just her voice was enough to set my blood on fire, enough to jumpstart my heart. "Sophie."

"I'm sorry I haven't answered," she said quickly, almost as if she'd been holding it in. "You were calling so late, and I've been so exhausted and going to bed early, and then by the time I woke up I knew you'd be busy already—"

"It's okay," I interrupted, a chuckle sneaking its way up my throat just from the reassurance that she was okay, that she didn't hate my fucking guts after Sunday night. "It's fine. Don't worry about it."

The silence hung heavy for a beat before she spoke again. "Your mom said you were worried about me."

I slid down the wall, my ass meeting the disgusting, gum-covered New York City sidewalk, but I didn't care. All I cared about was her on the other end of the line, talking to me. "Yeah," I admitted. "When you didn't answer two nights in a row, I got a little worried that something had happened."

"I'm sorry."

"It's okay, angel." I watched as a woman in absurdly high-heeled boots walked toward me, her body clad in a shimmering, bejeweled leotard and a feather boa around her neck. Between her lips, a cigarette hung loosely, held there by sticky lip gloss and little else. Every breath she took was smoke, every exhale a cloud. "How have you been feeling?"

"I'm okay. A bit nauseous, more so than last week. So very tired. Like, you have no idea how tired I am, Hudson." She laughed and I chuckled with her. The woman passed me, a dollar bill in her hand, and as her heels clicked against the sidewalk in front of me, the bill floated down, landing smack dab in the center of my lap. *Does she think I'm homeless? Do I look that sleep deprived?* "Your mom also said that Jamey misses me. Though she didn't mention anything about him missing you."

I snorted as I pocketed the dollar, making a mental note to give it to someone who actually needed it later. "Not surprised. He was not happy with me when I told him he'd be staying at his grandma's all week. He kept asking to stay with you instead."

"Aww, I absolutely would have let him if you wanted me to watch him."

"Nah, it's okay. You have enough on your plate right now. Plus, we wouldn't have been able to—"

"I told my parents," she cut in, her words so fast I almost didn't understand them. "I know we said we could do it together, but you told yours without me. So I guess we're even now."

"How dare you. I can't believe you went and did the exact same thing that I did. How unforgivable," I laughed, casting my face toward the sky as the sun peaked between the skyscraper buildings. "Yes, angel, we're even. That's fine. How'd they take it?"

She giggled as a *clunk* came through the speaker, what I could only imagine was her setting the phone down. When her voice returned, it was tinnier. Speakerphone. "Surprisingly well," she said, a steady hum picking up in the background. "They were a little surprised and kind of suspicious since they only just met you. But you know, I gave them the whole spiel."

"What whole spiel?" I asked, knowing damn well exactly what she told them but wanting to hear it from her mouth.

She hesitated, clearing her throat, and the hum in the background stopped. *Must be sewing.* "You know, the whole thing about knowing each other for two years and that we love each other, yada yada."

I nodded to myself, unwilling to show how her flippant use of the word *love* struck a chord in me. "Listen," I sighed, resting the back of my head against the hard concrete wall. "I won't be home until tomorrow night, now. I was thinking maybe, if you're up for it, you could come over when I get back and we can tell Jamey together. I know we're still in the danger zone but I just... I want to tell him. You're almost out of it anyway."

"Yeah," she said softly, bringing herself closer to the phone. "Yeah, Hudson, we can do that. Are you sure you're ready for him to know?"

"I'm sure. I've been thinking about it a lot the past few days, among other things. I'm ready for him to know."

"Okay." Silence, again. I wished I could settle myself into it, I wished it was comfortable, but with the amount running through my head and the intense noise of the hustle and bustle around me, I couldn't. "I hope he's not upset by it."

"He won't be," I reassured her. If she were in front of me, I'd take her face in my hands, kiss her forehead, her lips. Make her less nervous. "If you only knew how many times he's asked for a sibling, you wouldn't be worried in the slightest. He'll be over the moon, Sophie. He loves you."

"And you?"

My words caught in my throat. *What is she asking me?*

"Are you excited?"

My god, Sophia, you couldn't have been clearer? "Of course I am."

"Okay," she breathed. "Then yeah. Tomorrow night. Text me when you land?"

The way my chest clenched at the idea of her being at all nervous about my flight was foreign to me. "Yeah. I'll text you when I land. See you tomorrow."

"Bye, Hudson."

She hung up before I did, leaving me alone on the too-hot ground of West Forty-Eighth Street. I gripped the lanyard around my neck, giving it one swift tug and breaking it. I couldn't stand to be at the conference for another second.

I needed a drink, and I needed to think. I had to plan how I was going to tell her. It had to be tomorrow, no chickening out this time. I knew what I felt but all of it meant fucking nothing if Sophie didn't love me too.

Chapter 36

Sophie

Friday

The 'will he, won't he' was starting to get on my damn nerves.

I picked at my food as Hudson sat across the table from me. Takeout, again. I made a mental note to teach him some easy recipes if he was at all interested in cooking. I knew damn well he could afford takeout every night, could afford private chefs and charter jets and whatever the hell else he wanted. *A private chef could be a great idea.*

He'd rewarded Jamey's good behavior at his grandparent's with pizza. The food itself was great, so good that I could understand Jamey's intense excitement over it every time it was so much as mentioned, but it was so hard to concentrate when all I could think of was Sunday night and our phone call. He had to have feelings for me. Somewhere down inside that ice-cold exterior of his there had to be some warmth. I just didn't know when, or if, he would tell me.

Hudson met my gaze, a smile on his face from something Jamey had said that I hadn't heard in my daydreaming. "You alright with that, Sophie?"

I blinked at him, wondering what the hell the correct answer could be, noting Jamey's slack-jawed mouth. "Please, Sophie?"

"I'm sorry, I missed that. What?"

"Ice cream," Hudson chuckled, plucking another slice of pizza from the open box on the table. "I was thinking we could take Jamey down to Debbie's after we finish up dinner and do the thing."

Debbie's. He'd mentioned it so absurdly casually. Debbie's was a little ice cream shop down by the harbor, a mom-and-pop kind of place that had been running since well before either of us had been born. My parents used to take me and Aaron when we were kids whenever we had stellar report cards or even when we'd simply lost a tooth.

"Yeah, I'm definitely up for that."

Hudson grinned softly at me, his eyes fixed on mine. Jamey shouted something in excitement but I didn't hear it, and judging by the way Hudson watched me, he didn't either. It made those mindless butterflies take off again. Did he want to tell *me* something there, too?

"Perfect."

We fell back into silence minus Jamey's hasty chewing and brief outbursts about what kind of ice cream he wanted to get from Debbie's. Apparently, mint-chocolate chip wasn't good enough if we were going there. He wanted something even better.

"You okay, Soph?" Hudson asked, his grin sliding as his brows furrowed. His hand twitched where he'd left it on the table, almost as if he wanted to reach for mine. "You seem a bit distracted."

"I'm okay." *Lie. You're panicking. You're thinking of all the ways this can go wrong and wondering if you should just tell him how you feel, you idiot.* "Work's been a lot this week, so I'm just a little tired."

"Did you get everything you needed to do?"

I almost snorted. "No."

———

By the time Hudson parked the Range Rover at the harbor, the sun was hanging low in the sky, painting everything in deep oranges and pinks. I wished we were on the west coast so we could watch it set over the water, but I'd take a sunrise over a sunset any day.

Hudson picked up Jamey despite his protests of wanting me to lift him instead. He held him against his hip, high enough that he could see the menu as we stepped up to the little window to order. I watched as Hudson pointed out each option on the board, helping Jamey sound out each word, and the ache in my chest seemed to spread to my bones. He was such a good father, such a caring person and I loved to catch him off his guard. I wanted this side of Hudson, the side that I thought might want me in return.

But I also knew how much of an idiot I might be for wanting that.

"Which one are you having, Jamey?" I asked, coming up beside them. Jamey sat at my height on his dad's hip, and he giggled as he reached out and poked my nose.

"I think... maybe... uh..."

"You've gotta pick one, bud." Hudson chuckled as he shifted Jamey's weight on his hip.

"It's just so hard!"

"Well, *I'm* going to get rum-raisin. Why don't you just get your favorite?" Hudson asked, pointing to the mint chocolate chip on the board in big letters.

Jamey gasped as he looked at it, his eyes tracking further up than Hudson's hand. "Peanut butter! I want the peanut butter one. But I want chocolate on top."

Hudson laughed as he put him down, ruffling his hair. "Always full of surprises, aren't you, squirt?" His sights turned to me, that comfortableness settling between us, and he cracked a grin. "What do you want?"

I knew what I wanted. It was the exact same thing I had every single time I came to Debbie's, the exact same thing I'd gotten since I was a kid. "Orange and vanilla swirl."

"On it. There's a blanket in the back of the car," he said, nodding toward the Range Rover. "Why don't you and Jamey go lay it out on the beach and I'll meet you guys down there?"

———

I didn't notice Hudson joining us until his bare, sand-covered feet hit the blanket. He held three cones of ice cream in one hand as if he'd been doing it his whole life, effortlessly, as he sat down next to me. Jamey had already started working on building a sand mound, but the moment his dad arrived, he abandoned it for the treat.

I took my cone from Hudson, watching him carefully as he looked between me and Jamey. I wasn't sure what his plan was exactly—we hadn't discussed the finer details, just that we would tell him. The anxiety of it was eating me alive, and combined with Hudson's mixed signals, I felt like I was starting to panic a little.

"Can you tell him?" I whispered, leaning in just a hair closer to him. My shoulder brushed against his, and as he looked down at me, I swear I saw too much behind his eyes. Too much of what I wanted, not necessarily what he would give me.

"Of course." He closed the distance just for a millisecond, placing the softest kiss against my forehead, before turning back to Jamey. "Hey, bud. Sophie and I have something we need to tell you about but you've got to pay attention. Can you handle that?"

Jamey turned from the sand he'd been kicking, suddenly far more interested in what his dad had to say. "Okay. What is it?"

"So, you know how there's this one thing that you've been asking me for ever since you could talk?"

His little eyes grew wide as saucers as he looked up at his dad, peanut-butter ice cream melting over the side of his hand. "We're going to Disney?"

Hudson blinked, confusion marring his face. "You want to go to Disney?"

"Yeah! I saw a commercial for it at Grandma's."

I snorted, leaning more of my weight toward Hudson until my head rested on his shoulder. I was so damn tired and it wasn't even eight in the evening yet.

"Okay, no, this isn't about Disney. We can go to Disney if you want but this is something you've been asking for, not something you just found out about—"

"Oh my god, we're going to Disney!"

"Jamey, Jamey, hey." Hudson laughed, reaching out for his little arm and tugging him toward us. "Pay attention. This isn't about Disney."

"I don't get it."

"I know, bud. Just listen, okay?"

"Okay."

"You remember all those times you asked me for a little sister or a little brother?" Hudson said softly, pulling Jamey a little bit closer until he was practically dripping ice cream into his lap. "You remember how much you begged me for a sibling?"

Nausea churned in my gut as Jamey's eyes grew wide again, understanding slowly settling in. I wanted him to be happy more than I could even imagine; if he wasn't, if he was upset or angry, it would fucking shatter me.

"I'm going to be a big brother?" Jamey whispered.

Hudson nodded, plucking the cone from his hand before disaster inevitably struck. "Sophie's pregnant, bud. You're gonna have a sibling."

He looked between us, his little mouth open wordlessly. *Please say something. Please. Anything, Jamey.*

"Jamey?" Hudson chuckled.

"Oh. My. God!" Jamey shrieked, his little body finally moving. He threw his arms around mine and Hudson's necks, burying his ice cream-covered face between us. "Thank you! Thank you, thank you, thank you!"

The relief that flooded me was intense, washing me into shore like the waves before us. I'd felt like I was drowning, like I'd been swimming in a riptide that I couldn't get free of, but then that... that was enough to bring me to the surface. The backs of my eyes burned heavily, the tears building in the corners. "You're happy?"

"Yes!" He let go of us, backing up into the sand, raising his little arms above his head. "Did you hear that, world? I'm going to be a big brother! I'm gonna be the best big brother ever!"

Hudson laughed as he watched him, the smile on his face far too genuine for me to ever think it was fake. He wrapped an arm around my waist, pulling me in closer to him. "I told you he'd be excited," he whispered, placing a kiss on the top of my head. "There was nothing to worry about."

"Is it a girl? I hope it's a girl," Jamey gushed, collapsing on the blanket in front of us. He kicked his legs in the air, excitement and adrenaline flooding his system.

"We don't know yet," I chuckled.

"I hope it's a girl, too," Hudson beamed, reaching forward to tickle Jamey under his ribs. "Maybe we'll get lucky, bud."

I rolled my eyes at the two of them. "I don't care what it is. I just hope it's healthy." I met Hudson's gaze as I wiped my eyes, too many emotions rolling through me all at once. His eyes shone in the light of the setting sun, that same intensity behind them, and I laughed as another tear escaped. "Sorry, they're happy tears."

"Don't apologize." His thumb came up beneath my eyes, wiping the last that escaped away. My breath hitched at his touch, at how easy he found it to do in front of his son. "Don't ever apologize."

———

Jamey crashed out on the way home. His little snores were the only sound in the car, filling the silence. Hudson had only glanced at my hand once—I'd worn the ring, and now that I actually thought about it, I wasn't entirely sure why. We weren't pretending with Jamey.

"Come in," Hudson whispered, a sound asleep four-year-old in his arms as we walked up toward the house. The way he said it felt more like a request than a question, and I knew if I agreed, I'd either end up fucking him or falling asleep.

"I don't know, Hudson, I'm really tired..."

"You can stay the night if you want." He bit his lip, looking between me and the front door. "Nothing has to happen, Sophie."

"I know." Jamey was dead weight in his arms, his limbs flopped everywhere and his hair covering his face. Gently, I pushed the strands away. "I just need to get some sleep."

"Sophie..." Hudson sighed, taking the smallest step toward me. "Look, I... I know everything that's happened in the last week has been a lot for you. Hell, everything that's happened in the last couple of months has been a lot. I know you're overwhelmed."

Tears sprung to life in my eyes again and I took a step back.

"Just come inside. I'll put him in bed, we can just chat. We can talk about everything. All of it." He rolled his lips between his teeth, the words not there, not just yet. "Please."

I sniffled, wiping the tears from my face. "I need to go home. Unless there's something you adamantly need to talk to me about right this moment, I'd rather just go to sleep."

He sighed, shifting Jamey slightly in his arms so he could hold him with one hand. His other cupped my cheek, wiping away the tears as they escaped. "It can wait if it needs to. I'm sorry if this was too much for you today."

I turned my face toward his hand, keeping his warmth on me. "It's all just a lot. All of it. You and me, this child..."

"Then let's talk about it, angel."

I shook my head, stepping back from his small act of kindness. The night air hit my face, cooling it far too quickly with the dampness there. "I can't," I whispered. "Not tonight, okay?"

Jamey stirred in his hold, a little grunt escaping his lips. "Daddy?"

I nodded at him as I took another step back. "Put him to bed." I hated the feeling that ripped through with every step I took, from pavement to soft grass. But I couldn't just stay and watch him pull me in closer, I couldn't fall harder. I thought, stupidly, that he'd say something to me today. Maybe he'd tell me that he had feelings for me, that he wanted to give it a proper go, that raising this child would be easy as pie because we could do it together.

My condo was too warm, too uninviting. I didn't want to be there, I wanted to be next door, with him and Jamey, but it was pointless. Thoughts raced through my head; horrible, ugly thoughts that I couldn't do it anymore, that being fake engaged to him was far too hard when these feelings were building inside of me. I couldn't just pretend to be in love with him when I actually was. But the hardest part was I couldn't pretend to be his when I wasn't.

Fucking pregnancy hormones. That was all this could be. Just hormones. I'd get over it. I *had* to get over it.

Chapter 37

Hudson

Saturday

I chickened out.

I chickened the fuck out—again—multiple times now. Nathan was right. I was only hurting her in the process. I saw it on her face last night as she stepped away from me, as she declined my invitation to come in and talk, as the tears welled up in her perfect eyes and coated her freckled face. Forty-five had fallen. I'd actually managed to count all of them.

I wasn't going to chicken out today. I couldn't. I was going to lay every single card I had on the table, explain everything as well as I could. I was going to fix this.

I *had* to fix this.

The moment I woke up, as I shifted between the sheets searching for my phone, I decided that tonight had to be the night. If I forced myself into a position where I had to tell her, where it would be the only thing I could do, then I couldn't run away from it. I'd have to face it head-on, good or bad. I still wasn't entirely sure which was which.

I called my mom first and sorted out babysitting. She would take Jamey for the night, and though I couldn't explain exactly why, she seemed to handle it better than I thought she would considering she'd just had him for five nights in a row. Jamey wouldn't be pleased, but I needed him to be alone with Sophie this evening.

I called the caterers next. I booked a private chef for seven o'clock onward, instructing him to board my yacht before we arrived. It was too large to fit along the side of my house, so I paid the fees to keep it docked although I hadn't set foot on it in two years. The S.S. *Becks* would need a new name, but in the meantime, it would have to do.

I called the cleaners. Begged them at short notice to clean up the boat, change the sheets on the bed, and ensure the vessel was spotless after two years of avoiding it like the plague. I'd have done it myself if I had the time, but I didn't. I needed the day to prepare.

Nathan did like to say I was dramatic.

———

The traffic entering central Boston was absolute hell on earth. My satnav claimed there was a crash ahead and all four lanes of US-1 were stopped, inching forward at a snail's pace.

I pulled my phone from my pocket, double-checking around me that there weren't any police officers stuck in traffic next to me, and fired off a text to Sophie.

I need to see you tonight. I'll explain everything. Come over at seven. Wear something nice.

My hand shook as I hit the send button. I wasn't even sure if she'd respond. I'd told myself multiple times this morning that if she didn't want to talk to me, if she ignored my calls and messages, I'd go to her house and beg her to come with me if that's what it took. I wasn't going to let this fall apart again. I wasn't going to chicken out again.

My phone buzzed as I moved a centimeter forward in traffic.

Can we have crab legs again?

I chuckled, the back of my head falling against the headrest. That message was ten times better than what I was expecting. She easily could have told me to go fuck myself and even that would have felt like a relief.

Abso-fucking-lutely.

Okay. Will Jamey be there?

Nope. Just us.

———

My jaw nearly hit the floor like one of the animated characters in Jamey's cartoons when Sophie stepped through my door. I understood now why she wanted to know if Jamey was coming.

The tight, black dress she wore hugged every nook and cranny of her body. The neckline plunged almost down to her navel, thin straps held it up on her shoulders, and the back showed off so much of her skin that I thought I might actually not make it through the evening. I wasn't sure I'd be able to think about literally anything else other than what lay beneath the fabric.

"Don't stare at me like that," she grumbled, turning toward the nearest reflective surface as she pushed her stud earrings through the holes in her lobes. "You've seen me naked. Surely this must be nothing for you."

"That dress might just be on par with you, bare, underneath me."

She mumbled something under her breath, the little strands of hair hanging from her high bun rustling as she turned toward me. "Well, I figured soon enough I won't really be able to wear something like this for a while, so I might as well tonight."

"I'm not complaining."

"I know you're not."

"But for the record." I said, taking a step toward her. I brushed a wavy strand of hair from her face, my fingers gently swiping against her skin. It felt far too electric for my own good. "I'll still find you just as enticing when you're in your second and third trimesters. You can absolutely still wear things like this."

Her cheeks warmed beneath my touch, blush spreading out across her face. "I don't know if I should take that as a compliment or just a guy being pervy."

I chuckled as I dragged my fingers down along her jaw, lifting her chin so she'd meet my gaze. "Well, you'll have plenty of time to decide in the car. We need to get going, though. We're already late."

"Late for what?"

"You'll see."

. . .

Sophie didn't say one word to me the entire car ride.

Normally, her silence didn't bother me. I knew her too well by now to take anything bad from it. But for the thirty-minute drive out to the docks, I'd found myself white-knuckling the steering wheel, thoughts racing from bad to worse to catastrophic. I was nervous about getting back on the yacht after so long, I'd been spending my time on my smaller boat instead. I was worried that Sophie might get angry at me, might not feel the same way I did, or would just full-on have a heart attack from my openness.

A quick glance at Sophie's left hand as I pulled into the parking lot confirmed she hadn't worn the ring tonight. I almost wished she had, but she had no reason to and I had to remind myself of that. I didn't tell her she'd be impressing anyone, I didn't tell her there'd be anyone to fool.

I only hoped that when we inevitably left the yacht, there'd be one on her finger.

The rain slowed a little as I shifted into park, and her head lifted from the passenger window of my Mercedes. "Are we here?" She asked, a little yawn drawing her mouth open.

"Yeah." I leaned back between the seats, searching around on the floor for the umbrella I normally kept down there, but came up instead with an empty bag of crisps and Jamey's tiny raincloud umbrella. "Fucks sake," I breathed, groaning as I laid it out in my lap. "This isn't going to plan."

"It's okay," she said softly. "How far is it?"

"About a two-minute walk. But I don't want you to get wet."

"Jamey's umbrella should be fine." Her lips twitched upward as she looked at me, her eyes far too soft. "Don't worry about it. Have you got anything to cover yourself with?"

I shook my head no, pushing the door open with my foot. "Nope. I don't mind a little rain." The droplets began their ruination of my decently styled hair as I rounded the car, the pebbled parking lot crunching beneath my feet. My trembling hand shook as I reached for her door handle, slipping against the slick outer shell of my car, and I leaned over the empty space the door left behind to shield her from the rain. "Come on, angel."

She blinked up at me, Jamey's umbrella clutched in her hand, as she untangled the velcro close on it. "What's happening?" She chuckled as her heeled feet touched the rocks.

"We're having dinner on my yacht." I held out my hand, taking a step back as she unfurled the umbrella before grasping onto my arm for leverage.

"Are you taking me on a date, Hudson Brady?" She joked, elbowing me in the side as she found her footing.

"That's exactly what I'm doing."

"Wait, seriously?" Her eyes met mine, wide and full of a mixture of surprise and some hidden emotion.

"Seriously."

Placing my damp hand on the small of her back, I lead her across the gravel to the docks. She watched her feet the entire way, and I had to tell myself over and over that it wasn't because she didn't want this, it was just because her thin heels could get stuck in the gaps between the floating cement and wood. *It'll go well. It'll go well. It'll go well.*

"This is us." The S.S. *Becks* stood tall before us, the painted name on the side screaming at me in too-large letters. From the exterior, you'd never know that I hadn't stepped foot on it myself in two years, let alone anyone else.

It was the only thing that still filled me with anxiety, the thought of boarding. It made my throat close, my damp hands damper, that sinking feeling weighing me down and burying me beneath the water below us.

"You okay?" .

I blinked the rain from my eyes as I looked down at her. So fucking sexy in that dress, so fucking ridiculous with that raincloud PAW Patrol umbrella. "I'm fine."

"You look like you've seen a ghost," she said.

I chuckled lightly as I ushered her forward onto the ramp. "I did. You should've seen it. Big, see-through, scary. I think it had fangs."

"Fangs? I think you might be confusing ghosts with vampires," she laughed, folding her umbrella in as she stepped into the covered, lit area of the yacht. "Hudson?"

"Yeah?"

"Are you gonna... you know... get onboard?"

I stood at the edge where the ramp met solid, polished hardwood. The rain still fell over me, soaking me down to my bones, and that sinking feeling amplified tenfold. "Yeah," I breathed, staring down at the threshold. *It's a step. One step, and it's over. You'll have done it.*

A hand appeared in my field of vision, little raindrops hitting the skin and sliding down until they fell to the joining spot below. Painted nails, freckles. "Come on. You've got it."

My throat closed as I took her offer, grasping her wet hand in mine. She pulled me toward her with one quick burst, forcing me over the threshold and into the warm light of the cabin of the ship. I stumbled forward into her, her back hitting the black marble wall. I caged her in unintentionally, my breathing rapid, my heart pounding. I couldn't open my eyes, could only feel the water sliding off of me, dripping onto the floor and likely her face. I was onboard.

"Hey, hey," she cooed, her hand reaching up to cup my cheek. She wiped the water from my face, my eyes. "You're okay. Slow down your breathing."

Fuck, I loved her.

I did as she said, breathing in through my nose and out through my mouth to slow myself down. Finally, I forced my eyes to open, meeting her wide and worried gaze as she looked up at me. "Sorry," I mumbled.

"Ah, there you two are! I was beginning to worry."

I leaned back, putting that little bit of distance between us again and immediately regretting it. "Hey, Thomas," I said, forcing the most polite grin to my face as possible as I turned toward the chef. "Sorry we're late. The rain made it a little hard to see out there."

"No problem, sir. Your dinner should be ready soon. Would you like me to fetch you a towel?"

"Nah, it's fine. I'll get one. Thank you."

Thomas nodded before heading back off to the kitchen, leaving us in heavy silence. I glanced around the ship, taking in as much as I could see from the entryway. The cleaning crew had, I assumed, done a fantastic job. I didn't know the state it had been left in, didn't know how bad it had gotten over the years since, but it looked brand new again.

"Did you bring any other clothes? I can go grab them from the car," Sophie offered, her hand resting gently against my arm. "You're soaked straight through."

"I think I've still got some in the bedroom. I'll have a look."

. . .

The snort of a laugh Sophie let out as I walked into the dining room told me she could see just how ill-fitting the clothes I'd found were. They were two years old, and in those two years, I'd packed on a fair bit of extra muscle. I just had to pray that the buttons on my shirt didn't fly off into my food.

"Don't laugh at me," I smirked, plopping into my chair before her with one hand on the closures of my buttons. "It was all that was left in the closet."

"I'm not laughing," she insisted, one hand coming up to cover the growing grin on her face. "I actually kind of like it. Shows off *everything*."

"You have already seen me naked. Surely this must be nothing for you," I said, repeating her own words back to her.

Blush spread across her freckled face. "Shut it, Hudson."

Chef Thomas rounded the corner of the room with two bowls stacked on his arm and a small cutting board of bread. He set the bowls in front of us, clam chowder filled to the rim of the small containers. "Your appetizers."

Sophie snatched a piece of bread before he'd even set the cutting board down. "So what is it that you so desperately had to drag me all the way out here for? In the pouring rain, on a yacht, with a private chef. It must be good," she chuckled, dipping her bread into the chowder as the chef retreated back to the kitchen. "Or really bad, I guess."

My grasp on the spoon in my hand went slippery. "Maybe we should wait until after dinner to chat?"

"That bad, huh?" I watched as she stuffed a mouthful of bread between her lips.

"It could go either way." Dipping my spoon into the milky-white soup, I suddenly felt far too nauseous to eat. "And if it goes badly, then this date is going to be extremely awkward for both of us."

Sophie wiped the corner of her mouth with her thumb, her eyes studying me. "I don't think it'll go badly. If I didn't want to be on a date with you, Hudson, I wouldn't have agreed to come."

She had a point. She had to at least have some idea of where this was going, though maybe not how far.

"Can I guess?" Sophie asked, tearing another piece of bread as she watched me. I didn't know what to say, and she took my silence as a yes. "Okay, so, this is going to be even more awkward if I'm wrong. But I think you're finally going to admit that you have feelings for me. I think you're going to lay it all out there, the good and the bad, and tell me you want to give us a real shot."

I blinked at her, feeling far too much like an open book. The spoon in my hand dropped into the bowl, little droplets of clam chowder arcing up and landing on the wooden table. "That is... uh..." I cleared my throat as I grabbed for my napkin, hastily wiping away the specks of soup and fighting the urge to run away.

"Shit, am I wrong?" She asked around a mouthful of food, wide eyes getting wider, blushed cheeks getting redder. "Shit."

"No, you're not wrong." The words left me before I could even process them. "That's exactly what I'm doing, Sophia."

"Oh," she mumbled, hurriedly swallowing her mouthful of soupy bread. "*Oh.*"

I took a deep breath, forcing my racing heart to calm down, grasping onto the napkin so hard I was worried the fabric would tear. *Do it now. Do it now.* "I was going to wait until after dinner, but I might as well just do it now since you've already guessed." Another deep breath, in through my nose and out through my mouth.

"Take your time," she said. I nodded.

"You know parts of my story. Little glimpses here and there that I gave up, or that you shoved your way into. You know my ex-wife, Becks, left me and Jamey two years ago, and you know that I've been closed off ever since. I didn't see a future where I could find someone that made me feel again. But somehow, Sophia, *you* did. I don't know how. I don't know what witchcraft you hide under those adorable freckles, but you've weaseled your way in and fucking unfrosted my heart."

Sophie blinked at me, the bread in her hand crumbling into her soup.

"I think I might have known from the moment you ran across your yard barefoot and told your parents we were engaged," I chuckled, the words flowing a little smoother now, a little less frightening. "Or maybe when I caught you watching me from your window. From that moment I knew you'd be trouble at the very least."

Sophie's face grew redder, her hand covering her half-open mouth. "I'm definitely trouble," she breathed, the smallest laugh crawling from her lips.

"You are such fucking trouble," I chuckled, reaching across the table until my hand rested atop hers. "When you showed up in my office that first time, I wasn't sure if I was the luckiest or unluckiest man in the world. But I knew there was a pull between us, some invisible string tugging me toward you. I felt it pull when I saw you with Jamey that afternoon on the first day you watched him. I felt it pull when you asked me about Becks. I felt it pull that night that

I took you for the first time, felt it in the way I couldn't keep my hands off you, felt it in the way you breathed."

"Hudson..."

"I felt it pull harder when we fought. When I told you that sleeping with you was a mistake... that still fucking haunts me. I hated myself for that. I felt it pull when you hadn't spoken to me for days afterward, harder and harder each night, telling me to just go fix it. It pulled me so hard when I found out you were pregnant that I was honestly scared it might snap."

I took another deep breath, my mouth going dry, and tried to quench it with my glass of wine. It only made it worse.

"But throughout all of that, I was terrified. I still am. What happened with Becks, it wasn't like I saw it coming. We weren't fighting constantly, we were happy, we had a child. She was a great mom, not the best, but she was good." My hand spasmed from clenching the napkin so hard, dropping it from my grip. "The day before she left, the three of us went out sailing on *this fucking boat* and we had what I thought was the best day ever. Jamey fell asleep on the drive home. We were out late because we had a hard time docking, the water was a bit choppy. I carried Jamey up to bed that night and the look she gave me... I don't know if I should have suspected something was wrong right then and there, but it was different. Loving, but different."

Sophie's hand squeezed mine, and as I watched her, her eyes darted to the corner of the room. She held up one hand and shook her head before looking back to me, and when I turned, I saw Chef Thomas backing out of the room with plates full of food. "Is that why you didn't want to get on the boat?"

I nodded. "Yeah. When I woke up the next morning, she was gone. I haven't been on board since."

"Oh, Hudson..."

I sucked in air, needing to feel the sharpness of my lungs filling. *I'm okay, Jamey's okay, Sophie's okay.* "I didn't trust anyone after that for a while. I vowed to myself that I'd never let anyone get that close to me or Jamey again. But then you came along, and all of that went out the window. Or, rather, I've been fighting myself over it ever since. But this is different. This is so much more than what I've ever felt before, and we've only known each other, what, two months? If that?"

"Two years if we're going based on what we've told our parents," she joked, her hand squeezing mine again.

"Yeah," I chuckled. "It feels like two years, to be honest. It feels like longer. It feels like I might have known you my whole life, like I was just waiting for you to appear. I've fucking fallen in love with you, Sophia. I've torn down my walls for you. I've let you in, let Jamey get attached. I've gone against everything I told myself I wouldn't do for you. I'm only sorry that I've handled it all so poorly."

I watched as her throat bobbed, her eyes going glassy, tears beginning to form. She laughed lightly at herself as she wiped them away with the back of her finger, preserving as much mascara as she could. "I've fallen in love with you too," she sniffled.

I breathed out a sigh of relief, my grin far too wide to even try to hide it. "Good," I said, standing from the table and shoving my hand into the pocket of my slacks. I wrapped my fingers tightly around the little wooden box. "That makes what I'm about to do a lot less terrifying."

Chapter 38

Sophie

Saturday Night

What does that mean? What's happening? He loves me. He fucking loves me. I knew it. But why is he standing? The crab legs were coming. Doesn't he know that dinner is ready? They're going to get cold...

Hudson dropped to one knee and my heart nearly stopped.

"Hudson," I breathed, turning in my chair to face him. *He's tying his shoelace. It must have come undone. He was shaking his leg a lot, maybe that untied it? Oh my god, he has a box.*

"Sophia Elizabeth Mitchell," he started, his voice wavering as he held the little box on his knee. "No one, and I mean no one, has ever made me feel the way you do. I want to do this for real. I don't want to have to pretend with our parents anymore, and I don't want to keep confusing

Jamey." He laughed, sniffling as if he was trying to hold back tears, and opened the box.

In the center, on a neat little pillow, sat what may have been the most breathtaking ring I've ever laid my eyes on. It looked so similar to the one I'd been wearing. An oval cut diamond set within a gold band, smaller diamonds surrounding it. The ring was beautiful, perfect.

"I want to do everything with you. I want to raise our child together, I want to raise Jamey with you. I want to *marry* you. I will spend every day from here on out making up for every misstep I might take, every word I might fumble, every stitch of fabric I've made—and will continue to make—you mess up on. I will love you for as long as I have air in my lungs, for as long as you let me, and even longer after that. Will you marry me, angel?"

I didn't realize I was full-on crying until Hudson wiped the tears from my cheeks. It was all so insane, every piece of the puzzle slotting into place. I wanted this, I knew from the depths of my fucking soul I wanted this. We may not have known each other that long but I didn't care. Hudson was my person, my everything, and although I'd fought it the last few months I knew without a shred of doubt that this was where I was supposed to be. I didn't even care that his clothes were too tight or that dinner might be getting cold. *God, I was starving.* His proposal was perfect. "Yes," I choked, throwing my arms around him and launching myself from the chair. He stumbled backward on his knees, his ass hitting the polished hardwood, and we both laughed as tears streamed down our faces.

"Thank God," he said, one arm around my waist and the other holding his weight against the floor. "I was still a little worried you'd say no."

"Ahem. The crab is going cold, Dr. Brady. Would you like me to wait any longer?"

I lifted my head, wiping the tears as best as I could, and chuckled as I locked eyes with the chef. "Should we eat, Dr. Brady?" I mocked, plucking the ring from the box and sliding it onto my finger. Perfect fit.

"I'd rather take you to bed," he whispered, his shit-eating grin far too wide. "But yeah, let's eat."

———

Long after the chef had gone and the rain had stopped, Hudson cast off from the dock and captained the yacht out into the harbor. I watched as he steered, my legs laid out on the white leather chaise lounge just behind the wheel and a captain's hat on my head.

Chef Thomas had brought out a congratulatory bottle of champagne, and although I'd protested to Hudson, he'd insisted on one single glass. "One glass won't hurt the baby. I promise," He'd told me. After two weeks of not having a sip of alcohol, I could already feel the buzz seeping into my bones.

"Why are we leaving the dock?" I asked, swaying my bent knees as I watched him.

"Because I doubt the others that live on their boats will want to hear the sounds you'll be making tonight." Hudson chuckled as he turned to face me in my captain's hat. "Not going to lie, that hat only makes you look even more appealing to me right now."

"Then do something about it," I teased, pulling it farther down over my brows.

"Don't tempt me. I have to anchor first." He crossed the short distance to me, offering his hand. I took it gladly, feeling like a wet spaghetti noodle as he hauled me to my feet.

————

His hands were on me the moment we stepped through the door to the bedroom.

Fingers in my hair, tugging at the tie holding up my bun and releasing the wavy strands in one swift go. His lips met mine, gentle and soft but needy, and every little stroke was enough to set my senses on fire.

Hudson loved me. He'd said the words, he'd given them life, he'd *proposed*. I could feel the relief from him with every touch, every little movement he made as he edged me back toward the bed. Walls had crumbled, now a little pile of debris at our feet, and we'd clean it up tonight. We'd make it new. We'd build new walls together, not to keep one another out, but to build a life within them.

My back hit the soft, black comforter, my hands fisting the mess of his hair that he'd pushed back, dragging him down on top of me. "This feels so surreal," I whispered, watching the way his eyes softened as he looked down at me. His hands fumbled along the side of my dress, searching for the hidden zipper, and finally found it.

"I know exactly what you mean." One swift tug and the zipper was down, the fabric hanging loosely across my body.

"I wanted to tell you earlier. That night before my flight, actually. It was right there, on the tip of my tongue. I just couldn't find the words."

"I thought so," I chuckled, pulling him down and kissing him again. His mouth tasted of champagne and butter, his hair smelled like the ocean. I could stay beneath him like this for the rest of my life and be happy.

Wandering hands pushed the straps from my shoulders, baring my chest to him, and as I reached for the buttons on his shirt, one popped off in my hand. "I figured that might happen," he mumbled against my lips, grabbing his shirt by the collar. "Doesn't fit me anymore, anyway." One swift tug and the rest of the buttons popped. I laughed, happy nostalgia flooding me from the first night we'd slept together.

The two sides of his shirt hung limp around him. I couldn't stop myself from dragging my hands across his chest, from feeling every ripple of muscle, every bit of warmth seeping out from him. This was *mine. He* was mine, for as long as I wanted him.

It still didn't feel real.

"Hudson," I breathed, pulling back from the kiss enough to get some air. "Did you and Becks ever...?"

"On this bed?" He shook his head as he slid the fabric down my body, lifting me just enough to pull it off over my ass. "No. We didn't."

Okay. That's a million times better.

His lips met my neck, kissing softly on the tender spot beneath my ear. I sighed, raising my bare chest to meet his, relishing in the warmth between us. My hands wandered down to where his hips met mine, fingers toying with the latch on his slacks until it released. I could feel his cock pressing against the fabric, hardening beneath my touch. Sliding the zipper down, a groan of release escaped his mouth, warm air spreading out across my neck.

The length of him sprang to life as he pushed the fabric down. "No boxers?" I chuckled, wrapping my fingers around it.

"No," he grunted, his hands finding my skin once again as he kicked his slacks off. "There weren't any here and my other pair was soaked through."

"Is it bad that I think that's hot?"

"Definitely not." Lifting himself, he let the shirt fall off his shoulders and down his arms before throwing it off to the side of the bed. "God damn, angel. You look fucking unreal."

"Really?" I giggled. "I'm fairly sure I have mascara all over my face. You should have warned me to wear waterproof."

"Mmm, nah," he purred, reaching to the wall that ran along the side of the bed. He turned the knob that stuck out, dimming the lights above. "I think you look sexy with mascara running down your cheeks."

He settled himself between my thighs, one hand on my waist and the other beside my head. Warm lips met mine once again, hard and long and aching, a million words between them that had finally been set free. I kissed him back just as eagerly, fingertips drawing circles on his shoulder blades, hips bucking up, begging for more.

"I want to be gentle with you, angel," he mumbled against my mouth. "Don't make it hard for me this time. Let me just... live in this moment. Okay?"

I nodded. Within a second, my mind fogged over as his fingers met slick, damp flesh and his mouth closed over my nipple. Pleasure bloomed within me, spreading out through every nerve in my body. "Fuck," I breathed, tilting my head back and burying it in the plush sheets beneath me.

He circled my clit gently, taking his time, drawing me closer and closer with each little movement, each little lick and nip at my breast. He hummed his approval as my body took over, lifting and begging for more. "I almost want to keep you just like this," he grunted, his words muffled. "You look so pretty wiggling for me."

"No," I groaned, pressing my hips against his once again, the head of his cock just barely against me. "Please, Hudson. I need more."

He chuckled as he lifted himself, his fingers abandoning my most sensitive spots and wrapping instead around the thickest parts of my thighs. He pushed them up, opening me to him, putting me on display. "Since you asked me *so* nicely, angel..."

I gasped as he pushed inside, slow and tender, but the girth of him was enough to make my muscles burn as they loosened for him. I dug my nails into his shoulders, watched as he looked down at me with what I could only assume was passion.

Slowly, achingly, he settled. Every piece of him in me, every piece of me in him. "Fuck," he growled, lowering himself so he was only an inch from my face. "Why does this feel even better now?"

I took his face in my hands and lifted my lips to his. "Because you're not holding anything back now."

A small smile spread across his lips as he looked down at me with half-lidded eyes. "Yeah," he agreed. "I'm not."

His hips began to move, pulling back, dragging himself through me before burying himself once again. A rough moan escaped my lips; the sensation was far too heavenly to put words to. Over and over, he rocked his hips, finding just the right angle that sent me spiraling into myself and holding him there. He read my body language, he knew without asking exactly what I wanted, what I needed.

"Damn, angel," he groaned, his forehead falling to mine. "I want to keep you this way but I can't reach you like this. Hold on."

He pushed me further back on the bed, his length slipping from me, and crawled after me. "No," I whined, wanting that fullness and the brain fog it brought with it back.

"Come on," he chuckled, sitting back against the headboard and patting his lap. "Show me how well you ride for me, Sophia."

My mouth watered at his words, and I rolled, forcing myself up onto my hands and knees. I straddled him, hovering just above his cock and took his face in my hands. "Only because you asked so nicely," I mocked, throwing his words back at him.

Slowly, I sank onto him, filling myself back up and fogging up my mind. "Fuck, yes, angel," he groaned, one hand on my hip guiding me down until flesh met flesh. The fingers on his other hand snaked between us, finding that sensitive spot between my thighs and began to circle it.

I forced my hips to move, languid and slow, as my forehead dropped to his. I could feel the pleasure beginning to knot in my gut, could feel the telltale signs of a building orgasm deep in my bones. "Oh my god," I sighed, struggling to keep my concentration on the movement of my hips. Hudson guided them, helping every step of the way. "You have no idea how good that feels."

He chuckled as he looked up at me, his fingers moving just a little faster. "I have a vague idea." Briefly, his hand left my waist, pushing the hair back from my face so he could get a better view. "I love you."

I couldn't stop the smile that tugged my lips up. "I love you too," I mumbled, pressing my lips to his and holding him to me. No escape. No running away. I wasn't going to let that happen anymore.

Every circle, every little nudge of his fingers sent me plummeting over the edge. The climax ripped through me as his movements stuttered, taking everything and more with it, sending me below the waves that sloshed against the walls of the boat and drowning me in the most immense amount of bliss I'd ever felt. I couldn't hear the sounds I made, couldn't see through the fog, but Hudson's words echoed in my head.

I love you.

I love you.

I love you.

It wasn't the last time I'd hear it that night. It wasn't the last time we'd find our ends together, either, and when we'd finally exhausted every drop of energy we had left and couldn't last another round, Hudson pulled me to his chest and held me close. Our measured breaths filled the room, the waves barely noticeable, and as he turned the lights off and I drifted toward sleep, I could have sworn I heard him say, "Thank you."

Chapter 39

Hudson

One Week Later

A year ago, if someone had asked me if I'd be up at seven on a Saturday morning making breakfast for my fiancée and son, I'd have said they were insane. A year ago, I couldn't see myself being with anyone in a serious relationship for the rest of my life. A year ago, the thought of bringing a woman into Jamey's life would have never crossed my mind. A year ago, I wouldn't have been making chocolate chip pancakes. In reality, I still shouldn't be making chocolate chip pancakes. They were turning out horribly.

The soft pad of footsteps coming down the stairs told me that Sophie had woken up.

"Hudson?" She called, the tail of my name ending in a yawn. "What's burning?"

"Pancakes," I laughed. I flipped the one in the pan,

frowning as I was met with yet another nearly black bottom. "Didn't think you'd be up yet."

"Hard to sleep when the house smells like it's on fire." She saddled up to me, wearing one of my oversized shirts from my Harvard days that nearly reached down to her knees. "It didn't help the morning sickness."

I pulled her in under my arm, tucking her close to my chest. "I'm sorry, angel," I mumbled. I planted a kiss on the top of her head as she buried her sleep-coated face in my side. "Were you sick?"

"Just twice."

"Why didn't you call for me?" I dragged my fingers through her hair as I flipped the pancake once more, happy to see only a dark brown side instead of charcoal.

"Didn't want to distract you from the fire I thought you were putting out," she said, her voice muffled from where she nuzzled into me. "And I didn't want to wake Jamey."

"I'm already awake."

I looked over my shoulder, finding one very sleepy Jamey at the bottom of the stairs, one hand rubbing his eyes and the other clutching his teddy bear by the paw. "Aw, bud, you could've slept a little longer."

"I thought there was a fire," he grumbled.

I frowned as I looked back at the stack of cooked, mostly blackened pancakes. "Is it really that bad?"

"Yes," Sophie groaned.

Jamey's eyes blinked open, still out of sorts from sleep, and I watched as the realization settled into him. "Sophie's here? This early? Hi, Sophie!"

Sophie lifted her head, her mop of brown hair flowing back over her shoulders. "Hi, squirt."

"Did you and Daddy have a sleepover?" He asked, his

little eyes going wide as he looked at us. "You get to have breakfast with us!"

"I don't know if I'd call this breakfast..."

"Oh come on, Soph, it's not that bad," I said, turning back to the saddest stack of pancakes I'd ever seen in my life. "They're just that color because of all the chocolate."

Sophie snorted. "Nice try. Cereal, Jamey?"

"Yes please!"

I frowned as Sophie picked up the plate of pancakes and immediately dumped them into the trash. "It's okay, Hudson. Not everyone was made to cook," she teased, scraping off the scraps before plopping the dirty plate in the sink.

Jamey climbed his way up to the high-top seat, setting up his teddy bear on the counter so it was sitting facing us. "Daddy, I was thinking. A *lot*. Now that you and Sophie are engaged, like for real this time, I want to know when the wedding is."

"What?" I laughed, leaning onto the counter to get closer to him. "What do you mean, bud?"

"You haven't told me and I don't know why."

"That's 'cause we haven't decided yet, squirt," Sophie yawned. She pulled a bowl from the cupboard, sorting out Jamey's breakfast cereal before I'd even had the chance. It made the warmth in my chest swell and spread to see her mothering him like that already. "You'll be the first to know. Promise."

"I don't get it," Jamey pouted, turning his little bear toward himself. "Do you get it, Mr. Ted?" He nodded as if he were listening intently to nonexistent words coming from a stuffed animal. "Mr. Ted says he thought that the government decided when the wedding would be."

Laughter peeled from my chest at the same time as

Sophie, the absolute ridiculousness of a four-year-old's logic too much to handle. "No," I chuckled, reaching over the counter to ruffle his messy mop of dark hair. I almost wished he looked a little like Sophie. "That's not how it works. Sophie and I will pick a date, and then you'll know. You can even be in the wedding if you want, bud. Ring bearer, maybe?"

"Oh, I love that idea," Sophie cooed, plopping Jamey's bowl of cereal in front of him before sliding one over to me as well. "Maybe we can do it next summer? That'll give me time to fit into the dress of my dreams since the baby will be, like, four or five months old. Ooohhh, I could even make my own dress!"

"That sounds perfect, angel." Sophie's cheeks heated as I leaned toward her and pecked her on the cheek.

"Yeah! Ring bearer and summer wedding," Jamey chirped, his mouth full of cereal and milk, little droplets leaking out the sides of his lips. "Daddy, what's a ring bearer?"

"Only the most important job of the entire wedding." I made my eyes widen, trying to look as serious as possible. "You'd be bringing me and Sophie our rings. They're what makes the whole thing possible."

Jamey looked up at me in shock, his spoon falling into his cereal bowl. "I get to do *that*?"

"You sure do, bud."

"A summer wedding, a new mommy, and I get to do the best job ever?" His feet kicked against the marble breakfast island, his hands gripping the edge in excitement. "This is amazing."

Just the idea that Jamey was genuinely thrilled to have Sophie stepping in as a parent was enough to make my eyes burn with tears. It was something I'd wanted to give him for far too long, something he deserved, but something I hadn't given myself enough grace to find until now. The three of us —soon to be four—would be an actual family. My unit would be whole once again, and I had the most amazing woman I'd ever met by my side to bring that to fruition.

Heaven knows she'd already made my heart whole again, too.

Chapter 40

Sophie

One Year Later

"**M**om. Mom, calm down, you're going to ruin your makeup," I groaned, hastily grabbing some tissues and wadding them up beneath her eyes. "Alice spent so much time doing it for you. Don't make her regret it."

"I know," she said through choked sobs, her lower lip quivering. "I wasn't expecting to be this emotional."

"It's just a dress." I chuckled as I wiped away the little beads of black tears where they gathered in her ducts. "Save your tears for when I actually walk down the aisle, okay?"

"Come on, Leslie, pull yourself together," Lisa quipped as she gently slapped my mom on the back. "Time to put your strong pants on and face what's about to happen head-on, momma."

"I know, I know," Mom sighed, taking a deep breath and

fanning her eyes. "I'm good. I'm alright. Does Jamey have the rings? Lisa, did you check?"

"Of course. As long as he hasn't lost them, we're good."

"Who has Madeline? Sophia, where's your daughter?"

"Oh my god, Mom, calm down. Hudson's mom is watching both of them for the next..." I checked the time on my phone, my hands going clammy as I realized there were only five minutes until we were supposed to begin, "...five minutes. Oh, fuck, it's only five minutes. I can do this."

I double-checked my hair and makeup in the vanity, fixing any little imperfection I could find before stepping in front of the full-length mirror to get one last look at myself. The dress I'd made fit me perfectly—the deep V of the front sat flush against my skin, the lace sleeves hung loose and cinched in at my wrists. Lace over white chiffon hugged my waist before flowing out, the long slit up my front left thigh giving a little peek of a garter belt Hudson had insisted on. *I don't want to tear it off with my teeth in front of everyone. I want to do it alone with you in our suite afterward.*

I'd settled on having my long, wavy hair down in curls. I always felt more comfortable with it down, and Hudson liked it better that way too.

"You look beautiful." Lisa stepped up behind me, one hand on my shoulder as she looked at my reflection. "But it's time to go."

I nodded more to myself than to her. "How's Hudson? Have you seen him?"

"He's great." She grinned at me, her hand gently massaging the sore spots in my neck muscles. "He looks very handsome. He's all smiles."

I'd be a liar if I tried to say that a small part of me wasn't relieved to hear that. That same small part thought there might be the tiniest, minuscule chance that he'd run away,

307

that he'd realize how real all of it was and take off. To hear that he was happy, that he was excited made it so much better.

"Okay. Let's go."

———

From the back of the line, I could see Jamey and Madeline in the very front. Madeline was cooing, her chubby little hands stuffed in her bag of flower petals as she sat in the little wagon Jamey would be pushing. He was five, now, a little taller, a little smarter. Still looked exactly like his father even though Hudson liked to joke that he was beginning to look like me.

The doors opened and I watched as Jamey pushed his little sister forward, his feet bouncing in excitement. My empty hands shook. I'd opted to not go for a bouquet since I was having both of my parents walk me down the aisle, but I was beginning to realize the reason why brides probably carried them in the first place. I wanted something to hold on to.

One by one, I watched my bridesmaids and Hudson's groomsmen file into the room. From my vantage point, I couldn't see anyone at the far end, though I could hear Jamey's oohs and ahhhs and his little remarks to Madeline to tell her to watch.

Mom and Dad took my empty hands in theirs as the doors closed and we took our position behind them.

"You alright, bug?" Dad whispered, his clammy hand squeezing mine.

"Yeah," I breathed. "It all just became a little real."

The soft piano music hit its crescendo and the doors opened wide. I didn't see anyone, not a single soul, not the decorations our moms had spent so much time on, not the woodwork our dads had made together. I didn't see the flowers we'd picked out, I didn't see Jamey or Madeline or our friends and families on either side.

All I saw was *him*.

Decked out in his finest all-black suit, his hair back and away from his face, his stubble shaved. Madeline had been up all night crying, and I noticed he'd taken Lisa's advice and put on the smallest dab of concealer beneath his eyes, hiding the dark circles. He looked perfect—my person, the father of my child, my everything.

My heartbeat thrummed in my ears and suddenly I was moving, walking, running down the aisle. My hands were empty, my feet quick beneath me in my heels, and before the room and the people and the music filtered back into my senses, my arms were around his neck, my face pressed into his jacket. I didn't care if it left a makeup stain. It was *him*, and it was *me*. It was us and our children, and that was all I needed. It would *always* be all I needed.

———

As we stood in the courtyard of the Boston Public Library, the music from the reception filtering out through closed doors and the water trickling from the fountain before us, I couldn't help but feel like everything had gone too fast. The ceremony was perfect, the reception was perfect, the first dance was perfect. Everything had gone according to plan, but it went too quickly.

"I could do this every day with you," Hudson whispered, his arms squeezing me tightly from behind as he rested his chin on my shoulder. "Celebrate us every day, see you in this dress every day, marry you again every day."

I giggled a bit as I leaned back into him. "If only. It'd be a little hard to parent, though, if this was our every day."

"We could have another one though." He turned, kissing my neck gently. "Another wedding, I mean. Not another kid. I don't think we could handle three. But we could have one every anniversary, you could make a new dress every year, we could invite all our friends and family—"

"That sounds exhausting," I laughed. "Do you know how long it took me to make this dress?"

"Then I'll buy you one. Every year, a new dress. Consider it an anniversary gift."

"You're insane," I grinned, squeezing his arms. "But I love you."

"I love you, too." The music slowed, a cheesy love song blaring through the speakers, and through the glass doors, people milled their way onto the dance floor, arms around necks and easily swaying to the beat. Hudson swayed me along with it. "Thank you, Sophie. For everything."

"What do you mean?"

"You've given me everything. Another child, a thawed heart, the ability to feel again, to love again. You've given my son a mother and my life far more meaning than I deserve. You've given me a happy ending I didn't even know I wanted." He dragged his hand through my hair, turning my head to face him. "So, thank you. And I love you. And I don't deserve you."

His eyes were soft, his gaze so loving beyond anything I could have expected from him. It set off those stupid butterflies in my stomach again, spreading warmth throughout my body. I would never get tired of this feeling.

"You're welcome. I love you, too. And you *do* deserve me. You deserve every part of me, for as long as I live and far, *far* beyond that."

THE END

Hey Fabulous Readers!

Thank you for reading Accidentally Engaged. If you loved Sophie and Hudson's story, you'll love Can't Fake Twins: An Enemies to Lovers Romance, also part of my Single Dad Billionaires series.

Read on for a sneak peek.

The deal with Katie Martin was simple.
Play my fake girlfriend at my younger brother's wedding.
She's his ex.
But now for a whole weekend, she's mine...

She calls me her silver fox.
I call her my bambi who needs saving... from me.

She's not just another conquest.
My son adores her.
Her sunshine thaws the coldest of hearts.

I'll never forgive my brother for what he did to her.
I want to keep her safe, between my penthouse sheets.
But I don't do real relationships.
And now my plan has just one flaw...

There's nothing fake about our twins growing inside her.

Read now on Amazon.

Sneak Peek

Chapter One
Katie

I rubbed my hands up and down my thighs, pulling at the hem of my skirt as my boyfriend, Toby, looked over at me with a hint of irritation in his blue eyes.

"Don't be so nervous," he said. "It's just my family."

"Your family is important to you," I defended myself. "So, that means they're also important to me. I want to make a good impression."

Toby smiled. "Don't worry, they'll love you," he said gently.

I smiled back. Toby had been in a bit of a mood in the days leading up to the Christmas party, and I knew why. His brother was, by Toby's account, a total jerk.

"Is your brother going to be there?" I asked softly.

Toby sighed. "Yeah, him and his hellion kid. Don't worry about making a good impression to him."

"You guys don't really like each other much, do you?" I asked curiously. He didn't talk much about his brother,

other than a few disparaging comments. I didn't even know his brother's name. In fact, he rarely talked about his family at all. I could understand since his parents died in an awful accident a few years ago.

"He's my brother," he grunted, and that was all he would say about the matter.

I let it go. I didn't want to irritate him more than he already was. Toby and I had only been dating for three months; I liked him a lot and I wanted it to go further.

I was excited to meet his family and to get closer to him, I just hoped everything went well.

When we arrived, Toby put his hand on the small of my back, proudly introducing me to his uncles and aunt. All their kids were there, too, and some of the older ones introduced themselves.

I smiled at the kids running around. I loved being around children, and my job reflected that as an elementary school teacher.

Toby ignored the kids. I was sure he'd make a great father someday, but he didn't seem that interested in playing with his little cousins. I thought maybe he was just nervous about seeing his brother.

Toby disappeared into another room and when I peeked inside, he was playing poker and drinking scotch with his uncles. I chuckled. I guess I wasn't invited.

I wasn't much for poker or scotch, so I didn't mind. But I didn't particularly like being left alone with people I didn't know. I sighed, heading to the kitchen to try to find something to drink, preferably something with a little alcohol.

"You can't hit your cousins," a man said sternly in the kitchen as I walked in. His back was to me, and he had broad shoulders, his back muscles showing through the thin t-shirt he was wearing.

A little boy sat on the counter, pouting. He was blond with bright blue eyes, and I assumed the man was his father because his hair was also blond.

When I cleared my throat, the man turned to me, and I blinked once, twice.

His dirty blond hair fell over one bright blue eye, the same color eyes as the kid he was scolding. His jaw was strong and square, a light dusting of blond stubble covering it. He was so handsome that I was taken aback.

Katie, I told myself. *Your boyfriend is in the next room, and you're thinking how hot one of his relatives is?*

The man smiled, revealing a row of even, white teeth. "Sorry," he mumbled. "My kiddo sometimes doesn't play well with others."

I looked at the little boy who was still pouting but looking at me curiously.

"Hello," I said to the boy. "What's your name?"

"Colin," he answered easily, bouncing slightly on the counter. He looked back at his dad, curiosity seemingly sated. "Can I go play now?"

"Are you going to hit your cousins again?" the man asked.

"Not unless they're mean," Colin said, and I saw the man hide a laugh behind his hand.

"No hitting, Colin. I'm serious."

The young boy sighed. "Okay, Dad. Promise."

He held out his hand, extending his pinky. His dad did the same and smiled at his son as they shared a pinky swear.

The man put Colin down on the ground and he ran back off into the living room.

"I'm sorry," he said again, sweeping his hand through his hair to get it out of his face. "He can be a little gremlin when he wants to be."

I smiled. "No apologies. I know how kids are."

He chuckled. "Yeah, well, when he's good, I claim him."

I laughed, going into the fridge and grabbing a beer to sip on. "How old?"

"He just turned five," he answered proudly, and gestured to my beer. "Is there another one of those?"

I turned and grabbed one from the fridge, handing it to him.

"Thanks," he said softly, smiling at me shyly.

Dear God, he was handsome. Even more so standing face-to-face with him. His torso was shredded and his arms bulged in the t-shirt he was wearing. I'd never seen someone that attractive in real life.

Shut up, my brain said. *Toby's better looking.*

Of course, he was. He was my boyfriend. I was committed to him. So why did I feel like melting every time this man smiled at me?

"I'm Katie," I said dumbly, not knowing how to make small talk.

"Adam," he said, as he reached out his hand. I offered mine and he gripped it gently but firmly. His hand was soft and warm.

"You're related to Toby?" I asked, and he scoffed.

"You could say that" he said vaguely. I wondered if he could be one of the uncle's older sons which would make him Toby's cousin. They had a slight resemblance to one another in their eyes and the sexy shape of their mouths. Maybe that was why I found him so attractive—he looked a little like my boyfriend.

Adam didn't seem like he wanted me to pry, though, so I didn't ask him how they were related.

"I don't think you're one of my relatives," he said, looking at me with a smirk. "I'd remember you."

My face heated up. I knew I was blushing. Was he flirting with me?

"I'm just a friend of the family," I said hesitantly, and I didn't know why I didn't point blank tell him I was Toby's girlfriend.

Was it because I was so attracted to him? Toby and I, after just three months, had gotten so serious that there wasn't much flirting anymore. Maybe that was it. I was just enjoying the attention.

That wasn't so bad, was it?

"Good to know we're not related," he said, sipping his beer, still smiling and looking right into my eyes.

"And why is that?" I asked, my voice low. I felt a little nervous, looking around for Toby to come into the kitchen and find me flirting with one of his relatives.

I wasn't flirting, though. Was I? We were just talking. Making small talk was what one did at parties, right?

"Because you're too beautiful," he murmured, and I felt like my cheeks were going to catch on fire.

"I don't know about that," I muttered, leaning my back against the counter.

Adam leaned forward, close enough to me that he could lean down and...

Lean down and what, Katie?

What was I thinking?

I cleared my throat, looking up at him even though I knew I should probably look away. I wasn't used to that kind of conversation, Toby and I had been isolated in our own love bubble for the past three months. I had barely seen my family since I met him; socializing with anyone other than Toby had become foreign to me.

"Christmas feels like it might've come early, getting to chat with a pretty girl like you," he said in that same low murmur. His voice was a clear, smooth baritone and a shock like electricity went up my spine as he spoke.

"Don't rush it," I said with a smile. "I'm sure your son is looking forward to all the presents Santa is going to bring him." I made a gesture of quotation marks when I said Santa, and Adam groaned, throwing his head back. I could see a cord-like vein in his neck and for some reason, it made my lips hungry to kiss it.

"You're right. I hope Christmas comes as slow as molasses this year," he joked.

I looked into the living area to see if Toby had come out of the poker room, but he hadn't. The kids were running around the Christmas tree, some of them throwing tinsel on it. Others were decorating the tree with ornaments, and I smiled, finding it nostalgic.

"You like kids?" Adam asked me, and I looked back at him.

"Love them," I admitted. "I teach elementary school."

Adam raised an eyebrow. "You get better and better all the time."

I looked away from him, trying fervently not to have an obvious blush. I was pretty sure it was a losing battle.

"Where's your wife?" I asked, and Adam chuckled low in his throat.

"No wife. It's kind of a long story."

I was curious but again, not wanting to pry. I stood there awkwardly, not sure what to say. I didn't usually find it difficult talking to men, but I'd never met one like him.

Adam reached toward me, and for one hot second I thought he was going to put his hand on my hip, and pull me toward him, but all he did was open the refrigerator door and get another beer.

I let out a long breath.

"Katie?" Toby's voice rang out and I stiffened.

"Nice to meet you," I said, and Adam nodded.

"See you around, Katie," he said softly.

Saved by the bell, I thought, and rushed into the living room where Toby was frowning.

"Where have you been?" he asked under his breath.

"Sorry," I said, holding up my half-empty beer. "I just wanted a drink."

Toby gave me a look. *That* look, the one that told me he was annoyed with me, and my heart sank.

"You know I don't like it when you drink," he muttered, and I swallowed hard.

"It's just one beer, Toby."

"One beer turns into three and then I'm carrying you home over my shoulder," he snapped, and I sighed.

We had gone to a club when we first started dating and I'd had a little too much to drink. For whatever reason, it had really annoyed Toby. Ever since, he would make snarky comments any time I drank alcohol. He had never let it go.

"I'm sorry, Toby," I said softly, and placed the half-empty beer into a nearby trash can.

"They're about to put the star on the tree," he said, just as Adam walked past us, holding Colin in his arms.

"Oh, that's cute," I commented.

"The baby of the family always puts the star on top," Toby said, and for some reason it sounded like he was complaining about it.

Adam lifted up Colin and he placed the star on top of the tree with a big smile. It was a little crooked, but everyone applauded him anyway.

While I was watching Colin put the star on, Toby had trailed off somewhere else. I looked around but couldn't find him. I was trying to keep my eyes off Adam when a man approached me, smiling.

"Hello, there," he said. The man was almost the spitting image of Toby, just about twenty years older.

I smiled and reached out to shake his hand. "You must be one of Colin's uncles I haven't met," I said, and the man nodded.

"I'm Phil," he replied, and we chatted for a while about Toby's work as a carpenter and my career as a teacher. His family was warm and friendly, and I was having a good time despite my little tiff with Toby.

He's just nervous about me meeting his family. He'll be fine after this is over, I told myself.

The sound of arguing in the kitchen made me turn my head. Toby was standing there with Adam and poking him in the chest. They both looked angry.

I frowned, wondering what it was that had set Toby off. My boyfriend was sweet most of the time, but he had a hair-trigger temper.

I didn't know what was going on, but apparently it had incensed Toby enough that he was ready to leave, because he stalked toward me and grabbed my elbow steering me toward the door.

I waved goodbye to Uncle Phil, who still had a warm smile on his face, as Toby ushered me out of the house.

"What's wrong?" I asked. "Why were you arguing with Adam?"

"Adam?" he sneered. "You're already on a first name basis with my asshole brother?"

I blinked, surprised. "That's... that's your brother?"

"The one and only," he said dryly, opening the car door roughly and getting inside.

I got into the passenger seat, my heart in my throat. So,

320

the man who had flirted with me in the kitchen was Toby's estranged brother. It made me feel even worse for allowing it to happen, not to mention being attracted to him.

"What happened between you?" I asked, and Toby groaned.

"Katie, I don't want to hash out all my family bullshit right now. I just want to go home, have another drink, and go to sleep."

I looked at him. His face was flushed, and I wondered how many scotches he'd put down in the poker room.

"Maybe I should drive," I said quietly. He responded with a glare, so I shut my mouth, looking down at my hands.

Toby glanced at his phone, and his expression changed to something I couldn't put my finger on.

"I have to go into the office, it turns out," he said suddenly.

I frowned. "What do you mean? Why would you have to go into the office on Christmas Eve?"

"Why do you ask so many damn questions?" he muttered, and I looked down at my hands again, tears threatening at the corner of my eyes.

I was silent the rest of the ride home. Toby stopped for a moment outside the apartment and waited for me to get out. I walked toward the driver's side window, wanting a kiss goodbye, but he took off as if he didn't see me.

Tears began to roll down my face. I guessed it was some kind of karma for flirting with his brother, but to be fair, I didn't even know why Toby disliked him so much. And I definitely didn't know it was his brother when I met him.

I sniffled and walked into the apartment, my heart aching.

End of first chapter

Want to see how Katie and Adam end up fake dating? Order Can't Fake Twins on Amazon now.

"Loved, loved, loved Katie and Adam's story. A perfect amount of drama, emotions, love and spice." - Kristina

"There was just something about Katie and Adam's romance that seized hold of my heart and had me falling head over heels in love with them." Aunt G

A very entertaining, steamy, page turning, enemies to lovers, fake dating romance read with a happily ever after. Read Can't Fake Twins today—Free with Kindle Unlimited!

GET CAN'T FAKE TWINS

Made in the USA
Columbia, SC
25 March 2024